The Misfit Farm

Vanessa Junkin

Copyright © 2021 Vanessa Junkin
All rights reserved.
ISBN: 978-1-7782070-0-6

This book is dedicated to everyone who helped bring it to life.
Especially Will.

Although it was inspired by real people, places, and events—
the story is fictitious.

The Protest

"Let's remember our survival is at risk of self-destruction. It won't be due to any virus or natural event, it will be due to politics, religion, economics, or some other man-made construct."
-Keith Turner

In 2019, a pandemic began its sweep across the world—COVID-19. The coronavirus disease, caused by SARS-CoV-2, was first discovered in Wuhan, China. By 2021, over five and a half million people had died globally, while millions more suffered from the repercussions of "long COVID"—and those were just the reported cases.

As vaccinations rolled out, division surfaced between those who were adamant that global vaccination was the only way forward, and those who were equally steadfast in their refusal to put something in their body that they didn't believe in. Conspiracy theories erupted, fueled by social media. From their virtual podiums, individuals screamed the vaccines carried microchips to track people! Vaccines weren't safe, effective, or properly tested! Vaccination injuries were too great a risk! Blame 5G technology! Vaccines caused infertility in women! Vaccines *intentionally* caused infertility in women! Vaccines caused variants! Vaccines rewrite DNA! Vaccines cause autism! Natural immunity would protect us! It was just a flu! There wasn't really a pandemic!

By 2022, businesses were struggling after three years of revolving lockdowns. Inflation was rising. Food and resource shortages meant more than a few bare shelves in the toilet paper aisle. The creeping distrust of local governments and scientists was palpable, along with tension between unvaccinated and vaccinated neighbours. One side blamed the other for refusing to play their part in keeping society safe, while the other side rallied against the brainwashed "sheeple." The ensuing unrest was no surprise.

In Asia, protests began because the government wasn't doing enough to keep its citizens safe. France, a country historically willing to burn itself to the ground for the sake of a revolution, decried the impossibility of lockdown policies for those living in crowded public housing. In India, migrant workers demonstrated their outrage after being trapped by lockdowns without any government aid to keep them fed and housed. Soon after, a COVID testing centre was burned down on the Ivory Coast because protestors felt it was built too close to their homes. Then a German group held hundreds of protests, under the banner "World Wide Rally for Freedom," against government implemented COVID-19 restrictions. They touted #wewillALLbethere. And they were. Until they weren't.

A few months before the electrical grid went dark in Nova Scotia, a new strain of the virus was detected. There had already been at least twelve other notable variants of concern over the years, but this was different in that ground zero was a group of hunters in Romeo, Colorado. COVID-19 was known to infect white tailed deer, with an estimate of over half the population affected by the end of 2021. As hunting season approached, it was recommended that hunters wear a mask and avoid handling the respiratory system when butchering their kill. But in 2024, still not everyone had got the memo.

Sigma, as it would be named, was the result of COVID-19 infecting a population of deer, mutating, and then reinfecting humans. The genetic material it picked up along the way not only expediated the virus's spread, but also its mortality rate. By the time the hunters were identified as COVID-19 positive, their families and friends were also infected. By the time the hunters succumbed to the disease in hospital, the town's borders were completely restricted. Barricades and roadblocks were constructed for kilometers in every direction. The army began to air-drop supplies daily to the isolated citizens. However, within two weeks their service was no longer required—everyone in the town had died. Sigma had stolen thirty-five thousand people.

Under the instructions of the American government, a complete cull of the white-tailed deer population was authorized. They even went so far as to present their Canadian neighbour with an ultimatum: *"Dispose of your deer, or it will be taken care of for you."* To demonstrate their resolve, US troops distributed poisoned bait along the border and civilians of either nationality were incentivized with fifty-dollar payouts per kill. Sky high unemployment rates further contributed to the anti-deer frenzy that ensued.

Indigenous people on both sides of the border revolted against the sanctioned ecocide. As a marginalized group, they had already been harder hit by the pandemic than many others, yet their commitment to environmental welfare remained unwavering. They tried in vain to explain the ripple effect of removing such a large animal from the food chain. They believed that such a dramatic tipping of the ecological balance would result in even more disease, famine, and discord. I agreed there was a thin line between destroying ill deer and killing infected people. But to the First Nations there was no line, the deer were their people too. Their kinship was deeply rooted in their mutual survival. Killing the deer was synonymous with killing *them*.

On my last trip to Halifax in May of 2024, armed with my respirator, I attended a rally organized by the local Mi'kmaq to oppose the cull. I stood in quiet solidarity among the protestors, vowing to pay attention, to listen, and to stand beside them in their efforts. Even though I was a resolute lover of animals, I could not fully appreciate the depth of their frustration or their fear.

Part way through the ceremony, I watched as six, young, First Nations' women climbed onto a platform that had been erected outside the legislature doors. They each wore a red cloak with a collar of eagle feathers. I recognized them as the Defenders, local celebrities spearheading the Extinction Rebellion movement. The muted ambiance felt like a prayer, so I bowed my head. Somewhere a child began crying. When I peeked up, the six women had each thrown a thick rope over a rough-sawn beam that had been erected. Panic ignited inside my chest. Before I could form a cohesive thought, the Defenders had tightened their nooses and dropped from the gallows.

Cries of anguish, rage, and hopelessness rang out. Drums pounded feverishly. A group of men in full regalia charged the tactical police that had been standing by, looking bored, until then. A car fire erupted. Rubber bullets whizzed past.

I fled.

For decades, when commercial industries had contaminated local waterways, Indigenous people staged sit-ins. When zealous forestry operations cut down all but one percent of the old growth forest and endangered Nova Scotia's mainland moose, they circulated petitions. When the demand for oil threatened to poison the land, they handcuffed themselves to pipelines. For generations they eked out life on reservations while shouldering the loss of their language and their children in the name of assimilation. Now the United States government had signed a blank cheque to eradicate the deer population. For the Defenders, it was the match in the powder barrel. With attempts at peaceful protest willfully ignored throughout history, their martyrdom was their last gift of hope to Mother Earth and to their family—what remained of it.

Barricades were assembled around reservations and shots were fired at anyone who dared approach. Government officials on both sides of the border promised to meet to explore compromises and research alternatives, but when national public communication fell silent weeks later, as far as I knew, the cull was ongoing.

Part One

"The greatest fine art of the future will be the making of a comfortable living from a small piece of land."
-Abraham Lincoln

I

I stole a lipstick once. It belonged to my friend's mom. I saw it sitting in their bathroom and I casually slipped it into my overnight bag. I don't know why I did it, I didn't even wear lipstick—it always made me look like I was trying to be someone I wasn't. Her mom even asked me if a lipstick had "fallen into my bag" or if I took it "by accident." I lied. We all knew I lied, and I hated myself for the angry red stain it left on my character.

The sound of glass breaking shattered my guilty hesitation. I stuffed my bag with opioids, bronchodilators, epinephrine, antibiotics, antiarrhythmics, antipyretics, antifungals, and antihistamines. There didn't appear to be any antivirals left. Alex was working his way down the aisle toward me. He stopped to scan our surroundings every thirty seconds as I rummaged through what was left in the pharmacy cabinets for anything I recognized as potentially lifesaving.

Saline.

Burn cream.

Needles and syringes.

It wouldn't be long before traditional pharmacies no longer existed. *If stealing makes me a shitty person, this must be on the lesser end of the shittiness spectrum,* I justified. Then I grabbed every bottle of activated charcoal I could find, the "universal antidote" for many types of poisoning. Then it was my turn to scan the room for threats.

"Alex, we gotta go!" I hissed.

Two gruff men had smashed their way through the front window. They finished raiding the cash registers and were now heading in our direction. They had bandanas tied over half their faces and shotguns slung across their camo jacketed backs. It triggered a memory of the first time I had seen someone open carry. It was on my honeymoon in a café in North Carolina and it had made for an uncomfortable lunch for a pair of Canadians.

"Whatcha got there?" one of the men yelled, pointing at my bag which suddenly felt heavy. We weren't in a café in North Carolina—we were in a Shoppers Drug Mart in rural Nova Scotia. It was 2024, and we were stealing a whole lot more than lipstick.

Alex and I darted out the back door. Will, my husband, was waiting with the trailer loaded with supplies we had pillaged from the hardware store.

Shovels.

Pickaxes.

Plywood.

Rope.

Fencing.

Nails.

Oil.

Ammo.

"Go! Go! Go!" Alex hollered as we dove into our seats. Will peeled out of the parking lot. As I took off my respirator, my hands were shaking. After vigorously rubbing them with Purell, I stuffed them under my thighs and focused on deep breathing. A long line of traffic on the side of New Germany's main street slowed our escape, but the Camo Boys didn't seem to be following us. *They are probably too busy stuffing their pockets with leftover erectile dysfunction pills,* I thought snidely.

The lineup of cars led exactly where we suspected—the gas station. A full-blown fist fight erupted at one of the pumps between two women. The taller of the two had the other by the hair and repeatedly punched her in the face to the cheers of frustrated motorists waiting behind them. They stood in a pool of gas from a tipped over jerry can. The whole scene made me feel sick. Will caught my eye empathetically in the rear-view mirror. If it wasn't for the threat of the virus, we might have stopped to try and help. I couldn't wait to get back to the farm.

II

Lilies bloomed in the ditches along the gravel road. Ducks and chickens moseyed around the yard foraging for insects with a side of vegetation. Our three German Shepherds barked excitedly, and the alpacas looked up with feigned interest before continuing to graze. The June air shimmered with pollen—it was all surreal. If I didn't know any better, I might imagine that all was well in the world.

We parked behind bushes at the end of the driveway and Will retrieved the locked ammunition box we had stashed in the culvert. He took out a garbage bag, a jug of medical grade alcohol, a couple of rags, and a spray bottle. We used the rags dipped in alcohol to wipe down every item we had procured. Looking at it all laid out in the grass brought mixed emotions. I felt triumphant in relation to the medical supplies we had gathered, but everything came with an expiration date. The construction supplies brought a sense of relief, but also the uneasy reminder that this may be the last bucket of nails we would be able to find for a very, very long time.

Will stripped off his clothing. His body had already begun to change with the rationing of food. His muscles were more defined, and it worried me that what little fat stores he had were already being consumed. Alex placed our clothes into a bag where they would be kept for the next two weeks. We rubbed down our entire bodies with alcohol, painfully discovering every cut and abrasion along the way. Then we sprayed the interior of the car and wiped down the handles. We would keep the vehicle locked up for the next two weeks as well.

The car had been a gift from our neighbours who elected to head for their winter home in Florida before the borders were permanently closed. They were an older couple and they had joked that if the end of the world was coming, they'd rather get used to the idea while sitting on a warm and sandy beach. I couldn't blame them and although I would miss them, I knew that come winter their lack of physical conditioning would be a liability. Even if they survived the winter, their compounding medical issues would take their own tax by spring. I thought about the two backpacks full of medication we had just stolen and how quickly a chronically ill person could suck them up.

"How did it go?" Alex's partner, Steve, called as we headed up the driveway toward the house. Steve was gathering bruised drop apples with their young daughter. We had collectively agreed to bait deer to draw them away from the farm as a mitigation strategy. Every night after supper, Steve and Alex would take a pail of apples to a grove several kilometers down the road. So far it appeared to be working, the apples disappeared every couple days and fresh deer droppings were evidence that a few were still in the area. None of us agreed with the cull, so we had to learn how to live with the perpetual threat in our backyard. To continue our tactic through winter, we would soon have to put apples into storage. We were only a forty-minute drive from Berwick, the official "apple capital" of Nova Scotia, so the fruit was not hard to come by.

"Success," Alex said, placing his backpack inside the

back door of the house. "If we want to call it that."

"No gas though," I reminded him. We had already stocked up two three-hundred-gallon fuel tanks hidden behind our barn. We wanted to top up the car and fill the jerry cans we had just scavenged from the hardware store, but it wasn't worth the risk.

"We'll just have to make do. Right, Miss Norah?" I said, forcing a smile as I wrapped their six-year-old child in my arms. The adults at the farm walked a delicate line between keeping the children informed, while also remitting their fear. With things deteriorating minute by minute, it was difficult enough for the educated and experienced among us to understand. It was hard to imagine what must be going through their young minds. Luckily, there were plenty of chores to go around so idle worries were quickly redirected.

"What shall we have for supper, my girl?" I asked the little blondie, navigating away from the men as they caught each other up on the events in town.

"Eggs!" she said excitedly.

"Again?" I laughed. Currently, eggs were a staple thanks to our layer hens. Every day the Maran Sisters gifted us with enough eggs for breakfast, as well as the occasional supper. I was growing tired of so many egg-centric meals, but the novelty had clearly not worn off for Norah who had only recently moved to the farm. As the days shortened, so too would our supply of fresh eggs. One of today's "successes" at the hardware store was finding slaked lime which I would use to preserve some of the eggs for when the butt nugget babes took their seasonal reprieve.

"Hello, mommas," Norah murmured as she opened the coop door. She gently investigated each nesting box, stretching her tiny hand beneath ruffled feathers in search of her prize. I had taught her to keep her face and eyes well back from ornery beaks, but the hens never seemed perturbed enough to peck her. She also graciously thanked each one, mimicking my own ritual.

The late summer sun shone through the open windows of the coop, turning flecks of dust into sparkles. A light smell of smoke drifted in; someone had started the cooking fire. I could see the silhouettes of the men still standing in the yard with their furrowed brows and heavy conversation. Reliving the day's madness through story was tempting, but I looked away. Instead, I chose to step fully into the magic in the eyes of the little girl in front of me as she stuffed her bounty of smooth brown eggs into both of our pockets.

III

Alex had been living in his camper on our farm for the past six months. He was both a friend and a nurse at the South Shore Hospital. As Sigma cases skyrocketed, he had parked in our field to pre-emptively isolate from his family. Steve and Norah would come by on Alex's days off and have a picnic under the awning while he visited with them through the window. Steve would leave premade meals on the steps of the trailer for Alex to eat before heading back to the emergency department to work overtime. It was tough, but they made it work. By that time, everyone was used to making sacrifices.

When Alex's hospital became an out-of-control hot zone late in the spring, it was forced to shut its doors. There was no longer enough staff to keep it running—many had succumbed to the disease right on the hospital floor still wearing their scrubs. Those who didn't die eventually quit. The front-line war that had been waged for the past five years was conceded. A week later, Alex and Steve approached us about moving their family onto the farm permanently. They had quickly become claustrophobic in their townhouse in Bridgewater since they were all home together, all the time.

Alex was experienced in medicine but also enjoyed gardening and preserving. He had been instrumental in creating a community garden on the grounds of their townhouse complex. Steve was a hobby tinker and an excellent marksman who could provide protection if necessary. Norah, although only six, was a kind and helpful child who had taken an interest in caring for the farm animals. She had a way of reminding everyone to appreciate the tiny miracles of daily living, and in such a dark world that held its own special value. The family planned to live together in their trailer, but they would collaborate with us on things such as procuring food, cutting firewood, building and maintenance, and caring for the livestock. The merger made sense in many ways.

Next to arrive on the farm were Travis and his twin sons. Travis and Will had worked residential construction together until it was no longer safe to enter other people's homes. Travis was one of the hardest working people Will had ever met and, as someone who took pride in his own work ethic, his opinion meant something. Travis had a background in plumbing and heating and also knew how to use a shotgun. Along with his handy skill set, Travis had built up an impressive collection of tools and building supplies he was willing to contribute to our micro-community. Some of the items such as plywood and copper wire hadn't been on store shelves in months.

Travis recently lost his wife and mother of his children, Natasha. In early May, she contracted Sigma in the Long-Term Care Facility where she worked. He hadn't even been given the chance to say goodbye. One afternoon a phone call from an administrative official informed him there was an outbreak at Natasha's facility. There were no known survivors. In just twenty-four hours the devilish new variant had snuck in and murdered everyone—the residents, nurses and care aides, housekeeping, and kitchen staff. Everyone, except for those who had the privilege of working from home. No one was allowed into the LTC to retrieve the bodies of their loved ones—the risk of infection and further community spread was too high.

I've never heard a man cry the way Travis did when he told us the news. Primal. Guttural. Utterly devastated. Padlocks and warning signs were hung on the bolted facility doors, and a guard was hired to patrol the premises. Not long after, a fire mysteriously broke out on the ground floor. The few remaining members of the local volunteer fire departments—Travis included—were instructed by town officials to let the building burn.

Although Travis and Natasha owned a house not far from us, he knew he was going to need workable land to survive, as well as help raising his school aged boys. He never said it, but I think it was also just too hard to be in their home without her. Travis and the boys picked a spot to park their thirty-foot trailer in the field by our woodlot, near Alex and Steve's. We all agreed that one of the first major projects would be to build a barn large enough to house their trailers over winter. Technically, multiple residential dwellings on a single lot were not permitted in Kings' County, but the threat of a stop work order was now laughable.

Will and I were also anticipating the arrival of Jo-Anne, a vibrant, single lady in her seventies. She had been a staple in our lives since we moved to the province. Only two days after we pulled into our driveway for the first time, she had appeared with a basket of treats and home-cooked stew. From behind her mask, and six feet away, she was the first to welcome us to the neighbourhood. Without any family in Atlantic Canada, she took us on as her "kids" and she was our primary point of contact for a long time. We had informed the others that she would likely make her way to the farm if things got too uncomfortable in her own home. She, both stubborn and resilient, didn't want to impose, but we told her that if she decided to join us there would be a room waiting. Alex didn't know Jo as more than an acquaintance and he voiced concerns over her open invitation.

"What about her age? Don't you think she'll be a liability? What will she even be able to contribute? Do you think we have enough resources to support another person?" He peppered me in particular. While I appreciated his bluntness, I also felt defensive. Not only did I love Jo-Anne, but I also still felt the farm belonged to me and Will. Alex's remarks felt like needles piercing my freedom of choice and autonomy. At what point did Alex and his family stop being just guests and transition to equal members of the farm's democratic process? Had they already earned that right? I made a mental note to reexamine the concept of ownership, and its pending obsoletion, at another time.

Luckily, having Jo-Anne at the farm would have very real advantages, childcare being one. She was also a talented forager and had experience with naturopathy. The biggest asset though, in my opinion, was that she was an excellent cook who could make a dry piece of leather palatable. Feeding the people she cared about was her love language and so far, to my great annoyance, kitchen related duties kept being furtively passed off to me. Will and I were typically grazers that would maybe eat one big meal a day, but it had quickly become apparent that three meals were now expected—plus snacks! Thankfully, the kids were usually eager to help me harvest the ingredients, but I found myself becoming a tad resentful toward the other adults. Kitchen attendant was not the role I would have assigned for myself, but when grumbling bellies became grumbling mouths, *somebody* had to do something.

One afternoon in late July, Jo-Anne parked her old gold Taurus at the end of the farm's driveway. We had recently barricaded the entrance with a large pile of logs to prevent vehicles from driving up to the house unannounced. If someone wanted to come by, they would now have to do the last two hundred meters on foot, which gave us more time to determine if they were welcome or not.

When Jo-Anne arrived, Norah and I happened to be on the porch colouring together. We waited patiently for Jo to emerge from her vehicle so I could explain the disinfection protocol we had established, but she didn't get out of the car. I beckoned to her, but there was still no motion.

"That's odd," I said to Norah. "Wait here, ok?" I was about halfway down the driveway when Jo honked at me. I could see her waving her arms from the driver's seat. It was evident she was trying to tell me not to come any closer.

"Are you ok?" I shouted. With the sun beating through the windshield, I couldn't get a clear view of her face, but I thought she looked paler than usual. "Everything alright, Jo?" I asked again, although I could now see that she was writing something. Moments later she held a piece of paper out the window, a limp white flag. It had one word scrawled on it that punched my heart into the pit of my stomach.

SICK.

IV

"Go down to the camp," I shouted to Jo-Anne. "I'll meet you there in a bit." The gold Taurus slowly retreated down the gravel road. Years ago, we had partnered with Nathan, Will's childhood friend and the best man at our wedding, to purchase a small hunting camp a few kilometers away. We planned to turn it into a rustic retreat, envisioning budding writers and recently divorced hippies finding solace in exchange for help on the farm. Nathan lived in Ontario with his long-time girlfriend, but every six months or so he would come to visit us in East Dalhousie for a "workcation." With the project put on hold by the pandemic, the property was now overgrown. The cabin was barely visible nestled among thorny raspberry bushes and aggressive poplar saplings. It had a rudimentary water capture system, a fire pit for cooking, and a rocket stove for heat, along with a comfortable bed and an extensive library of outdated books.

"Norah?" I said, returning to the blissfully unaware child sprawled out in a puddle of sunshine on the porch. "Can you go find Will, please?" Puzzled by the tone of my voice, she looked up hesitantly just as one of the tears I was fighting fell onto my cheek. Abandoning her crayons, she threw her arms around my waist, giving me a quick squeeze before dutifully marching off toward the men who were clearing ground for the new barn.

When Will came up to the house he found me standing at the kitchen table sorting through medical supplies. I was putting together a broad spectrum of medications and equipment I thought might get Jo and I through the next two weeks.

"What's going on? Didn't I see Jo's car pull up?" he asked, placing his hand steadily between my shoulder blades.

"Yes. She's sick. I don't know any details, I just told her to go to the camp." Will eyed the packages of personal protective equipment stacked beside me. In what felt like a very different lifetime, I was a paramedic. I had been transitioning out of my career when COVID hit. A PTSD diagnosis had leaked the air from my tires and, although I was in recovery and able to get back behind the wheel, I knew that the demands of the job were no longer healthy for me. I wanted something different for myself, and for my marriage, so I took my final leave several months into the pandemic. Although I missed some aspects of the job and was thankful for the experience, I had no regrets. Plus, I had been gifted a bunch of expired supplies on the way out the door. Aside from tending to the various cuts and scrapes that farming inflicts, this was the first time I had been called back to duty. My mouth was suddenly dry.

"What's the plan?" Will asked, turning me to face him. I wasn't entirely sure, but I knew I had to do something, and we had been married long enough for Will to know better than to suggest otherwise. Over the next hour we hashed it out together. I would take our old canvas tent, thankful that the nights were still warm enough for camping to be feasible. Alex and I would allot a reasonable portion of the medication for Jo, accounting for the predicted needs of the rest of the group. Will would check in on us every morning and bring down the day's food and firewood. I would go down to care for Jo for two weeks but would adjust the timeline once I knew more about the trajectory of her illness. All that was left to do was to tell the others.

As evening approached, the adults gathered on the porch. Travis's twins, Chris and Ryan, had engaged Norah in a rousing game of soccer on the front lawn. The boys, both twelve years old, were lanky and tall for their age. When they arrived on the farm, we weren't sure if they would have any interest in playing with Norah, but they seemed to have developed a soft spot for her. Despite their borderline trash talk, the boys would let her score every time. Pinching his nose, Ryan transformed into a nasally announcer and gave the audience play-by-play commentary. Even the most reserved adult felt an upward tug on their lips.

I doled out a fresh pot of tea I had made from my herb garden, complete with dandelion honey. Mint was used for a nutrient boost and to help with digestion, and anise hyssop for a licorice twist. I saved some in a thermos to take to Jo later as it was also known as an expectorant, capable of clearing congestion from the lungs. Jo had taught me that herself.

"There's been a development," I began, massaging the fine lines on my forehead. "Jo-Anne is here. Well, not "here"—I sent her down to the camp." Everyone turned to look at me and Will. "She's sick. I'm not sure with what." My words were only met with silent concern, so I continued. "My plan is to go down and look after her." The silence turned to grumbling. I could tell Alex was searching for a worthy dispute to sink his teeth into.

"I knew this was going to be a problem," he said. "She hasn't been here two minutes and is already leeching our resources without any contribution."

"Whoa," I said, frowning. "You see that fencing over there? We got that from Jo-Anne when she downsized."

"Seems like an awful big tradeoff for wire mesh," Alex retorted.

"You interrupted me. See that blonde alpaca? She brought him here when another farmer needed to rehome him, and he's been out there making premium manure for our garden ever since." Alex clenched and unclenched his jaw.

"So, some fencing and some bullshit? Nice. Now it makes sense." He rolled his eyes passive-aggressively.

"*Alpaca*shit," I quipped back, refusing to be railroaded. "Half the books about the local flora and fauna on our bookshelf are from Jo—the knowledge she's shared with us over the years is invaluable. I wouldn't know half the natural remedies I do now if it wasn't for her." Alex shrank back into his seat with a combined look of annoyance and defeat. I softened my voice. "I can appreciate your concern—you're just trying to protect your family. I'm scared too, Alex, but Jo-Anne has been contributing to this farm long before we were even friends. She might not be related to me or Will by blood, but she's the closest thing to family we've got. Imagine this was your grandmother? Would you turn her away just because she hasn't "contributed"?" Alex sighed and shook his head.

"*GOOOOAAALLLL!!!*" Ryan shouted through cupped hands at the emerging moon. Chris hoisted Norah up onto his shoulders and proceeded to race around the yard as she pumped her little fist into the air. Hopping onto the porch, he carried her past the adults as we high-fived our congratulations.

"How long will you be gone?" Steve asked quietly when

they were out of earshot again.

"My best guess is two weeks. We know that's the general timeline for the virus to be contagious if that's what she has. I'll know more when I get down there. Will can update you all after he drops off firewood in the morning."

"Stay safe," Steve said, giving my shoulder a gentle squeeze as he walked by. "I'll tell the kids." He headed off toward the trailers to start Norah's bedtime routine with Ryan and Chris in tow.

"Anything I can do to help?" Travis was the last to speak on the matter. I had always seen Travis as a reincarnation of Smokey Bear—cute and cuddly, but with six-inch claws. He was the sweet and tender father he had never known himself—but could also likely throw a shovel across a lake if he thought it would accomplish something.

"Just try to keep things running as normal as possible up here," I replied. "I'll know more tomorrow. Try not to let the kids worry."

"Don't you worry about us either," he said. "You just focus on getting Jo better. We'll see you when you get back. Might even have a couple barn walls up by then."

"What are you taking for supplies?" Alex asked pointedly, rejoining the conversation.

"I was hoping you could help me put together a medication and IV package. We've already packed the camping supplies. I'm also going to take my dog for protection, and company." Being put in control of a task seemed to lighten Alex's mood a little.

"It will be getting dark soon," he said as he headed into the kitchen. Will sighed, placing his hand over mine. I rested my head on his shoulder.

"It's going to be weird here without you," he said. Between the demands of farm life and the pandemic, it was very rare that we had been more than a stone's throw away from one another over the past five years. Although maintaining space and independence are the keys to some happy marriages, we had discovered that we worked best within arm's reach. I breathed in his earthy scent with an overtone of sweat. "I can't believe it will almost be time to start fall harvest when you get back." We sat there together for a few more minutes as the outline of the moon grew clearer.

"May the odds be in our favor," I said wistfully. I planted a kiss on my husband's stubbled cheek before going to meet Alex at the makeshift pharmacy in our kitchen.

V

The solar motion light above the cabin door announced my arrival, but there was no sound to greet me. I felt a pang of sadness as memories emerged of Nathan, Will, and I clearing trails, having beers around the fire pit, and scheming about the eco-tourism empire we would create. I peered in the window to see Jo sleeping beneath a stack of fleece blankets. I tapped quietly on the glass, not wanting to startle her. She slowly propped herself up on one elbow.

"How ya feeling, Jo?" I called, smiling at her familiar face. Familiar, but also pale and dull with darkness beneath her eyes.

"Old," she replied, followed by a raking fit of coughing. Her hands trembled as she searched for a mug on the bedside dresser. She gasped for air between sips.

"We'll get you sorted out," I reassured her as she sank back onto her pillow. Will was getting a fire started so he wouldn't have to set up my tent by moonlight. I got busy preparing a decontamination station on the picnic table outside the cabin door.

Sanitizer.
Wipes.
Garbage bags and can.
A spray bottle of medical grade alcohol.
Soap.
A basin of water.

I also lined up the various medications and medical supplies I might need, then I methodically donned my personal protective equipment.

Booties.

Gown.

Scrub cap.

Respirator.

Face shield.

Gloves.

I wouldn't have the luxury of using the single-use PPE items as intended. I had taken three kits, leaving the last three at the farm in case they were needed. I planned to cycle through each kit, drenching them in seventy percent alcohol and then isolating them to dry between uses.

"I'll see you in the morning!" I called and waved across the yard at Will.

"I'll see you in the morning," he echoed. "I'll tie Remmi up beside the tent before I go. Be safe, ok?" I nodded, blowing him a kiss.

As I entered the cabin, I left everything outside except the tea, Tylenol, tissues, and a mixture of eucalyptus and coconut oil, so nothing would be unnecessarily contaminated before I knew what I was dealing with. The cabin itself was only one room hosting a double bed, a dresser, a rocking chair, stool, and a well-worn library. I set the items I brought on the dresser and placed a gloved hand on Jo's cool forehead. I hoped that she couldn't feel me shaking.

"When did it start?" I asked.

"Five days," she wheezed. She was in bad shape, each word visibly draining her.

"Were you in contact with anyone?" Jo nodded.

"Karl brought me a chicken. He's gone now." Karl was

Jo-Anne's neighbour. He was also elderly and widowed, and although no romance was shared between them, they had always looked out for one another. When I asked her about it one time, Jo-Anne said the dealbreaker was Karl's incessant smoking. I didn't blame her; I couldn't even picture him without a hand-rolled smoke pinched in the corner of his mouth.

"Karl's gone?" I pressed, not wanting to fatigue her but also needing the information.

"Went looking for his daughter. In New Brunswick," she squeaked, followed by another long fit of coughing. It sounded wet. Handing her a tissue, I encouraged her to spit out anything she brought up. Steam wafted from the thermos when she could finally hold it up to her lips.

"Mmm," she sighed gratefully, her chest rattling.

"Can you smell and taste the tea?" I asked her.

"Yes, I can. Thank you," she crackled, laying back down. *Good,* I thought to myself, scratching symptoms off my mental COVID screening checklist. I rubbed some of the eucalyptus and coconut oil mixture on her upper chest. Eucalyptus, one of the best multipurpose essential oils, would help relieve her pain and reduce inflammation. Jo also taught me that it promotes circulation in the respiratory system while inhibiting hypersecretion. As she began to relax, I felt for the pulse at her wrist. It was weak and fast, but present. A palpable radial pulse also suggested that her blood pressure was above eighty systolic, a good sign, but when I pinched the skin on the back of her hand, it was slow to return to normal. Her gums looked dry too.

"I think you're dehydrated," I told her. "I'll need to start an IV." Jo nodded her consent. She likely hadn't been getting enough fluids between the coughing, and fatigue, and no one to care for her. I wondered how she even managed to drive to the farm. *At least there weren't many vehicles on the roads these days,* I thought, ironically.

I continued my assessment on the tiny, white haired treasure in front of me. Her ordinarily plump cheeks looked flat and drawn. She usually kept her hair short, but I had to brush back her bangs to get a look at her pupils. They reacted normally to my exam. There was more good news—no sign of discolouration on her fingers or toes. Jo also confirmed that she hadn't been vomiting or had diarrhea. Her pain was generalized aching accompanied by a sharp twinge between her lower right ribs when she coughed. When I investigated the tissue that she had been coughing into, I found thick greenish-yellow sputum. I was beginning to feel confident that whatever was going on had a bacterial component. That didn't mean she wasn't carrying Sigma or some other vintage variant—it could very well have been the catalyst for a secondary bacterial infection taking advantage of her weakened immune system.

But there was hope.

"I'll be back in a few minutes," I told Jo as I pulled the blankets back up to her chin.

Outside in the cool night air I organized my thoughts. My working diagnosis was bacterial bronchitis, possibly brought on by her visit with Karl and his chain of cigarettes. At this point, antibiotics and intravenous therapy were a reasonably aggressive course of treatment, considering Jo's age and the fact we were cut off from any formal health care system. I removed my gloves and sanitized my hands before carefully picking out a litre of normal saline, IV supplies, and five days' worth of Azithromycin. As I turned to go back in the cabin, Remmi whimpered impatiently

from where she lay tied beside the tent.
"Not much longer, Remmington," I reassured her.

VI

I woke the next morning to Remmi—who had been my soft black pillow just moments before—barking at something outside the tent. Will's shadow was illuminated by the early morning sun.

"Good morning," he said softly, placing a thermos of hot coffee in the dirt by the tent door. Not a morning person, I grunted at him in appreciation. We were rationing the last bag of beans at the farm. Coffee was not part of the local supply chain and had quickly disappeared off store shelves. Luckily, I had planted coffee chicory last season. The root could be roasted, ground, and brewed for a coffee flavored beverage, although unfortunately without the caffeine kick. So, just like New Orleanians during the civil war, we had started mixing the root with our real coffee beans to stretch them out.

I got dressed in the tent as Will went to start a cooking fire for me and Jo. He dropped off a bundle of wood to get us through the rest of the day, along with some canned food in a reused feed sack. Remmi looked confused when I tied her to the nearby tree again, preventing her from going to greet Will. She whined her displeasure. Throughout the pandemic we learned that all kinds of animals could contract COVID-19 but, so far, there was no documentation of dogs transmitting it. Before the deer, there were only a few cases of mink having spread mild cases of infection to humans. We had decided to isolate Remmi along with me, just to be safe.

"What's the verdict?" Will asked in a hushed voice from across the yard, as not to disturb Jo. He stirred a pot of porridge for us to share. It was a sight I could get used to.

"I think she has a chest infection, and she was a bit dehydrated. She came down with it after visiting with Karl. I'm hoping, *hoping*, it's just bacterial. Whether or not she responds to the treatment over the next few days will give me more info to work with."

"Friggin' Karl," he replied, rolling his sandy blue eyes.

"Ya, friggin' Karl. Anyway, she's been sick for six days so we should be in the clear in about eight more. That is, if she isn't symptomatic and if everyone is on board with that timeline of course." Alex flashed across my mind. At this point any hostile contagion, not just COVID, could jeopardize the farm's micro-community and limited stock of medications. If the virus taught us anything, it was the fragility of the elaborate welfare systems that had normalized triple digit birthday cards in the first world. Prior to things like manufactured medication, commercial agriculture, and social security programs, people were lucky to see past their twenties. This phase of the pandemic was like a giant reset button had been pushed, and the survivors were just ticking time bombs, especially with the degradation of traditional survival skills. Will and I agreed to play the farm's self-imposed isolation parameters by ear.

"I actually had an idea." I changed the subject. "You know that old cast iron tub we always meant to do something with?" Will nodded. "Well, I think it's time we did." He agreed to get someone to help him bring it down the next morning, along with extra firewood, much to my delight. I wanted to give him a hug so badly but resigned myself to blowing a kiss. This husband of mine had been going along with my crazy ideas ever since we met. I missed him the moment he went back to the farm to start his own day. The men were hoping to start digging in posts for the new pole barn by the afternoon.

Before turning my attention to Jo, I gave Remmi her breakfast. She was accustomed to eating raw dog food, thankfully. With only one processed pet food plant in Nova Scotia, it had also quickly gone the way of the coffee bean. Feeding the dogs and cats raw food simply meant we had to keep more fowl. We also supplemented with veggies, not because their diet required it but because the dogs liked them. They could regularly be found helping themselves in the garden. I always had to keep an eye on the first snap peas of the year or Remmi would eat the whole crop herself, right off the vine. When she was finished eating, I put out a blanket for her under the big yellow birch beside our tent. I pressed my forehead against hers, thanked her for her companionship, and reminded her to stand guard.

"How are ya today, Jo?" I asked as I entered the cabin in my new set of PPE.

"A little better," she croaked out a lie. I put down the porridge Will had warmed over the fire and checked her pulse. *A little stronger, but still fast.* I pinched the nail on her pointer finger and circulation bounced back to the blanched area in about two seconds. *Promising.* I didn't need a stethoscope to listen to her chest—it sounded like she was breathing through a soggy pile of garbage.

"You've gotta try to cough that out," I gently scolded her to which she nodded, her white hair falling across her face. I was concerned about her lack of energy. It was hard for her to eat more than a half spoonful of porridge before coming up for air. It occurred to me to try something I had read about a long time ago called "pulmonary toileting." I think the concept stuck with me because of its weird name. As an ex-paramedic, emergency care was my specialty, whereas definitive care was left to other professionals. The technique would be outside my formal skill set.

After her pitiful breakfast, antibiotics, an IV infusion, and another eucalyptus rub, I asked Jo if I could try moving her into a couple of positions. She told me she trusted me completely, and I was immediately reminded of the weight that carried. From what we knew, we were probably all she had left. I couldn't remember the postures exactly, but it seemed intuitive. What I also couldn't remember, which bothered me significantly more, were the risks.

For our first attempt at pulmonary toileting, I tried sitting her forward and clapped my cupped hand lightly on her back. We would pause when the coughing shook her body so hard that she started to gag. I grabbed the cabin's garbage pail and asked her to let whatever came up drain into it. Bile accompanied thick green mucus. I felt like we might be getting somewhere so I tried moving her into a prone position, face down, with pillows under her legs to get a better tilt. Jo's arms flailed like a panicked swimmer, so we aborted as I apologized profusely. I felt bad for causing her distress, despite her reassurances that she was no worse for wear. It did leave her in need of a nap though, so I left her semi-reclined, face up. I was ready for a break too.

As I opened the cabin door, I could hear Remmi's low growl coming from beneath the tree where she was tied. Her hackles were fully raised, sharp black blades among the morning shadows. I stopped in my tracks and tried to follow her pointed gaze. Whatever it was, it was around the back of the cabin, out of my line of sight.

Well, shit. Pleeease don't be a bear!

The unwashed pot from this morning's porridge sat guiltily beside the fire pit, a symptom of my distraction. Pretending I forgot something back in the cabin, I unsheathed the hunting knife that we kept on the window ledge. I didn't want to cause Jo any more undue stress—Remmi felt the same way about raccoons as she did about bears. Regardless, I wasn't about to let my favorite dog take on a fight by herself—it was part of our unspoken pact.

I tried to steady my breath as I approached the corner of the building. Remmi's growling intensified. Twigs snapped ominously. As I peered around the corner, I wondered if anyone at the farm would be able to hear me screaming. Remmi's vocalizations turned to excited yips as a great set of antlers rose from the brambles. Tawny hide flowed over the animal's throat and chest muscles. Its dark eyes were piercing with inquisitiveness. It was the Great Prince of the Forest, come to graze. The flood of relief I felt subsided as quickly as it came.

"Get out of here!" I roared unnecessarily. Remmi had already scared the buck back the way it came. Two flicks of its white tail and it had vanished. "Good girl, Remmi! Good girl!" I clapped, jumping up and down, encouraging her barking. I normally reinforced her desired behavior with treats or pats, but I still needed to decontaminate.

I suddenly caught a glimpse of myself in the reflection of the cabin window. My blue surgical gown flapped around me, and my face shield was starting to fog up. My long brown hair hadn't seen a hairdresser in over three years and poked out haphazardly from beneath my scrub cap. My respirator looked especially ridiculous, alien even, in the middle of the Acadian Forest. If someone had tried to tell me in 2018 where I would be on this day, I would have questioned their sanity—if that same person saw me today, I am certain they would be questioning mine.

I poked my head in to let Jo-Anne know what had happened. She cracked a half smile before falling back asleep. Then, after deconning, I took Remmi out for a walk as a reward and to look for bait apples—but not before I did the dishes.

VII

Using our compact tractor and a complex system of ratchet straps, Will brought down the old cast iron tub the next afternoon.

"What did you say you wanted this for again?" he asked, shutting down the machine.

"I didn't," I replied with a grin, wiping my dirty hands on my jeans. After tending to Jo, I had spent the morning cleaning out the old herb garden I planted back when we had very different plans for the cabin. Now barricaded by ferocious cane berries, it would be easily overlooked if a person didn't know it was there. With a little sweat, perseverance, and a bunch of angry welts, I had given light to lavender, mint, lemon balm, thyme, oregano, chamomile, and rhubarb. Despite the overgrowth, the hearty perennials had done fairly well left to their own devices.

Will spoke with a slightly furrowed brow. "Just so you know, Alex and Steve weren't happy about me bringing it down here."

"Weren't happy about it? Why would they even care?" I was flabbergasted.

"They think you're wasting gas," he shrugged. "And time." There it was again, the ever-prickly issue of personal ownership. I wanted to remind them it was *our* tractor, and *our* gas, and *our* time—but I hesitated. The approach felt wrong—a sharp fragment of the ultra-independence that western culture hung its hat on. I knew things were going to get more difficult, much more difficult, as the months went on. A committed community with a wealth of skills and knowledge was our best chance of survival. That meant individual interests and pursuits would, as a necessity, be secondary to the needs of the group.

"What do *you* think?" I asked the tall, rugged husband of mine standing across from me in the yard. "Honestly."

"You know I back you one hundred percent, my dear. It's always been you and me, and it will always be you and me, until the end." He motioned if it was ok to start unhooking the straps. I nodded.

"What about Travis?" I pressed, hoping for a majority rule.

Will chuckled, "Who do you think helped me get this thing loaded?"

Friggin' right.

"But seriously, what did you want this chunk of iron for?" he asked. The tub had come to rest haphazardly near the fire pit, which was perfect.

"A redneck hot tub," I told him, without a hint of comedy. Will burst out laughing anyway.

"Oh boy, maybe we should come up with something different to tell Alex. If he thinks you're down here hot tubbing..." He trailed off as I shook my head vigorously, fiery sparks igniting in my veins.

"You know what? Screw him! If Alex has a problem with it, he can come down here and tell me to my face. It's not even for me. It's for Jo." I explained to him the difficulty I was having managing the congestion in her lungs. She still couldn't say more than a couple of words at a time before the effort exhausted her. The steam from a hot bath should help get things moving. I also pointed out that if Alex, or

Steve, or any of us, ever got sick, then maybe the time and effort I was "wasting" would be better appreciated.

"Jo's also a little, you know, *ripe*," I mouthed to him, waving my hand under my nose. I doubted she'd been able to have a shower or bath since falling ill, perhaps even longer with the power having gone out. I knew her house didn't have a water source in proximity like we did with the spring fed pond at the farm, or a passive rain capture system like we had at the cabin. Beyond the fact that having a bath would simply make Jo feel better, it was also an important way to keep other hygiene issues from weakening her further. The last thing she needed was an opportunistic yeast infection, or something more menacing like C-diff. I was worried that another layer of infection would be too much for her.

"I'll explain it to them," Will said, holding love in his eyes for me. "I wish I could help. I miss you. Yes, *and* you," he said to Remmi who hadn't stopped staring at him since he arrived. She sighed and put her head on her paws, resigned to her own strange new isolation routine.

Changing subjects, Will filled me in on the slow progress on the RV barn. I figured he would be ready to pull his hair out, and he was. He was working with a mixture of reclaimed and freshly sawn wood, plus two inexperienced carpenters—Alex and Steve—on his crew. But, despite the frustration, he and Travis had managed to get the frame of the structure halfway to completion. I was also happy to hear that they were all impressed with Travis's boys who were keeping Norah occupied—or perhaps it was her keeping them occupied. The little girl had been my unofficial sidekick since moving to the farm and I missed my little shadow.

"How many more days?" Will asked rhetorically as he

fired the tractor back up. I held up seven fingers above my head and then made them into a heart for him.

The threat of climate change had been the original catalyst for our move to the farm and our survivalist lifestyle. We chose Nova Scotia because of its long growing season (for Canada), and cheap real estate. It meant we had enough time and money left over to devote to becoming more self-sufficient outside the demands of the middle-class grind. Having "come from away", we quickly discovered that the changes brought on by global warming were magnified on the coast. Hurricanes were more frequent and intense and were often happening outside their regular season. Last winter, snow had been on the ground for a total of five days, which might sound nice if it wasn't accompanied by incessant one hundred kilometer per hour winds. When the pandemic began to create supply chain issues beyond toilet paper and Rice Krispies, we were already starting to buckle down on bushcraft education, sustainable resource acquisition, and long-term survival planning such as permaculture. That was how I came to learn about redneck hot tubs, of course.

The concept was simple in theory but significantly more arduous in practice, like many things worth doing—writing a book, starting a business, or raising a child, for example. The foundation and platform for the tub would consist of large rocks, which first had to be collected and carefully assembled. I reminisced on all the stones I had cursed while picking them from our farm's field, as I now cursed these stones for being so sparse and out of reach. I was most certainly a difficult woman. After a couple of hours of work, I was mostly satisfied with my creation, a kind of hollow rock pyre. My next task was to drag the cast iron tub into its elevated position. It nearly did me in, despite the muscular physique I had developed over the past few years of physical labour. The thought of Alex chastising me for wasting time and resources was the final motivation I needed to make it to the top.

Afterward, I sat in the shade with Remmi for a few minutes. She was clearly laughing at me inside her dog brain, but also very content licking the salt from my sweaty skin. I groaned realizing I still had to get water into the tub and start the fire beneath it. *Whose idea was this anyway?* Thankfully, there was a length of hose hanging beside the barrels that were constantly replenished from the cabin's eaves when it rained. When the water was brought up to hot tub temperature and the fire had settled down, I added the herbs I had collected from the garden. I reveled in the aromatic steam washing over my face. Lavender to relieve congestion and reduce inflammation, chamomile to calm the mind and promote rest. I was a little jealous that I wouldn't be the first to try out my contraption, but I knew the look on Jo's face would be worth it.

VIII

As Jo regained her strength, she was eventually able to hold more than a few words of conversation. I was relieved the day she said she thought she could make it to the outhouse without support. My interventions appeared to be working as the light returned to her eyes and pink returned to her cheeks. By the sixth day at the cabin, she felt well enough to sit in a lawn chair in the shade and watch as I hung hand-washed laundry out on the line. It turned out that the redneck hot tub was multipurpose. We were having a wet fall and a storm had replenished the water capture system yesterday. I had used the tub to wash our clothes after Jo had her daily soak.

"The breeze feels good," Jo said with a content smile on her face. "All I need is a glass of wine, and the day would be almost perfect." I wondered if there was a word to describe that emotion—having a wonderful time in the middle of the mass extinction of your species. We had spent the morning discussing the last pieces of news we heard before the black outs gradually evolved from intermittent in May, to permanent in June.

Initially the areas hardest hit by COVID were, as usual, the poorest. Without access to reliable media, let alone public health, some communities were wiped out before they even knew what struck them. The Sigma outbreak had begun in Romeo, then spread to Chama, before exploding across Colorado. Aerial footage had been leaked of roads littered with bodies, and no one left alive to bury them. Lockdowns were swiftly put in place but, with an American president who had a clandestine dedication to business as usual, it was only a matter of time before a businessperson carried Sigma to South Africa.

The week we heard of the first cases identified in Canada was the same week the Happy Valley slum was bombed into oblivion. The democratically elected South African government had suffered a monstrous coup by far-right militants. On television the self-appointed "leaders" declared that their weaponized actions were heroic—a desperate attempt to save the more affluent residents of Cape Town. Their heinous act was a distorted echo of the Defenders at the Halifax protest—we were no different than animals. As a fact. As an atrocity. As a marvel. And the bombing was, of course, futile.

Despite being next door to ground zero, Canadians received a smidgen of lead time over Sigma thanks to the heavy-handed governance of interim Prime Minister Roy Bluehorn. In a surprising show of force, he had fully deployed the military to police Canada's borders by air, sea, and land. Impassioned by his Plains Cree bloodline, Bluehorn's words rang clear across the country: "Canada is closed." No one was allowed in or out of the country under the threat of immediate detainment or, if met with resistance, lethal force. As the American endorsed deer cull amplified, tension mounted at the border and fatal skirmishes became a daily occurrence. Jo-Anne, coming from a military family, said that hearing the full callout was the most scared she had ever felt.

Canada was not the only country to find themselves on the eve of civil war—devastating conflicts erupted across the globe as blame, misinformation, and fear permeated civilization. Some outlier religious communities took fate into their own hands and began hosting suicide parties to escape the devil, otherwise named Sigma. I didn't tell Jo about the Youtube videos that circulated showing children and livestock being sacrificed to atone for the sins that brought the virus to the world.

In true form, the reaction of rural Nova Scotia was a little quieter. Residents were asked, originally, to remain in their home communities except for essentials such as groceries. With most businesses closed and many shelves empty, there was not much incentive to go anywhere anyway. Even if there was, provincial gas regulations had been abandoned and fuel quickly rose to over fifteen dollars a litre.

On May 22nd, days after I attended the Halifax rally, Nova Scotians received a forty-eight-hour notice to remain on their own properties and within their own homes for the foreseeable future. With the quiet disbandment of local government and police forces, the notice was more of a suggestion that appealed to Nova Scotians' deep sense of duty to the common good. Of course, not everyone was on board and reports of neighbourhood militias, looting, and citizen-led trials were the last sprinkles of local news we'd heard. Humanity at its finest.

Our conversation had hung heavily in the air. After so many years of traumatic daily news, case counts, and conversations dominated by the virus, the information blackout had bizarrely offered a reprieve. Although no news in this case was not good news, it was still more soothing to the nervous system than the incessant bombardment of terror. Jo's only wish was that she knew how her children and grandchildren were doing in Alberta.

Although I was not close to my family, divided by opposing philosophies and priorities, I often wondered about them too.

After getting Jo settled back in the cabin for an afternoon snooze, I took Remmi for a walk. Our earlier conversation had made me anxious and that had a way of spiraling into paranoia, depression, and anger. Through my mental health journey, I learned that finding my way back to baseline as soon as possible was the best prevention. There was no magic wand to wave, although Health Canada's regulated potions had been helpful on occasion. Commanding the driver's seat in my own brain took deliberate, consistent practice. Peace, quiet, natural beauty, and gentle exercise with someone who loved me was usually what the doctor ordered—bonus points if they liked belly rubs and kisses on the snout. It sounds simple but, as anyone who has suffered knows, just picking up the dog's leash can be an impossible task somedays.

Remmi and I hadn't seen the buck, or any large wildlife for that matter, since we started baiting a kilometer or so away from the cabin. Birdsong and the chattering of squirrels were the only things to greet us as we swam our way through the forest. I had an idea where I might find a patch of late berries, and I was hoping there might be enough for a small batch of wine to surprise Jo with one day.

IX

On our ninth day at the cabin, I believed Jo was well enough for us to return to the farm. Thinking back to the days when Rapid Tests were given out by the handful at every local library and health centre, I couldn't help but feel a twinge of anxiety returning without a negative result. Between hoarding and misuse, the supply of self-tests had quickly disappeared. I knew I would never forgive myself if I was the decision maker who got someone else sick. Or killed. After fully sanitizing the cabin yesterday, Remmi and I had spent the night on the floor, sans PPE. It had been unseasonably chilly and since we had now passed the two-week mark since Jo's symptoms began, I decided to be my own guinea pig. When I woke up I felt great, aside from a stiff back.

I told Will in the morning that we planned to come back early afternoon. If anyone had any misgivings or apprehension, he would come back and tell us. So far there had been no word. Jo and I busied ourselves getting the cabin tidied up and we harvested herbs and rhubarb from the garden to take back. After repacking the sterilized PPE and unused medical supplies, I took Remmi on an extra-brisk walk in the woods to calm my nerves. I was excited to see everyone, I just hoped we received a warm welcome.

Remmi, Jo, and I piled into her Taurus. I finally got an up-close look at the things Jo had packed for herself during her illness. Among the stacks of sweaters and t-shirts there was a crockpot, snowshoes, a large oriental fan, a bag of yarn, canned food, and an empty cat carrier.

"Oh no, Jo!" I said as something suddenly occurred to me. Jo had a habit of feeding feral cats. She couldn't help herself—it simply wasn't in her heart not to put something out for them to eat. Without the funds to get them fixed, her habit was known in the community for having taken on a life of its own. Once in a while, a cat would warm up to her enough for her to lure it into her home. Most nights at least one or two could be found begrudgingly sleeping in her basement. She'd let them out in the morning to join their umpteen brothers and sisters.

"Oh, don't worry," Jo said, patting my hand. "I had Sam in there, you know, the scruffy tabby? But he cried so pitifully on the way to the car I let him go. I just didn't have the energy to put the carrier back in the house."

"Whew!" I replied. "I'm sure he'll be just as happy fending for himself with the others," I reassured her, noticing the wrinkle of concern on her forehead. Will and I didn't really endorse her crazy-cat-lady-routine, but it seemed to give her a sense of purpose. We were also certain that Karl, her farmer friend across the road, never lost any of his feed to mice.

We parked in front of the log barricade at the entrance to the farm. I explained the sanitation protocol we had established as I dug the ammo box out of the culvert.

"You guys think of everything, don't you?" Jo said fondly. I smiled, trying to fend off my impending sense of dread. No one had even come to the front porch to greet us. In fact, the whole farm was quiet. *Where is everyone?* I wondered. *Maybe they didn't want us back after all. But then, where was Will?*

"They must be working back in the woods," I told Jo with thinly veiled panic.

"I can't wait to meet everyone," Jo replied. "Especially the kids. It's always nice to have their youthful energy and enthusiasm around." I nodded, scanning the front garden for any signs of life. After being wiped down, Remmi ran off in the direction of the alpaca pasture to find her two packmates.

As we approached the house, a soft strum of guitar strings could be heard. Will and I had a small solar radio we had purchased for backcountry camping—someone must have left it on. Just then Norah opened the kitchen door shouting, "*Wait!* You have to get changed first!" She grabbed both my and Jo-Anne's hands. I tried to explain to her that I already washed our clothes at the cabin and that we were clean, but she insisted. Jo laughed with delight as the six-year-old pulled us through the door with all her might.

"Nice to see you too," I said, bending down to give her a hug. Her little body was vibrating with excitement.

"I picked out your clothes," she informed us, pointing at the kitchen counter. I noticed that the harvest table usually occupying the middle of the room was missing.

"What's going on, Norah? Where is everyone?" I asked her. She crossed her arms, an insolent pout on her lips. "Alright," I shrugged, agreeing to play along. On the counter were two neatly folded outfits. I recognized the dress I wore to my engagement party ten, no, eleven years ago. Tears threatened as I held the material against me. It still smelled like the Tru Earth laundry detergent I used to use.

"But how..." Jo trailed off, picking up a tailored pantsuit I vaguely remembered her wearing one Christmas. Norah shrugged, giggling as she ran from the room. Jo and I shared a look of bewildered amusement. After changing, Jo smoothed the front of her suit with her hands.

"You know what?" she chuckled. "I wouldn't recommend getting sick as a weight loss solution, but I didn't think this fit anymore!"

"You look beautiful." I squeezed her hand. "And I'm so glad you're ok." My voice cracked.

"Take a lot more than bronchitis to kill this old bird," she said, squeezing back. Just then the kitchen door opened, and the twins walked in. They each wore buttoned up shirts and dress pants that hadn't quite kept up with their growing adolescent bodies. They held out bouquets of wildflowers. Unable to contain myself any longer, I burst into tears.

"Seriously, what is going on?" I sobbed, holding onto both boys at once. "Nobody died, right?" Laughing they shook their heads, neither betraying the aura of mystery. "Alright then," I relaxed my shoulders and patted my face dry with a dishtowel. "Keep your secrets."

Ryan extended me his elbow, as Chris did for Jo. Taking the cue from our adorable escorts, we followed the boys out of the house toward the newly erected barn. My husband had done it again. His industriousness was one of the reasons I had chosen him as my life partner. When it came to construction, I was the dreamer and the designer, and he was the doer—yin and yang. Most days.

The sound of music increased as we reached the door. Inside, Will, Travis, and Alex stood behind a buffet table draped in my bright white linen, overflowing with delicious looking dishes. Steve was playing his classical guitar, standing at the head of the beautifully set kitchen table.

"Ok, did *I* die then?" I whispered to Ryan, who laughed.

"No, we just missed you," he replied, leading me to the buffet.

"Rooster or ham?" my husband asked, a mischievous twinkle in his eye. He was wearing the suit from our wedding, looking just as good as the day I married him.

"Both, please," I said, leaning over to kiss him long enough for the kids to start making faces of disgust. The men proceeded to fill our plates. There were salads overflowing with crisp slices of cucumbers and sweet peppers from the hoop house, accompanied by homemade oil and vinegar dressings. There was soup made with butternut squash which must have just ripened, and toasted pumpkin seeds to top it. There were steamed beans, mashed potatoes, and fresh bread. When we couldn't fit a single thing more on our plates, the boys accompanied us to our seats and pulled our chairs out for us.

Our best dishes had been brought from the house, and the space was wonderfully lit by candles. Flower arrangements, matching our bouquets from the boys, dotted the table and standing in the middle was one bottle of wine and one bottle of whiskey. When we were all seated, Alex rapped his knife against his wine glass and cleared his throat.

"Times are tough," he began, looking at me directly. "It would be easy to let fear get the best of us, to divide us, like we watched unfold in so many parts of the world. It might seem easier at times to turn inward, to barricade our families, to cut away our friendships, to remove ourselves from any differences of opinion. But that is not a world I want to live in because that is not a way of life that inspires *living*—and we are going to need a lot of inspiration in the months to come. I realize now that if we are to survive, we must be gracious in holding space for each other. More than that, we have to find reasons to be thankful and to celebrate. We have to remember to use the good china from time to time, because tomorrow is not guaranteed. Perhaps one day, with the right combination of hard work, love, and sense of purpose, we will do more than survive. We will *thrive*." He uncorked the bottle of wine and stood to pour each of us a small glass. Even the kids received a thimble's worth in their cups. Norah sniffed hers before making a face and promptly handing it back, stirring amused smiles among the adults.

"I want to apologize to you, Vanessa, for not being as kind as you deserve." Putting my hand on my heart, I nodded my acceptance. Alex then turned to Jo. "And I'd like to formally welcome Jo to the community here on the farm. I look forward to getting to know you more. Will and Vanessa have only had wonderful things to say about you and it sounds like you will be an asset to this bunch of misfits."

"May we thrive," said Jo, lifting her wine. Glasses clinked as we all raised a toast. Ryan pressed play on the solar radio and songs from Will and my wedding album spilled out. Under the table, Will stroked the back of my hand with his thumb.

"Was this your idea?" I whispered to him. He shook his head, nodding in the direction of Alex. "And Jo's suit?"

"He thought of that too," Will whispered back. "He took the boys on a bike ride to her place to find something. Did you know she left the basement door open for the cats?" I stifled a grimace.

After fully stuffing ourselves and cleaning up just enough to prevent attracting wildlife, the party moved outside. Alex and Steve started a bonfire and the kids danced to music of their own choosing from their now obsolete phones. The adults shared funny stories, childhood memories, and covertly dirty jokes, while passing the bottle of whiskey between us. When a rousing spinoff of "We Are Family" by Alvin and the Chipmunks began to play over the speakers, Alex boosted Norah onto his shoulders. She roared with laughter as he masterfully delivered infamous moves such as the "Shopping Cart" and the "Sprinkler."

"I love *partiessss!*" she squealed, her tiny hands wrapped tightly beneath her father's chin. It dawned on me that this might be the first party in Norah's remembered history. Her surrogate mother had only given birth to her a year before the pandemic began, and Alex and Steve had been very explicit in their family's isolation since. As if reading my thoughts, Alex winked at me, and I realized that the celebration was about much more than just my and Jo's return from the cabin.

After the kids went to bed, Travis produced a baggy with individually rolled joints for each of us. I watched the sparks from the fire float up into the night sky, and I was awed by the twinkling masterpiece above us. Without any light pollution, the stars were truly as bright as they had ever been.

X

The end of summer went by fast and slow all at once. With the camper trailers moved into the new barn, attention was turned to harvest, seed collection, and winter storage. Although I got a few late succession plantings in the ground, the looming winter season made me nervous. It was the first time there would be no trips to the grocery store, and our little acreage wouldn't be sustaining just Will and me. There were ten of us now on the newly designated "Misfit Farm", including three growing children, plus various livestock who also required feeding. Both a blessing and a curse, our Berkshire sow had farrowed eight healthy piglets in the spring. Having quickly run out of pellets from the feed store, we extended their pasture into the forest so they could forage naturally, and I supplemented whatever I could from the garden. Caring for the piglets was a chore the kids were delighted to take on, even teaching them how to sit, stay, spin, and shake hooves. But when their food sources dried up in the winter, we'd harvest them. It wasn't something any of us looked forward to.

In late September I had two pivotal ideas—both would increase our food production, and both involved thievery. One night as the adults sat around the kitchen table after supper, I pitched my first proposal—another recon mission. In agreement, Steve pointed out that we should try to find anything we thought we might need before the snow fell, and not just because there would be no plows to clear the roads.

"If there are other survivors," he started, "some of them are probably about to have a very difficult winter if they aren't properly prepared. Desperate people do desperate things, and if they were able to follow our tracks in the snow back here..." He trailed off. He wasn't wrong, but what he was suggesting made my stomach churn. The virus was one monster but trying to survive a Canadian winter off-grid was quite another.

We started putting together a wish list, fuel being at the top. At the moment, the farm's fuel tanks were still over half full as our consumption had been cautious. It was mostly used for the portable sawmill, compact tractor, chainsaws, and the generator to power the oven on special occasions. We would also need to use the generator to run the well pump over the winter. An ice-free hole in the pond was always a backup option as a water source, but my second idea would work a whole lot better if I had running water. Plus, the luxury of on-demand water simplified so many things like cooking, hygiene, and livestock husbandry—not to mention its positive impact on psychology. Of all the factors related to endurance, a person's mind most impacts their chance of survival.

My second idea also required us to find as many double paned windows as we could salvage—I wanted to try to build a winter greenhouse. I had investigated extending the growing season with unheated structures before, such as our hoop house and various cold frames. It worked in that it prevented cold tolerant crops from dying, but growth was stunted until longer daylight hours and above freezing temperatures returned. I hadn't tried supplementing light and heat because the cost of proper infrastructure and hydro was prohibitive, but I figured there was no time like the present to experiment.

The additional lighting I had in mind wouldn't require fuel thanks to my—somewhat extremist—solar light collection. Any given time of the year, our property was lit up like a fairy rave. Strings of lights and lanterns dripped from trees and fence posts. The solar-lit figures of bees, chameleons, and flamingos were scattered throughout the gardens. It wasn't by design—it's like when somebody's aunt overhears that they like chickens and suddenly everything they get for Christmas is covered in cocks until the end of time. I had been crowned the solar light lady of the family. I wasn't sure what the sum of lumens would work out to, or if my idea would even work at all, but I imagined moving them all inside one greenhouse would be pretty bright.

With the light issue theoretically addressed, the last piece to obtain was a heat source and there was an old wood stove behind the alpaca barn waiting for reassignment. I reminded everyone at the table that, to keep the plants from freezing, we would have to take turns keeping the fire stoked overnight. Travis thought his boys might enjoy that job, especially if we set them up with hammocks and a promise that they wouldn't have to wash dishes for the winter. We decided we could all live with that arrangement. With the right combination of light, water, oxygen, fertile soil, and commitment, we might have fresh greens over the winter. As the other avid gardener in the group, Alex seemed even more enthusiastic about the project than me.

With my requests added to the recon list, we delved into what else to keep a lookout for and what might be needed to obtain it.

Canned food.

Flour. A flour mill? Where would we find one?

Salt. Sugar. Vinegar. Canning jars.

Goats, sheep, or cows for dairy? When Travis pointed out the hilarity of putting entire live animals on what was essentially a grocery list, I no longer doubted if we were a "real" farm and not just something Will and I had been playing at.

More ammo.

Batteries.

More medical supplies? Vet supplies.

Water treatment chemicals in case the well went bad. A hand pump for the well.

Clothes, and especially boots, to fit the kids as they grew.

Pig and poultry feed.

More hay. We'd need the hay trailer. Wheat and hay seed for the spring.

Tools to remove the windows for the greenhouse.

A hose to siphon fuel from abandoned vehicles.

And a loaded gun, just in case.

A route was planned with key stops at a veterinary office on the outskirts of Bridgewater and any previously operational farms along the way. It was decided that Steve, Travis, and Will would complete the mission the next day while the rest of us stayed put. The merits of going out during the day versus the night were carefully weighed. Although the darkness would hide their movements on private property, the vehicles' headlights would draw attention as they travelled the highway. The night would also limit their own vision as much as it would prying eyes, all the while slowing down their activities on unfamiliar ground. They would leave early in the morning, just as the sun rose, to afford them the most time to scavenge, secure their load, and return home before sunset.

Alex raised the question of what should be done if they did come across other survivors. Steve suggested that if they encountered someone who knew them, they would try to establish what resources they might have and what kind of situation they were in, without giving away too much about our own. Perhaps one day it would be safe, or even necessary, to expand our social circle, so it would be good to know who was still in the area. If they came across someone who needed help, they would bring the information back to the group to be tabled. Strangers, if they asked, would be given a vague address a couple of towns over. Any hostility that could not be resolved verbally from a distance would, unfortunately, be met with force. It was agreed that they wouldn't return until they were certain they weren't being followed.

The next morning the men, minus Alex, loaded their tools into the two farm trucks along with ratchet straps, empty totes, and jerry cans. Two trucks would burn more gas than one, but they could also bring more home, and it provided security in case one broke down or got stuck. Steve's shotgun case sat ominously in the back window of the rusted-out GMC. Jo had packed them each a sandwich, an apple, and a thermos of weak coffee while Norah and I whipped up a batch of oatmeal cookies. It was so nice to have another skilled pair of hands in the kitchen.

We tried to keep the atmosphere of the pending mission lighthearted. Ryan and Chris had drawn up their own wish lists which they made sure were not forgotten.

A basketball.
Fishing rods.
Their own canoe.
Sour gummy worms.

Chips.

Comic books.

The adults kept their hugs and kisses quick, making sure their voices didn't shake as they said their goodbyes and good lucks. The men promised to be back before nightfall.

XI

"Can you tell me why we're building the root cellar here?" I asked Chris and Ryan. They opted to help Alex and me while Jo-Anne spent one-on-one time homeschooling Norah. A full day of Physical Education sounded much more appealing to them than Math and English at the kitchen table. I also hoped the novel experience would distract them, as well as myself, from ruminating on the dangers the men might face while away on the supply run.

"Because we forgot to build the cellar before the barn!" Chris yelled, looking back mischievously for my reaction as he wheeled a load of dirt outside. His shaggy light brown hair shone as he stepped into the sun. Both he and Ryan had grown about three inches since the spring. I found it hard to believe that this fall we would officially have teenagers on the farm.

"Ha. Ha," I replied sarcastically, shooting him an evil eye. When he brought back his empty wheelbarrow, I continued the conversation. The boys may have been given a pass from Jo's formal teaching for the day, but that didn't mean they weren't going to learn something useful.

"Because we won't have to shovel off the door in the winter!" Ryan chimed in, his head popping up from the eight-foot by eight-foot pit that was nearing completion behind the trailers in the barn.

"That's part of it, yes. Building it in the barn will protect it from snow and ice." I nodded encouragingly. "Why else?"

"Ummm, because it keeps the food close by?" Chris added, patting his flat stomach.

"True," I nodded, "Convenience played a part in the decision. How do you think putting it inside the barn will affect the temperature?"

"It's a lot cooler in here than in the sun," Chris said, wiping his brow before wheeling another load of dirt away.

"That's right, the shade will keep it cooler inside, like a fridge. It will help stop nasty microorganisms from wrecking the things we store." I stopped to take a breather from piling cinder blocks nearby that we would be using for the walls. Will and I had been collecting the materials to build a root cellar for a few years. The blackout had now forced our timeline and frankly I was glad to have the extra hands to complete it. It was difficult and dirty work.

"And as an added bonus, this one didn't fill up with water," Alex said, rolling his eyes. Before deciding to build the cellar beneath the barn, we dug a test pit close to the house. We must have disrupted a spring because the next morning it was full of water, so the site was abandoned. The soil was sandier where the barn was built, and the men had also proactively installed two French drains around the foundation. Even as we reached the desired ten-foot depth, there was no sign of seepage.

"Definitely a good point," I confirmed, refilling everyone's water bottles. "Have you ever seen what happens when an apple gets left out on the counter too long?"

"It gets all wrinkly?" Ryan said, topping off the last wheelbarrow load.

"That's right. We're digging into the ground to preserve

humidity, so we won't have to eat wrinkly fruits and veggies this winter."

"That's something I didn't even know I had to worry about," Chris said incredulously, making everyone laugh. The next hour was spent digging in an exhaust pipe, cutting rebar, and getting the footer prepared for concrete. With perfect timing, Norah appeared in the doorway announcing that lunch was ready. It was a good time to take a break because once we started mixing the concrete, we wouldn't be able to stop. The finite amount of mix we had did not leave much room for error.

I still hadn't got used to the feeling of using the "just in case" resources and amenities we had squirreled away since moving to the farm. Logically I knew this was the right time to use them, but there was also something uncomfortable about dipping into our emergency stash knowing we may never be able to replace it. Fuel was the biggest concern of course. Life was going to be a lot more difficult once it ran out or expired. *More difficult but not impossible,* I reminded myself, beating back the negative pattern of thoughts that had been creeping up on me lately.

Jo-Anne and Norah had lunch waiting on the picnic table beside the alpaca pasture. An ancient apple tree provided shade, still loaded with so many apples that they hung in clusters. I suspected that it was a soft mast year which, on top of Alex and Steve's daily baiting, explained the lack of wildlife seeking food around the farm.

"Look Vanessa," Norah said as I approached, turning her attention away from KLee who she had been treating to carrot pieces through the fence. KLee was our big, brown, alpha-female alpaca, and Norah had taken a shine to her just like all the other animals. "I set the table all by myself! Jo showed me how to do it proper!" she proudly informed me. Jo-Anne smiled at her, covertly straightening a fork. She was the central force preventing me from going on kitchen strike and all of us devolving into cavemen. As Jo would say, "food is the glue of society", and her meals were certainly something we all wanted to be part of.

On the menu today was cold lettuce soup, which tasted much better than it sounded. For dipping, there was sourdough focaccia with edible wildflowers baked into the top. There was also a chef salad with cubes of ham, hard boiled eggs, chopped cucumbers and tomatoes, and grated carrot. For dessert, oatmeal cookies.

"Honestly, I eat better now than I did when I was making stacks of cash working in the ER," Alex complimented Jo. "Isn't that ironic?" She humbly waved him off, but I could see that she was blushing as she heaped salad onto the boys' plates. He had never complimented my cooking like that. I supposed it had something to do with the different secret ingredients we used—Jo, love, and I, antipathy.

As I looked around the table at the happy, sun kissed children, the strong, lean bodies of the adults, the beautiful meal we were sharing, and the clean line of laundry swaying in the background, the nagging bits of fear from earlier were completely abated by pride. We were really doing it. It had already been four months, an entire season since the final lockdown order was broadcast. Our rag-tag group would probably never have been voted most likely to survive: an old woman, a gay couple and their young child, a recently widowed father and his twin sons, and Will and I—a couple of naïve, self-proclaimed farmers. We weren't family by blood, but now we were family by design.

Light in the barn was starting to fade by the time the waterproof membrane was installed in the cellar and the concrete footer was poured. All that was left was to lay the cinder block walls, construct the stairs, and install the door. I couldn't wait to show Will as he almost always spearheaded the labour-intensive jobs. Satisfied with our progress, I led Alex and the boys out to the front lawn for cool down stretches. There was no time to be delayed by sore muscles so, with kindness, we tried to hold each other accountable for taking care of our bodies. Even Norah and Jo came out to join us, having completed their lessons for the day and put dinner to simmer on the stove. After, the kids ran off for a game of hide-and-seek while Alex headed to his trailer to unwind. Jo positioned herself for a nap in one of the hammocks by the flower garden while I leafed through a copy of "Edible Plants of Atlantic Canada."

Just as I was starting to worry, I saw the ears perk up on the dogs who were lazing beside me on the porch. Minutes later running lights shone through the tree line, and I realized I had been holding my breath. As the Dodge rounded the corner, I could see that its box was filled with neatly stacked windows, and the flat deck trailer it towed was piled high with square bales. As Will parked at the end of the driveway to prepare the decontamination ritual, he waved from behind the steering wheel. His furrowed brow and pursed lips were illuminated by the setting sun. Like a sucker punch to my gut, intuition told me that something had happened.

The old GM was not far behind, totes and pallets crisscrossed with ratchet straps filling the truck bed. Steve and Travis stopped at the end of the driveway to roll the log blockade back into place. The men barely shared a word between them. From the size of their haul, they should have been buzzing with congratulatory excitement.

The dogs and I ran to meet Will in the parking area

behind the house. As he stepped out of the truck, I leapt into his arms like I hadn't seen him in months.

"I missed you too," he mumbled into my hair.

"How did it go? Are you ok?" I demanded.

"Yes, and no," he replied, his tone alarmingly serious. "We have news."

XII

After quickly storing the hay before the dew began to settle, everyone took up a space in the living room to share Jo and Norah's stew. Wolfing down their supper, Chris and Ryan begged to know whether any of their wish list items had made it home. Travis and Will tormented them with shrugged shoulders, impish smiles, and vague tidbits. Finally, to get them out of their hair and the room so the adults could talk privately, Travis told them to go look behind the driver's seat of the GM. Although she hadn't asked for anything herself, Norah followed behind the boys in their trail of excitement. A moment later the distinct sound of children playing and a basketball slapping against the driveway floated in on the nighttime air.

"So…" I prompted, eager for my own tidbits of the outside world.

"The best news is that we saw Keith and Tracey," Will said, my jaw dropping to the floor. Keith and Tracey had been fellow Farmers' Market vendors in New Germany. They owned a goat farm and an apiary and sold a beautiful range of finely curated honey, cheese, and soap products. We had bonded over the anomaly of being childless, middle-aged, first-generation farmers.

"Oh my god!" I exclaimed when I was finally able to speak. "How are they?!"

"Managing," Will replied. "We discussed trading a

breeding pair of goats for a pig." I nodded enthusiastically, encouraging him to go on. Will explained that Tracey's father had died shortly after learning of the devastating Sigma outbreak at his wife's Long-Term Care Facility—the same place Natasha had been working. Tracey and Keith lived beside her parent's home just off the highway between New Germany and Bridgewater. When they hadn't heard from her dad in a couple days, they went over to check on him. They found him in his recliner with a quilt his wife made pulled up under his chin, his favorite cat asleep on his lap. They believed he died of a broken heart. I caught a glimpse of Travis rubbing something from the corner of his eye.

"I'm so sorry to hear about her dad. Where did you meet up with them?" I asked, changing the subject.

"They hadn't heard a vehicle on the highway in weeks, so they were curious when they heard the trucks. They recognized us as we went by, so they flagged us down on our way back. We were the first people they had spoken to since June, aside from Tracey's dad. They watched as traffic on Trunk 10 slowly dwindled away, eventually stopping all together, until they saw us."

"Amazing," Alex and I breathed simultaneously. Will went on to tell the group that they had also discussed the merits of moving closer together to support each other. He suggested to them that our neighbour's home, with its surrounding orchard, blueberry fields, and river frontage, currently sat vacant. However, it was decided that it didn't make logistical sense this late in the season. Keith and Tracey already had their hay in for their sixty goats, their firewood stacked, their bees moved to their winter location, and the process of winter food storage underway. They agreed to meet again in the spring to reevaluate, if possible.

"Amazing," I said again. "Did you see anyone else?"

The room fell silent as the three men suddenly found their own hands remarkably interesting. I stared at Will pointedly, but he was committed to picking at a piece of dirt wedged under his thumbnail. It felt like an eternity had passed before Steve spoke up, his voice quavering.

"The first...the first farm we stopped at...Oh, God... help me..." he looked up at the ceiling in search of divine guidance. "I...I had to hurt somebody," he finally spat out, massaging his lips with his fingertips as if they might smear away a bad taste. Jo gasped in shock, clamping her hands over her heart. Alex put his arm around his husband supportively, a grave look of concern clouding his face. Travis checked out the window to make sure the kids were still preoccupied by their game in the driveway.

"I wouldn't put it quite like that," Travis said empathetically. "She forced your hand. Don't be going and blaming yourself. What happened was not your fault." I fought to keep a tight leash on the torrent of questions zipping around in my head.

"The smell..." Steve visibly cringed, obviously still struggling to put his experience into words.

"Do you want me to tell them?" Travis asked kindly.

"Thank you...but no. I need to acknowledge this myself, I think." Steve took a deep breath. "We stopped at the first farm because it had a bunch of brand-new windows leaned up beside the house. They must have been getting ready to replace the old ones. Anyway, while Travis and Will were loading them up, I was poking around the property to see if there was anything else we could use. There was this...smell...coming from out back, so I went to investigate. What a mistake..." He cleared his throat before continuing. "I found the farm's owners. An older couple. I guess the husband died a few days ago and his wife had drug him out back to bury him. But she was too weak from the virus herself, I assume. There was only a couple of marks from her shovel on the ground beside them." I took Will's hand in my own to stop him from picking his cuticles raw—and to keep myself grounded.

"She was still alive?" Jo-Anne whispered perceptively. Steve nodded slowly.

"I thought she was dead at first. She was sitting against an old hazelnut tree with his body across her lap. He was all bloated. I don't know how she could stand the smell. It's like it's burnt inside my nostrils," he went on. "Her breathing was so bad she could hardly speak. When she saw me and my gun though, she asked me to "take her." Begged me actually— to make it quick. Said she couldn't do it herself."

"Oh, honey," Alex murmured, kissing the side of his husband's head.

"It's not what you think." Steve's eyes were wide as he looked around, appearing to gauge the group's reactions. "I told her I couldn't help her. *No way!* I couldn't do it! I was about to go get Will and Travis, but she pulled out a shotgun. I guess it was lying behind her husband because I didn't see it at first. She couldn't even lift it up, she was so weak— but she had it pointed right at me from her hip. She said something like, "check the barn" or "in the barn" ...and then I heard her take off the safety..."

"Oh no!" Jo and I exclaimed in unison.

"And that's when I shot her. It was...instinctive. Oh, good god. I shot a sick, little, old lady," Steve confessed, abruptly facing the unsavory reality all over again. "I didn't hurt her—*I killed her.*" His face pale, he slumped against Alex and devolved back into silence.

"Oh, honey!" Alex repeated, wedging Steve tightly against him as if he might relieve his husband's suffering by absorbing it into his own body.

Taking their cue, Travis and Will began filling in the details that followed. Although they would have liked to give the couple a proper burial, they simply couldn't risk the exposure to Sigma. A sliver of salvation, if there was one to be had, was that they were able to fulfill what they imagined was the woman's last wish. When the men looked in the barn, they found five ornery draft horses. The animals had kicked holes in the walls in frustration and chewed their empty water buckets into pieces. The manure piles on the floor suggested they had been confined for a week or more. After freeing them from their stalls, the men also opened the pasture gates—gifting the animals the ability to determine their own fate.

"I am so sorry you had to go through that. What a horrific tragedy," I told Steve. "But Travis is absolutely right, *it was not your fault.* If you had made any other decision, you might not be sitting here with us now. I'd even go so far as to suggest you did her a great kindness." Steve breathed deeply and briefly met my gaze with tear-filled eyes. "If you ever need to talk, I'm here—we all are. You don't have to carry this alone."

Exhaustion, shock, and sadness weighed on the shoulders of everyone in the room. With so much focus on survival, we hadn't allowed ourselves the space to process everything that happened since the pandemic came to a head. Immersed in day-to-day busyness, we had collectively avoided facing our pain. Because the scope of devastation was almost too enormous to comprehend, we had buried our grief beneath endless to-do lists. Travis and the boys hadn't even been able to have a funeral for

Natasha. I suspected that, like a growing pile of dirty laundry, it was going to become increasingly difficult to ignore. Maybe it was time to air it all out—to acknowledge our new reality before it overwhelmed us. Perhaps it was time to help each other find the words to say goodbye to the lives we would never know again.

XIII

A few days later, we took the afternoon off to hold a celebration of life. I challenged everyone to write a letter, or letters, to the people or things or moments they had lost due to the pandemic. There were no rules, only a suggestion to reflect on any unspoken or unresolved feelings, and a promise to hold space for each other. I wasn't a religious person but, while recovering from PTSD, I learned that sharing difficult experiences within a supportive community could facilitate healing.

Steve played "Amazing Grace" on his guitar as everyone gathered in a circle around a ceremonial fire. Following a moment of silence, everyone was invited to read what they had written, ask someone else to read it for them, or to simply place it into the flames. Since it was my idea, I said I would go first which was met with audible sighs of relief from Chris and Ryan.

My letter was not addressed to anyone, but instead explored all the things Sigma had so ungraciously taken from me. I would never be able to repair the fractured relationship with my parents and, although I doubted it was ever a real possibility, I was sad the opportunity had now been stripped from my hands. I grieved for all the friends I would never see again, including Natasha with her infectious laugh and the sweetness she brought to everyone's lives. Although we had come from away, we had quickly integrated into the local community steeped in the salt of the earth. It was the first place Will and I had felt inspired to put down more than temporary roots. Now the multi-generational lineage that had quietly built this beautiful corner of Nova Scotia, had been extinguished. I expressed the guilt I felt as an outsider and a survivor, and the fear I felt of what lay ahead. I was also ashamed of how little I appreciated the luxury of going for a drive whenever I wanted, or hot water on demand, or attending festivals, or ordering take-out. I regretted not turning all the privilege of convenience I had into more joy. I placed my letter into the fire, exchanging it for a smoking bundle of rosemary and thyme which I slowly waved over my body, cleansing the space where my essence kissed the universe.

Will went next. He expressed his grief over not seeing his niece and nephew grow up, or his parents grow old, even if it was just over Skype most of the time. He would not be able to take us on the trip to South America that we had dreamt of since before the pandemic began. He also joked that he wished he ordered one last Big Mac, which cracked a few smiles of solidarity. He then folded his letter into a paper airplane and flew it into the heart of the fire, before picking up his own bundle of purifying herbs.

Next, Travis carefully unfolded his letter. "Dear Natasha..." he started, his voice catching. The circle patiently waited. "Dear...Natasha," he started again. Ryan started to cry softly, leaning into his father's side. Sighing, Travis refolded his letter, looking up at the sky.

"Natasha, I never have and never will love someone as much as I loved you," he said, speaking from the heart. "You know I will do the best I can for our boys. I talk to them about you every day, and every day I hate that you aren't here. We've got good friends to help us, but right now, the best part about every day is that I'm one step closer to being with you again." Travis scrunched up his letter into a ball and tossed it into the fire, followed by Ryan who chose not to read his.

Chris seemed inclined to follow suit but hesitated before passing his letter to Jo-Anne. Jo held the letter to her heart and looked deeply into his eyes in acknowledgment before reading it aloud.

"Mom," she began. "I'm sorry for all the times I was bad. I'm sorry I didn't give you a hug or tell you 'I love you' before you went to work that day. I didn't know you wouldn't come home. I wish you could see all the cool stuff me and Ryan have been doing on the farm. Every day we feed the pigs and the alpacas, and make sure their pens are clean, and that they have fresh water. No one even has to ask us. We do Jo-Anne's lessons without complaining, most of the time. Sometimes I think I can feel you watching me, and it makes me want to do my best. I love you, Mom. Love, Chris." Her face wet with tears, Jo reached out to squeeze his hand before passing him back the folded paper.

"Do I have to burn it?" Chris asked, looking over at me. I shook my head no and he carefully placed the letter back into his shirt pocket. Jo read her letter next which she had written to her grandchildren that she loved immensely despite only getting to see them on summer holidays. She wished she could see them grow up and fall in love and travel and build careers, or whatever they felt called to do with their lives. Alex's letter was addressed to the colleagues he had worked doggedly beside in the ER to the very end, and Steve's was addressed to his parents in Maine who he missed desperately and regretted not spending more time with. As he placed his into the fire, I noticed a second letter that he didn't mention was folded within the first. I suspected it had something to do with the woman with the horses and I desperately hoped that it brought him some closure.

Norah was the last to share, and she revealed that Jo had helped her write two letters as well. She had also drawn pictures for the words that were too hard to spell. The first was a collage of all the things she missed: her old bedroom, Timbits, going to her favorite beach, and the friends she had briefly met at the special daycare that had been organized for the children of the South Shore Hospital staff. The second letter, she told us, was all the things that still made her happy, because writing the first letter had made her too sad. She depicted collecting eggs from the chickens, kissing KLee on the nose, playing soccer with Chris and Ryan, having a feast in the barn, hugging the big dogs, cooking with Jo, and listening to her dad play his guitar. When she was finished, she demanded to know why everyone was crying, crossing her arms, and stamping her foot in disappointment that she had not been able to cheer us up. It resulted in a weird symphony of laugh-sobbing as everyone began exchanging hugs.

To conclude the ceremony, Steve took to his guitar again, this time accompanied by Jo who sang a beautiful rendition of "You'll Never Walk Alone." For a while everyone sat staring into the flames in quiet reflection. It reminded me of something I had heard one time about televisions being the modern caveman's shared fire, a focal point to gather around in the spirit of community. I sighed, privately mourning movie nights curled up on the couch with Will, and the dogs, and a bag of All Dressed chips. The memory felt absurdly bougie now.

"Alright," Jo said eventually, breaking the pensive trance. "Who wants sausages?"

"Meeeee!" the boys shouted in unison.

XIV

I pinched a faded marigold to see if the petals were dry, which would tell me if the seeds were ready to harvest. The orange frills were one of my garden staples, a flamboyant natural repellent of pests like whitefly, root knot, and root lesion nematodes. The seeds were easily kept year after year and brought a joyous pop of colour to the garden's sea of green every summer. Satisfied with the crinkling between my fingertips, I set about plucking the hearty flower heads into my basket.

The men had taken the boys with them to cut and buck hardwood. It would take a whole year before it was properly seasoned. Like so many things on the farm, it was a chore that had to be planned long in advance. The sound of their chainsaws echoed across the field, carried on a warm October breeze.

Jo and Norah were on the porch taking a break between lessons. Norah coloured in a workbook while Jo napped in a gravity chair, the wind thumbing through the pages of a drugstore novel on her lap. I breathed in the peaceful solitude deeply from where I was crouched among my plants. Learning to relax into the constant buzz of activity, and voices, and needs of everyone now living on the farm had been a big adjustment. It was important for me to carve out these uninterrupted moments. It allowed me to recharge my internal battery and untangle my thoughts.

An hour or so had passed when a fuss stirring in the chicken coop drew my attention. The alpacas ran to the nearby fence line, their ears pointed toward the perceived intrusion. Willow, the eldest and keenest alpaca, began sucking wind in and out of her belly, activating her squealing alarm. Following her gaze, I thought I saw a large shadow move across the nesting boxes. Norah, her eyes filling with concern, mouthed, *"What is it?"* Pressing my finger to my lips, I motioned for her to stay quiet on the porch while I investigated.

Grabbing a pitchfork that leaned against the side of the building, I peered into the coop. In a dim corner I could make out the figure of a stranger. The man was struggling to stuff a chicken into an empty feed sack that was already squirming with another unhappy hen inside. An egg fell from his pocket and cracked on the floor which, as he turned to look, led him to catch my eye.

"Can I help you?" I asked, my voice loaded with equal parts assertion and confusion as I stepped fully into the doorway. I positioned myself so the man either had to answer me or find a way to get across the chicken run and hop its five-foot fence before I caught up with him. As my eyes adjusted to the light, the condition of the man's body suggested he wasn't going anywhere too quickly. I pointed the pitchfork at him anyway, establishing a formidable barrier of wrought iron tines between us.

"Hungry," the skeleton mumbled, placing the sack of irate chickens carefully on the floor and raising his hands above his head in submission.

"Vanessa?" Jo called, having been woken by the commotion.

"I'm in the coop," I yelled back. "There's a man in here!" I heard the door to the house open and close as Jo ushered

Norah inside.

"Where did you come from?" I asked the man as Jo made her way to my side. I didn't recognize his gaunt face, long unkempt hair, or stooped stature, as anyone from the area.

"I'm just..." the man swayed, "hungry..." He collapsed in a heap on the floor. Jo and I looked at each other in bewilderment.

"Have you seen him before?" I asked Jo, who had not.

"He looks unwell," she whispered. I agreed, he looked like he was starving. Watching closely, I could see his ribs were still moving beneath his thin and dirty plaid shirt. Confident he was still alive, we backed out of the coop and locked the door behind us, giving ourselves space to think.

The men weren't expected back for another couple of hours, and it seemed cruel to leave the stranger face down in chicken shit, especially in his obviously weakened condition. My duty as a former medic to help any person in distress simply would not let me turn away, despite the risks. I decided we would set up the large canvas tent that had been repacked in the hayloft after Jo's illness. It would serve as a temporary emergency room. Jo busied herself putting the poles together in the shade while I went in the house to gather medical supplies.

"Is something wrong?" Norah asked, appearing from the living room. I searched for the best way to explain what was happening, wanting to be truthful while also shielding her from any unnecessary stress or fear.

"There is a man here who Jo and I don't know. We think he came here because he saw that we have lots of food. He seems very hungry and tired. I'd like you to stay inside while Jo and I get him settled in the tent in the yard, which will be like his own private hospital room, ok?"

"Is he sick?"

I told her I wasn't sure, but on the last recon mission the men had found a handful of COVID rapid test kits in a desk drawer at the veterinarian's office. I checked the expiry date as I pulled one out to show her. 2024-11-16 it read, still good for another month. We'd have our result shortly.

"I'll make him a get-well card, just in case," she replied, hurrying back to her markers. My hands expertly tied the strings of a surgical gown behind my back without a thought. *Here we go again...*

"What's his name?" Norah called from the living room. I told her I wasn't sure, but hopefully we would know that soon too.

Assuming dehydration and possibly hypoglycemia, I prepared a D5W10 infusion. Inside the tent I hung it from a coat rack turned into a makeshift IV pole. Jo prepared the army cot I once used on overnight EMS shifts, thoughtfully adding blankets and a pillow. The only thing left to do was get the unconscious body onto it. I didn't want to risk Jo being exposed, so I explained to her the tarp-drag technique I was familiar with. It was straightforward and I was fairly confident from the stranger's diminutive stature that I would be able to manage his extrication on my own. Cautioning me not to hurt my back, Jo went inside the house to watch from a safe distance, and to keep Norah distracted from the distressing scene that was about to unfold.

In the chicken coop, I was able to roll the man's limp, but breathing, body onto the tarp with ease. He was even lighter than I imagined. I could feel each bone delineated beneath his skin. His dark eyes fluttered as I dragged him out into the sunshine in the direction of the tent. I gave a thumbs up in Jo's direction, but a scene from Breaking Bad reflected at me in the sliding glass doors. I lifted the man onto the cot like a parent might put their child to bed. He moaned as his head came to rest on the pillow. Opening the COVID test kit, I swabbed his nostril in hopes of establishing some peace of mind. Minutes passed and only one line appeared. He was negative.

With a sigh of relief, I began a full assessment. On top of being thin and filthy, the man's pulse was weak and thready, and his pupils were slow to react. His jeans, about two sizes too large, were tied with a length of frayed binder twine. The breath emanating from his scraggly, grey striped beard smelled sweet and fruity and raised my suspicion of starvation ketoacidosis. Confident with my predetermined treatment choice, I initiated a conservative management plan which would require careful monitoring moving forward. Starvation wreaks havoc on all body systems and refeeding syndrome would be a real risk. Too much kindness too quickly could kill him.

When I stepped out of the tent to decon, the distant sound of chainsaws had fallen silent, so I suspected the men were heading back from the woods. I walked out to the edge of the field to meet them, catching up with Will, Steve, Travis, the boys, and the dogs.

"Where's Alex?" I asked, preferring to explain the situation to everyone at once.

"Oh," Steve said with a puzzled brow, "he said he wasn't feeling great, so he was going to lie down in the trailer. I thought you would have seen him." I shrugged my shoulders, indicating I hadn't, before launching into the segue.

"I did see someone else though." Everyone stopped in their tracks. I filled them in on the morning's events and their reactions transformed from surprise to alarm. We decided to have a meeting over lunch to discuss the next steps. Steve went to fetch Alex, and Travis took his boys back to their trailer to get cleaned up. Will and I put the dogs in the pasture with the alpacas. As we walked back to the house together, he asked the obvious but uncomfortable question.

"Do we have enough food? Could we support another person over the winter?" I truly wasn't sure. The end of the fall harvest was still underway, and some hardy greens were just starting to mature in the newly built winter greenhouse.

"Maybe."

It was the best answer I had.

XV

"You wasted a rapid test on him? Without asking anyone?" Alex's accusation was met with looks of puzzlement around the kitchen table.

"Alex, honey, I think Vanessa has shown us she is quite capable of sound judgement when it comes to medical matters." Steve came to my defense while still placing his arm around his husband's shoulders. Alex brushed him off. He had been increasingly edgy and aloof as of late.

"She could have waited," he continued his one-man protest.

"*She* doesn't need *your* permission," I retaliated, unable to locate the kill code to my automated defense system. Alex's critical attitude had finally pushed one too many buttons. "I am very tired of your constant backseat driving. Nothing I ever do is good enough—despite everything Will and I have done for your family. They aren't *your* test kits, *you're* not my superior, and this is not *your* farm."

"I guess I should just go fuck myself then, eh? So much for 'living in community' as you're so fond of telling us," Alex snarled. Jo shushed him, waving indicatively toward his daughter who was sound asleep on the couch in the next room. Ryley, the youngest of the farm dogs, was curled up beside her. Both of their mouths were open with soft snores emanating from them, and Ryley's tongue was hanging out. It looked like an illustration by Norman

Rockwell. I suddenly wanted to crawl into a hole myself.

"I'm sorry, I take it back," I said, grinding into reverse. "I regret what I said—about this not being your farm. That was a mistake. We offered you a space here unconditionally. We want you to make it your family's home. But—I'm really grappling with the cynicism you keep throwing in my face. I feel like you don't trust me, and I don't know why. I'm trying my best, Alex." As he rolled his eyes at me yet again, I began to embrace the notion that whatever was going on with him possibly had very little to do with me, even if I was his favorite choice for target practice. It seemed that in the absence of grease, the squeaky wheel was now treated to Alex's boot.

Looping back to the matter at hand, I calmly explained that the kits expired in a couple weeks, and we hadn't even used one since we found them. The validity of my decision was echoed in a collective nodding of heads, and Alex begrudgingly stood down. After Jo and I reiterated how we came to find the stranger in the chicken coop, and the condition he was in, the question on everyone's mind was—what do we do with him now?

"I'll tell you what we should do with him!" Alex ominously slammed his hand down on the table. "He knows we are here, and he knows what we have. He might tell someone! They might try to rob us! Or worse." His concern rang a little hollow although men had certainly been killed for lesser reasons than being in the wrong place at the right time.

"I don't know about where you come from," Travis countered, his arms crossed in front of his chest, and his soup uncharacteristically untouched, "but that's not how we treat our neighbours around here. At least, not before we get to know them." Chris and Ryan sat taller in their seats, also crossing their arms in perfect mimicry of their father. They would make a formidable trio when the boys were a little older.

"I don't know if you've noticed, but the *'around here'* that you grew up in doesn't exist anymore!" Alex exploded. "Are you goddamn bleeding-heart liberals trying to get us all killed?"

"Why don't we take a walk…" Steve suggested, but Alex stood up and blasted out the door before his husband could finish his sentence.

"He hasn't been himself," Steve patiently tried to explain. Steve himself had also seemed chronically tired lately. He was rarely heard playing his guitar outside of music lessons with the kids, and laughter was almost never heard coming from their shared trailer. *Perhaps it's time for a neck-up check-up with those two,* I thought to myself.

"What do you think, Will?" Travis asked, getting the conversation back on track.

"My concern is food. If he wants to stay here when he wakes up, can we support him? We've got a lot of mouths to feed this winter—and not just human ones." Will looked to me for an answer as I was the head grower. Even with careful rationing and the winter greenhouse, it was going to be tight. "Or maybe he doesn't even want to stay. Maybe we offer to give him a hen and send him on his way? I think we could spare a hen and a rooster. Or maybe he doesn't even wake up? Maybe he's too far gone, is that a possibility?"

"He's in pretty bad shape," I acknowledged. The mystery man's recovery was not guaranteed, especially with our limited resources and without access to a lab. Besides, if Alex thought it was wasteful to use a rapid test on him, he was definitely going to have an opinion about using any more than the bare minimum of supplies to rehabilitate him.

"Would you like the opinion of an old woman?" Jo chimed in. We all turned to her expectantly. "We don't have many luxuries," she began, "but we do have one. Time. Why don't we wait to hear his story? Keep him as comfortable as you can, Vanessa, but, and I don't think I need to tell you this, it is not exactly the time for heroics. I fully expected when you cared for me down at the cabin that if you came to realize I wouldn't survive, you would have had the gall to end my suffering." She was right, I tried to be mindful of the big picture when I made these kinds of decisions. Although letting her go without pulling out all the stops would have been the hardest thing I ever did, it also would have been the right thing to do. I chased the darkness from my mind.

"Would you like the opinion of a young man?" Chris piped up, a humble grin creeping across Travis's face. "I agree with Jo. Let's see if he wakes up, and if he wakes up let's see what he has to say. Seems like a no-brainer to me." He casually shrugged his adolescent shoulders, his astute words proving that we had made the right decision to begin inviting the boys into some of the more "adult" conversations. They had shown such maturity since coming to the farm, from helping care for Norah, to pitching in on difficult tasks without being asked, to sudden outbursts of wisdom such as this. We were all incredibly proud of their resilience and the sort of young men they were proving themselves to be. I wished with all my heart that Natasha was here to witness it.

"I guess that settles it," Travis said. "We wait." Everyone at the table agreed and attention was turned back to lunch—a hearty bacon and potato soup. After the kitchen was back in order, Steve pulled me aside.

"Do you think anyone would mind too terribly much if I took the afternoon off? I'd like to spend time with Alex, just the two of us." I told him I thought that was a great idea and suggested that they go down to the camp for the night. It had been a while since anyone had a date night. Norah would stay for a sleepover party with me and Jo. We'd do DIY face masks and stay up way too late playing games and eating popcorn, I promised him. Relief filled his eyes and, after giving me a quick hug, he went off to find Alex.

As I got ready to go look for a small propane heater for the stranger in the tent, Will caught my hand, turning me toward him.

"That was nice of you," he said, "what you did for Steve and Alex just now." I relaxed against my husband's strong body for a moment.

"It's what I would have wanted someone to do for us," I told him, "when we were struggling."

"I know," he said, "that's why I love you."

XVI

When I woke the next morning, Jo already had Chris and Ryan working on their science text books in the living room. A teacher and a pack rat in her past life, Jo had revealed the volumes of textbooks and workbooks she had stashed in her basement. After she recovered from bronchitis, we drove over to her house to collect them, along with some of her other belongings, and to check on the cats. Much to her relief, the felines were fine, and the learning materials were still in good condition despite having sat in unopened boxes for several decades.

Norah stood on a stool in the kitchen, carefully leveling a cup of flour with the back of a knife. Her newest responsibility was to feed the sourdough starter Jo taught her to make. She was always quick to point out her role in the beautiful breads, pancakes, pizza doughs, and cinnamon buns it provided. Jo and I joked that sourdough starter would be the next generation's Chia Pet.

"I guess I slept in," I confessed sheepishly to the room.

"I guess you needed it," Jo replied, empathetically handing me a fresh cup of tea. "Will and Travis have gone to the woods to mark trees for milling. And your patient is awake." Glancing out the back window I saw the stranger slumped in a lawn chair outside the tent, staring into a steaming mug in his hands.

"Did you..." I started to ask.

"No, I told him to ask you what he could have to eat this morning. His name is Paul Joudrey and he came from his camp, way in behind Crossburn," she filled me in. "I didn't want to ask too many questions in case I tired him out. He's just had a cup of tea with dandelion honey, same as yours. I didn't get too close or anything." I hugged her in appreciation before hurrying out to officially meet Paul.

"Hello, Paul." I approached him slowly, bringing along my own lawn chair.

"Hello," he said weakly. "I'm sorry if I scared you."

I assured him he needn't be sorry—we were all just trying to survive these days. An aura of shame or sadness clung to him. The fine wrinkles about his eyes sagged under the weight, like evergreen boughs after a snowstorm. He didn't offer anything else, so I went about introducing myself and telling him a little bit about our—tongue in cheek—Misfit Farm. After a pause, he shared that he had actually heard about the "new farmers" on Alton Road a couple of years ago. He couldn't help but notice the addition of the alpacas when he drove past sometimes—they had been the talk of the neighbourhood.

"I like what you've done with the place," he offered. "I always meant to stop and say hello. This isn't quite the introduction I had in mind." We had a small laugh together, at his expense. He was visibly tiring so I shifted the conversation to more important medical business. Paul confided that he hadn't had a real meal in over a month. He'd been surviving off whatever fruit trees he could find.

He knew he needed to find a better source of food, or he was soon going to die, especially with winter approaching.

I sensed there was more to the story but didn't want to press if he wasn't ready or didn't have the energy to share. We agreed that he should try a half cup of oatmeal with a few berries to see how it went down. If it sat ok, I'd fix him a half cup of soup for lunch. I explained that I believed he was truly starving and that we would have to reintroduce food very slowly, so his body didn't go into shock. He nodded, his gaze falling back to the earth between his feet.

"One more thing before I leave you to rest," I said, retrieving Norah's get-well card from my back pocket. "The little girl who lives here wanted me to give this to you." Paul's hand shook as he took the piece of purple construction paper. On the front she drew a chicken holding a vibrant bouquet of flowers, the words *'Feel Better'* scrawled underneath. Inside Jo had helped her to write:

Dear Mister,
I like to eat eggs when I'm sick too. Jo will make us real good ones if we ask nice. Hope to meet you soon.
Your new friend, Norah.

Paul mopped up a stray tear with the collar of his shirt. "I almost forgot how nice it was to have someone to talk to," he said. Just then Norah, who had come to watch us from the kitchen window, tapped on the glass to get our attention. She waved enthusiastically, hopping up and down, unbrushed curls bouncing on her head like a Jack-in-the-box. Paul tipped his imaginary hat in her direction, the first sparkle of light gracing his dark blue eyes.

XVII

Now that he had a face and a story, Alex's attitude quickly changed toward the wannabe chicken thief. Overnight he transformed back into the passionate and dutiful nurse still living beneath the shadow of trauma that threatened to smother him. He was much more suited to treat the effects of starvation than I was, having completed a nursing practicum at the Mokolo District Hospital in the Far North of Cameroon, West Africa. After evening chores one night, Steve and I shared a pot of homemade tea in the kitchen while Alex assisted Paul in having a warm sponge bath.

"How's Alex doing? Truly?" I asked.

"I know he is still ruminating about what happened in the ER." Steve strained the hot tea into our mugs. "It's hard to get him to talk about it, but sometimes I catch him saying things under his breath when he thinks I can't hear. He wants to be strong for us, but I keep telling him that the wall he's fortifying is keeping the people who care about him on the outside too. I think with everything he's been through he just doesn't have the emotional capacity to accommodate anyone else right now. Even us, his family. The only time he seems to relax is when he's taking care of others on his own terms. That's when he feels in control. That's when the world makes sense to him."

"We had a fight about it once," Steve continued. "I

wanted us to get a bigger house a couple years ago, so I was looking at ways to re-budget our income. You know how much he was still sending to Cameroon every month? Two hundred dollars. Every month, two hundred dollars to the SOS Children's Villages. I asked if he would consider scaling it back to fifty— not to stop all together, just to pare it down while we saved for a bigger place. I wanted to have a spare bedroom for when my parents came to visit and maybe a fenced yard so we could get a puppy for Norah. You've seen how much she loves dogs. Well, you'd think I asked him to cut off his own damn arm. He said I didn't understand and that I was being selfish." Steve shook his head sadly. "It's part of what made me fall in love with him, his commitment to putting others first. I didn't realize at the time that it came at the cost of not having any love left over for himself. I wish I had gotten him help back then. I wish I'd seen the red flags for what they were. Then with the pandemic, everything just slowly got worse. Now his moods don't swing—they ricochet."

"We only accept help when we're ready," I reminded him softly. "I'm not sure Alex is ready, even now." Steve sighed. I wished I had a magic wand to lend him.

In the yard, Alex opened a bag he had put together for Paul. On the recon mission the men had found clothes that would fit the boys as they grew over the next few years. Some of it looked like it might fit Paul, so Alex had washed and folded a couple of outfits for him. Paul shyly held a navy Acadia University sweatshirt in front of his chest to show him it was an appropriate size.

"It's like 'Queer Eye: Pandemic Edition'," I joked.

"He's a really good person, you know," Steve said. "I just worry about how his outbursts will affect Norah. I hope she doesn't think his anger is her fault. She's so sensitive." I didn't tell him, but I was concerned about the same thing having grown up in an emotionally unstable home myself. Being forced to walk on eggshells as a kid is not a path to developing a secure relationship attachment style (according to the many self-help books sitting on my bedside table). If I had to guess, it probably also worried Alex. He had to be aware on some level of the example he was setting for her, even if he felt unable to control it. Kids are always impacted by caregivers who can't or won't do the work to take care of themselves, no matter the reason.

"And what about you?" I probed. "How have you been doing, with everything?" Steve sighed deeply.

"I don't know, Ness. I try to be a good partner to Alex but he's so unpredictable. One minute I'm his angel but the next, well, I might as well take myself out with the trash." Steve snorted awkwardly. "Sorry, it just occurred to me that we don't do that anymore—take out the trash... Anyway, as much as I think I've made peace with the "suicide-by-bystander" incident, I keep having this nightmare—but it's my parents sitting under that tree, waiting to die. I think about them all the time. Needless to say, neither of us are getting much sleep."

"I'm so sorry for everything you are going through," I told him. "Thank you for sharing it with me. I wish there were something I could do to help."

"Me too. If I could roll us all up in bubble wrap, I would," he replied.

Paul had just reemerged from his tent fully dressed in a pair of properly fitted khaki cargo pants and his new-to-him hoodie. Alex made him do a spin before giving his nod of approval and sending him off to bed with a spare pair of his own pajamas.

"Tomorrow, a haircut," Alex said, joining us in the

kitchen. I went to the cupboard to get him a mug and put together a plate of the soft pretzels Jo made that day. When she presented Paul with a piece earlier, he said he had never tasted such a thing. The way he smiled at her looked a little like love when he took his first bite.

"He's looking much better—steadier on his feet too," Steve praised his husband, clinking their pretzels together.

"Sad story there," Alex informed us. Everyone on the farm had been patiently waiting for Paul to feel comfortable to share how he came to be alone in the backwoods of Crossburn with no food for the winter. It seemed that Alex's attention and care had picked the lock.

Paul wasn't alone at his hunt camp at first. He had moved there with his wife, Anette, in June. Anette was a Type 1 diabetic and, when the pharmacies all closed, she had no way of renewing the insulin prescription she needed to keep her alive. Anette was adamant that she wanted to spend their remaining time together on her terms where she had always felt the safest, and happiest. The last drops of gasoline in their jeep had taken them to the door of the camp that had been in her family since the Springfield Railway began operating in 1906.

Anette and Paul had spent the early summer working on a small garden, fishing in their canoe along the river, and watching the birds from their screened in porch. They played cribbage and every night before they went to bed, Paul would read her poetry from their collection of Canadian writers.

After a week of increasing illness, Paul woke one morning to Anette's lifeless body beside him. She had died in her sleep, holding the hand of her beloved husband. Although it was exactly as she wanted, Paul's heart shattered with the loss of his best friend. Unable to move for two days, he thought he'd will himself to die right there beside her. But death wasn't ready to call Paul home, so he eventually set about digging his wife a grave. He buried her beside the garden that had brought her so much joy.

And then he sat.

Weeks went by and, besides cooking a can of beans or soup over the woodstove, Paul sat in their screened porch looking out where his wife—his life—lay in the ground. Squash bugs raided the tender plants Anette had so patiently tended, knowing they were only meant to feed her husband over the winter. Lettuce greens bolted before they were harvested, and nighttime creatures greedily snapped off the tops of the carrots and parsnips. Before he knew it, fall had arrived and yet his body still refused to betray him.

He didn't even remember making the decision but one day found himself walking away from his cabin with the last can of soup in his bag on his back. It was a couple more days before he stumbled upon our neighbour's home. In their orchard he was able to find a few good apples still clinging to the trees. Finding the door unlocked he had looked through their kitchen but came up empty handed, not knowing that they had gifted Will and me with anything they weren't taking to Florida. That night, he smelled Jo's cooking fire from down the road at the farm. The irresistible prospect of fresh, home cooked food was what led him staggering into our coop the next morning.

"That poor man," I mumbled from between wet fingers.

"But that's not all," Alex went on. "Paul's a Red Seal electrician. He used to install solar energy systems."

XVIII

"If you could go to one store, any store, but only one—where would you go?" I asked the twins as we got the winter greenhouse ready for their inaugural sleep over. The number of daylight hours had begun to dip below ten and the occasional light frost had begun to settle over the garden. It was also the boys' thirteenth birthday, October 30th, and they wanted to have a party. During their biweekly art classes, Jo, Norah, and I had helped them make festive leis for everyone from dried hydrangeas. Then, last night, the boys had commandeered the kitchen with a strict no-adults policy and the promise of a tasty surprise for the celebration.

"Sports Check!" Ryan answered as he hung another strand of icicle lights from the trusses. "I miss intramural sports, and our soccer ball is going flat."

"Does the Imax count? It's not really a store I guess but man, could I ever go for a movie on the big screen." Chris straightened a bright pink solar lit flamingo.

"That's because you miss your girlfriend, *Ammmanda*," Ryan pointed puckered lips in his direction, making kissing sounds. Chris threatened to throw a garden spade at him.

"Will can help you with the soccer ball," I told Ryan. "Just ask him to show you how to use the air compressor. He can hook it up to the generator."

"Oh, awesome!" Ryan carefully placed a mysterious tray

draped in tea towels on one of the potting benches. "No peeking!" He wagged a finger at me. I crossed my heart. "What store do *you* miss the most?" he asked.

"Lush," I sighed dreamily, which was met with puzzled looks. "My favorite bath and body store." They nodded but clearly did not truly appreciate the luxury of fresh, ethically sourced, and cruelty free bath bombs and bubbles.

After I showed the boys how to light and maintain the woodstove, they went about rounding everyone up for the party. I gingerly stashed my own surprise for later in the lean-to woodshed we built on the north side of the structure.

"It looks like a gingerbread house on steroids!" Paul exclaimed as he stepped into the brightly lit reception. "Did you boys get a permit for this?" he joked. Following Alex's strict prescription of rest and healthy, easily digestible food, Paul was on a steady path to recovery. He had moved out of the tent in the yard and onto the living room couch. Norah had enlisted him in her morning chicken care routine and, although Alex mandated that he take lots of breaks, he had been helping the boys stack the firewood for the greenhouse. He had also taken it upon himself to wash and dry the dishes after every meal, insisting that Jo put up her feet and have a cup of evening tea. I often overheard her giggling as they visited.

The boys wanted to be the ones to tell him that the group decided to invite him to stay on The Misfit Farm as long as he liked. Alex had been the one to suggest we extend a formal offer, an olive branch for his reaction when Paul first arrived. The vote had been unanimous, further solidified by his scheme to bring solar power to the farm as soon as he was well enough. If we had solar power, I was certain we could grow enough food for everyone in the off-season.

"Happy Birthday to you twooo," Jo sang as she swept into the room, placing a lei around each guest's neck. Travis handed each of his sons a small square package wrapped in Christmas paper I saved last year. Tearing them open they found KitKat bars which Travis had kept hidden from them since the last recon mission. They hugged their father ecstatically, vowing not to eat them all at once—before promptly eating them all at once.

As his gift, Steve had charged the boys phones using our old solar powered radio. He worried all week that they wouldn't be ready in time as, in true east coast fashion, the sun failed to cooperate, but by lunchtime today he excitedly informed me that the batteries read fully charged. Using an auxiliary cord, he rerouted Avicii from one of their playlists over the speakers. The sound slightly shook the glass windows, much to the boys' delight. With the dance party under way, I decided to reveal my own contribution—homemade wine.

"I call it *'Berry Good'*!" I shouted over the music to the mixed reaction of applause and groans. While caring for Jo at the cabin I had found enough late berries to make exactly one and a half bottles. Having already cleared it with Travis, the boys were able to have a half glass each, graduating from the splash they received at the dinner party. Once again, Norah emphatically refused a taste of the "gross juice." This prompted Chris and Ryan to unveil their mystery tray so she would have something to enjoy too. A dozen dipped candy apples glistened under the multicoloured lights.

"Very impressive!" Jo complimented them, having been the one to find the recipe among the farmhouse's plethora of books. Cooking was Jo's favorite way to teach the children a variety of skills: fractions, chemistry, reading comprehension, and of course, culinary arts. She whispered to me that she was apprehensive letting them work with hot sugar unsupervised but opted to encourage their independence. "Besides, Paul was doing the dishes!" she laughed, elbowing him in the ribs.

Eventually the adults prepared to retreat, leaving the kids to a game of truth or dare while relaxing in the newly hung hammocks.

"*Wait!*" Ryan shouted, putting a pause to the cleanup. "Do you want to live with us, Paul?"

"Ya, Paul," Chris added, not wanting to be left out. "Do you want to live with us, *forever?*" A grin spread across Paul's face. With his new haircut and fresh hand-me down clothes, he was almost unrecognizable from the day he arrived.

"Well...I wouldn't want to intrude..." Ryan, Chris, and Norah sprang up to hug him, insisting in unison, *"Pleeeeease!"*

"I guess it's decided," Will said. "Welcome to the homestead, Paul." Released from the clutches of the children, Paul shook everyone's hands, thanking each person in turn.

"I'm sorry I don't have a gift for you, boys," he said, turning to face everyone. "But I think I'm well enough now to share a gift with you all. I'll need help, but what do you think about getting the power back on around here?" Claps, tears, and cheers ensued.

"You know what this calls for?" Ryan shouted, whipping off his shirt.

"*HIPPIE DIP!*" Chris answered as they both streaked from the greenhouse and jumped into the pond. Will looked at me mischievously before grabbing me and throwing me over his shoulder like a sack of potatoes as I screamed in protest. Before long almost everyone found their way into the water in various states of dress.

"Best birthday ever!" cried one of the boys, playfully splashing their father. A chilly end-of-October water fight ensued. Unable to stand it any longer, I clambered from the pond in pursuit of a towel. Standing on the bank, exposed only by the moonlight, I caught a glimpse of Paul and Jo quietly holding hands.

XIX

"We'll be down to half a tank." Steve looked up from the calculations he had been working on after dinner. "We won't have enough to run the generator through the winter if this doesn't work."

"I understand what you're saying, but the gas has likely already started to degrade. Who's to say it will even be usable in two or three months from now? Plus, we can see if there's anything left to siphon on the way. Although, I think the shelf life of any gasoline at this point will be questionable." I added my two cents. "How confident are you that we can pull this off, Paul?"

"I've had gas sit in jerry cans for two years that could still run a chainsaw," Travis interjected. "I know that's the exception but don't forget, we have fuel stabilizer. It should help."

"As long as the system hasn't been poached or damaged, and we can get to it, I'm ninety percent confident we can get enough power for the farmhouse, the barn, and maybe even the winter greenhouse. I'm telling you—the place is a bona fide mansion. No cost was spared by these folks."

"What if they are home?" I was worried. The quick trip to Bridgewater a few months ago somehow felt very different than this trip to Truro. It was two and a half times as far for starters, and we weren't as familiar with the route.

"If they survived, they're probably hunkered down in a

fancy-ass bunker, waiting out the apocalypse with glasses of champagne in their hands," Paul tried to assure me. I snickered at the visual, but it did little for my anxiety. "They were barely ever home—they've got five more places just like it. Oil money or something."

"No risk, no reward," Travis piped up. "Honestly, if we pull this off, it has the potential to take us from surviving to thriving, as Alex would say. The fuel is going to run out eventually one way or another. Whatever solutions we come up with now is an investment in ourselves for years to come." His optimism was infectious.

"Why didn't you have a solar system installed yourself, Paul?" Will wanted to know.

"The shoemaker always goes barefoot," Paul sighed. "Anette had other health problems on top of her diabetes. When we lost our son, Jerry, her mental health really challenged us. She couldn't work or anything. There never seemed to be enough money."

Will and I could certainly appreciate the financial aspect of what he was saying. Even with the provincial government rebate, the upfront cost of a solar system had been prohibitive for us too. Whenever we managed to save a couple of bucks, an emergency would swallow them up whether it was the tractor needing fixing or the septic bed needing to be replaced or flights home to see Will's grandpa before he died. There just never seemed to be enough cash on hand. We kept hoping for the day when sustainable options were more accessible to the little guys.

"I didn't know you lost a son," Jo said, covering his hand on the table with her own.

"It was a long time ago now, but talking about it, well, it still feels like yesterday. He was a scallop fisherman, just starting out. Stolen by the sea," Paul explained before changing the subject. "So, who is going to be my all-star crew?" Will, Travis, and Steve were the obvious choices. Alex had opted out of the meeting due to a headache but had already said he'd stay behind to look after the kids with Jo.

"I'd also like to go," I spoke up. "I'm not the handiest but I like to think I'm a good project manager. I can help keep things organized so we are in and out faster."

"Aka: bossy," Will teased.

"Hey, in the words of the late RBG, women belong in all spaces where decisions are made!" I quoted back at him.

"I'm just kidding," he said, pulling me close. "I'd love to have you riding shotgun, and I know you miss road trips." My husband knew me too well.

"It might be my last chance."

The rest of the evening was spent getting packed up for the morning.

Tools.

Ladders.

Ropes.

Tie downs.

Jerry cans.

Although we had made fun of Travis's forty-eight-foot extension ladder when he brought it over (and mercilessly debated if it was compensating for something), it was suddenly a key piece of the puzzle. Even collapsed it still hung out the back of the trailer by several feet. Out of habit I tied a piece of red flagging tape to the furthest rung.

Goodbyes were again kept short in the morning. We would have less than ten hours of daylight and almost five of them would be consumed by driving. Paul told us that the install had taken him and two other experienced guys about six hours. If everything went perfectly, he figured we would have it disassembled in three or four. That only left us with a two-hour buffer to get it loaded plus any other stops to look for gas. At least we probably wouldn't have to worry about traffic jams, the route we were taking up Trunk 14 never posed that problem even when the province's population had topped out at one million.

I giggled a bit as Will pulled up to the stop sign at the end of our road.

"What?" he asked.

"Nerves more than anything," I replied. "I was just wondering who you thought you were stopping for?" He reached over and patted me on the knee reassuringly.

"Aren't you the one who always says integrity is doing what is right, not what is easy, even if no one is around to see it? By the way, Ryan lent us his phone for the drive, why don't you set us up with some tunes?" he suggested. Alone in our truck with music playing over the speakers and a bag of trail mix between us, it felt like old times for a moment. I pretended that the lack of traffic and the empty homes we passed were just folks on vacation. It was such a nice day, everyone must be on the lake.

What was harder to imagine away were the hastily dug graves that filled the churchyards we passed. Even under normal circumstances, families without life insurance would be hard pressed to cover the cost of one sudden death, let alone multiple burials at once. Folks promised each other they would hold receptions and services at a later date, "when this was all over." When the police department was still operational, there were reports of people being charged for illegally burying their loved ones in cemeteries at night, with nothing more than a blanket and a shovel. Alternatively, some bodies never had a grave dug at all. Homes were simply adorned with scraps of caution tape, or hastily scribbled *'Do Not Enter'* signs—entire families succumbed to Sigma inside.

"Want to get a coffee at Tim Hortons?" Will joked as we turned onto the main stretch of highway. Unable to maintain the façade, I burst into tears. "Oh Ness, I'm sorry." He motioned for me to move into the middle of the bench seat so he could put his arm around me.

"It's just so sad!" Tears streamed down my cheeks. "Sometimes I forget, you know? We will probably never see your parents again. All our friends—gone! All of this...waste!" I gestured out the window as we passed a little strip mall, its store front windows smashed and knee-high grass growing up through the cracks in the sidewalk. I quietly hung onto him for the rest of the trip, remnants of the old-world streaming by us like a deranged horror film.

When we arrived at the address of our solar powered dreams, Travis and Will got to work cutting the lock on the iron gate across the driveway.

"That was tough to see," Paul said, stepping up to the passenger window of our truck. "Living in the bush, you can't really appreciate what happened to people in town until you see it for yourself. There was no escape for them."

The pandemic was fuel to a fire in terms of the global housing crisis. Economically blessed folks were gobbling up rural real estate at exorbitant prices, even places that had sat rotting on the market for years. Many of them were also landlords and as they cashed out, their homes and apartments were bought up by large corporations and turned into Airbnbs. The average tenant, completely priced out of the market by industry closures, had nowhere to go.

Tent cities had exploded in downtown cores around the world, the perfect breeding ground for community transmission. It is always the poor who pay the most.

The grand gate swung open allowing us access to the beautifully cobblestoned driveway. Fancy iron lampposts dotted the lane and, although unkempt, the landscaping had clearly been magazine worthy at one time. As we approached the mansion, two palm trees waved at us from where they grew beside decorative columns framing the front door. Curved stairs wrapped around twin stone turrets that led to the first of two balconies. The entire home was stylish grey brick with white trim, and the roof was slate-grey steel. Paul was right, no one appeared to be home.

"Where are the solar panels?" I asked. Paul motioned for us to follow him around back. The rear of the home was south facing, and its entire roof was filled to the brim with a rail-less solar system. It was truly a thing of beauty, although maybe not in the esthetic sense.

"If you guys want to set up the ladders, Vanessa can help me find a way in. Once I make sure the system is offline, we should probably work on loading the batteries while we are all fresh. They aren't light." Everyone set to work on their assigned task. Using a crowbar, I pried open a garage window where the inverter, batteries, and controls were housed. Sirens started blaring as I made the breach.

"Guess it still works!" Paul shouted at me over the noise with an enthusiastic grin. My eardrums protested in pain, no longer accustomed to such intense decibel levels. The sound also callously gifted me with a flashback of a 911 call in a distant city. I gritted my teeth against the unwelcome intrusion. It had been a while.

Once inside the garage, Paul quickly deactivated the alarm system and my blood pressure settled back toward baseline. Sunlight flooded in as he opened the main garage door, illuminating our workspace. The batteries were much larger than I envisioned, and there were five of them.

"About two hundred pounds, each," Paul said, answering my unasked question. After we backed up the hay trailer as close as possible, I did some stretches while Paul went to collect the others. It took a little over an hour before we got them all loaded and secured. Everyone was sweating and, although we could each feel the clock ticking, I encouraged a quick water and electrolyte break. We didn't have a lot of time as it was, so we definitely didn't have time for easily preventable mistakes or injuries. The men dutifully ate the apple slices I handed out, accompanied by Jo's homemade hazelnut butter for dipping.

Under Paul's guidance and the knowledge of knots that Travis had gained volunteering with the New Germany Fire Department, surprisingly quick work was made of bringing the forty-five solar panels safely to the ground. By two o'clock the entire eighty-thousand-dollar system was fully loaded. Seeing the hay wagon filled with the strangers' possessions, I was overwhelmed with a mixture of guilt, gratitude, and sadness. It would have taken a whole year's worth of wages to purchase ourselves. Of course, it didn't make sense on so many levels to let the system sit and rot just because it wasn't "ours"—but only one short year ago theft over five thousand dollars had up to a ten-year prison sentence in Canada. Integrity was getting tricky. I decided to leave an apologetic note to the homeowners in case they ever returned. Then, with some effort, I manually closed the garage door behind me.

"So raccoons don't get in," I justified with a shrug to Will's cocked eyebrow.

A couple of quick stops on our way home enabled us to refuel the trucks and replenish the jerry cans. The initial shock of the journey having worn off, I couldn't help but wonder if, as a species, we would have done anything different if we knew before what we know now. If communities were designed with a basic level of independence, could we have beaten the virus in a long game? If access to uncrowded housing and nutritious food was stable—maybe even a right—could everyone have "stayed the blazes home"? Would the masses have played boardgames with their kids and eaten too much bread while scientists sought a solution instead of combatting misinformation? Was there any universe in which humans collectively had the foresight to prepare for a threat of this scale?

I had my doubts.

The likes of Jane Goodall and David Suzuki had beaten their chests about climate change for decades, and they were essentially ignored. It appeared we were destined for demise, one way or another. Sigma had just beaten the acidification of the ocean to the punch.

As we turned back onto the last stretch of road home, a pink and orange sunset had begun to fill the sky. It reminded me of an article from India that read, thanks to COVID lockdowns, the Himalayan peaks could be seen from one hundred kilometers away for the first time in decades because of the reduced pollution. Perhaps what we saw as human devastation was Mother Earth, or God as some would call her, correcting herself.

Part Two

"I am not what happened to me, I am what I choose to become."
-Carl Gustav Jung

I

I thought Jess would leave me for sure the day I began digging up the backyard. She was an optimist and saw the bunker as a bad omen. We had already spent many nights arguing over the potential trajectory of the pandemic, her on the side of science, and I on the side of intuition.

"They say Omicron will establish herd immunity. That's the last hurdle before the pandemic becomes an endemic, like the flu," she told me. "We just have to be patient and follow their recommendations." I was never certain who "they" were, and I didn't trust them. First it was two weeks of lockdowns, then it was two, no, *three* shots, then the final third wave became the fourth and fifth waves. As I watched the shelves at local stores become increasingly bare, with fewer and fewer cashiers working to ring up orders, something triggered inside me. My gut was screaming that things were about to get a whole lot worse before they got better.

In Afghanistan in 2012, my squad was caught in the middle of tribal crossfire during a community patrol. Forced to abandon our damaged Light Tactical Vehicle and unable to establish communications on our radios, we were in acute danger of being pinched off by the warring factions. During the struggle, my team leader was hit by shrapnel resulting in an open femoral fracture to his right leg. He was unable to walk, and we couldn't relay our location to the rest of our platoon. After securing a tourniquet, a decision was made for our gunner and driver to make a run for support while I stayed behind to tend to him. Night began to fall and there was still no sign of a recovery mission. Although we were semi-hidden under an apricot tree behind an old garden wall, it was a miracle we hadn't been discovered. The sounds of boots and shouting and gunfire were only a few feet from where our backs rested.

Unexpectedly, the owner of the garden, an Afghan father named Aadhil, spotted us and waved for us to enter his home. Quickly weighing the risks, we decided to trust him. I made sure he saw the Canadian flag sewn to my shoulder as we approached. So far, we had been well received by neutral locals in the area. I must have had four leaf clovers firmly planted in my asshole that day because Aadhil saved my life by hiding us in his homemade bunker with his family.

Deceptively concealed beneath an old Turkman carpet on their living room floor was a hatch leading to a large underground room. It had cots, a bunk bed, and shelves carved into the sandy earth that were lined with homemade preserves and bottles of water. The floors were warmed with prayer mats, and a qibla compass hung on the northeast wall.

For two days and three nights we waited out the firefight, the ground rumbling around us with exploding mortars. My team leader passed in and out of consciousness but aside from keeping him warm and comfortable, there was nothing more we could do. To pass the time and preoccupy our minds, I taught the family's young son, Aaban, to play tic-tac-toe by etching the game into the earthen floor with the side of a fork.

When the firefight finally ceased on the third morning, I was unable to wake my team lead. Evidently, he had died in his sleep, likely from internal bleeding. Numbly, I snapped off the dog tag around his neck and put it in my shirt pocket in case we got separated. Retrieving his beautiful Turkman carpet from above, Aadhil helped me roll up the lifeless body inside it for transport.

As the family and I somberly emerged from their bunker, we found the town heavily damaged. The east side of their home was now rubble, but it did not draw their attention away from helping me reach safety. I suspected the task of rebuilding was an anticipated intergenerational curse. Aadhil, a mechanic by trade, was able to retrieve a semi-functional van from the wreckage of his shop across the street. We loaded his family, along with the body of my team leader, into the oil burning heap of burgundy steel. As he sped off toward the Canadian base, dust billowed from rusted out holes in the floorboard between my feet. After carefully navigating the theatrics of approaching the Canadian base in an unmarked civilian vehicle, I made sure Aadhil and his family were well compensated. For many years after, Aaban and I would exchange letters at Christmas and Ramadan, but I hadn't heard back from him since Trump organized to pull the last of the American troops from the area in 2021.

Since moving back to Peterborough, I hadn't exactly made friends with my neighbours. I decided to retire after my last tour in Syria and the noise of their daily lives kept me on edge—children screaming, dogs barking, music playing, lawnmowers backfiring. I got in the habit of sleeping during the day, with pharmaceutical support, and staying up at night when the neighbourhood was quieter. So, when I first stuck my shovel in the ground on a late

May evening in 2024, no one bothered to ask any questions—except for Jess.

"Are you seriously doing this, Nathan? People are going to think you're nuts!" she nagged me, clearly dissatisfied with my indifferent response. Maybe "they" would be right, maybe I was nuts. They would probably be a little mad too if they experienced the sights, smells, sounds, and tastes forced upon me during combat. I hadn't adjusted to civilian life as well as Jess, my family, or my team of therapists, hoped. All I knew was I had the same feeling in my gut as the day I decided to trust Aadhil. It was a feeling I couldn't shake, much less explain. Instead of beating myself up for not meeting the square peg criteria everyone demanded, I got busy fortifying my round hole.

II

"How are things on the East Coast, Willy?" I asked my brother-from-another-mother. Thanks to the Atlantic lockdown bubble, it had been years since I could get out to see him and his wife. I missed my friends and their dedication to a quieter, more methodical way of living. I especially missed the heavily wooded barrier between them and the rest of the world. In my Peterborough subdivision, the air always seemed to buzz with busyness and anxiety, but in East Dalhousie the call of a loon or rain on the steel roof was a quick salve for a troubled mind.

Their home was the first place I'd been able to sleep through the night since retiring from the military. It was only a few years back that everyone thought *they* were the crazy ones tossing lucrative careers aside and moving to the middle of Nova Scotia where they didn't know a soul, to farm of all things. But I understood—sort of. When your own fleeting mortality repeatedly slaps you in the face, it no longer makes sense to live another day without clear intention. At least, that was how Vanessa explained it when she decided to leave her career in paramedicine. I guess to the world of consumerism it would appear insane—trading in the luxury of fingertip convenience just for a little peace and calm. For them, there was also no pressure to keep up with the Joneses because the Joneses didn't even know where East Dalhousie was.

"Not good, Nate," Will's familiar voice replied. "Vanessa's on her way back from that rally in Halifax. Did you see it on the news? About the Defenders? It's pretty messed up man, I imagine she'll be rattled when she gets home." He had to fill me in about the deer cull and the ensuing suicides as I had sworn off social media, including the news, for the time being. The fear mongering and constant negativity just got me too amped up, and my lack of focus rapidly led to a lack of function. My disordered hypervigilance was like having adrenaline constantly pumped straight into my brain and it was exhausting, especially for a guy that hardly slept on a good day. My nervous system and I were on a need-to-know basis.

"Give her a hug for me, will ya?" I told him. "In other news, I'm probably just a few buckets of dirt away from being single myself." When Jess got home from work yesterday, she saw the size of the hole I had dug and then promptly didn't speak to me for the rest of the night. I wasn't sure if it was the hole itself or because I forgot to put dinner on, again. My parting gift from the service was revolving temporary memory loss so meal planning— ok, planning in general—was not my strong suit. Either way, she was pissed off. Again.

"When was the last time you did something nice for her?" Will asked.

"Technically the bunker *is* doing something nice for her. She's the only one I'm letting in if shit hits the fan!" Will laughed at my weak defense.

"Just because *you* think it's something nice doesn't mean *she* thinks it's something nice. Maybe try doing something else? Like, plan a date or something? Light some candles? You know, the stuff women like—and I don't mean like the women you bunked with overseas!" He expertly shot down my next argument. It was hard to get anything past a buddy who knew you since you were kids. He was right though, I needed to do better. Besides, Jess had been pulling doubles and triples as staff slowly stopped showing up to the facility where she worked. I asked her to quit several times but her loyalty to the residents she worked with was less like professional courtesy and more like love. I tried hard to understand that too. She had been assisting the disabled—or rather, "folks with disabilities" as she would correct me—for over ten years. They were now more like her family than her actual family.

"Guess it will still be a while before we can work on the cabin again, eh?" I changed the subject.

"Looks that way," Will confirmed. "But if you ever get tired of bunker life, you know the address. Door is always open for you both." I was reluctant to hang up the phone, but also knew I should try to make up with Jess before she headed back in for another shift. I decided to pack her a wholesome lunch and even thought to include a sexy note with the promise of a back rub and a bubble bath. I also set an alarm on my phone, so I'd remember to give her a hug and a kiss before she left. I knew I wasn't perfect, but at least I was a work in progress?

III

The next Wednesday Jess was hastily sent home from her job at Bonny Acres for the last time. The residents' families had been called to pick them up and management assured staff that arrangements were being made for those without a place to go. Rolling electrical blackouts had begun in the area and the skeleton staff could no longer safely run the place.

Jess was absolutely devastated.

The people she worked with were vulnerable, many having suffered various forms of trauma from discrimination to exploitation to neglect—the entire spectrum of abuse. The pandemic was especially hard on them, not only because of the strict isolation protocols at Bonny Acres, but because the whole concept demanded abstract reasoning. Jess felt like she was being forced to abandon them when they needed her the most. If their families were unable to support their unique needs at the best of times...After finding me in the backyard to inform me she added her name to the list of potential adopters, she quietly picked up a shovel.

"You look like you're digging your own grave, not our passport to survival!" I joked, trying to lighten her mood. Her retort—*"Might as fucking well be!"*—told me exactly where the jest had landed. So much of how she identified was tied to her work. There were countless birthday parties, weddings, Christmas mornings, and New Year's Eves she had missed because she couldn't, or wouldn't, take time off. Bonny Acres was chronically understaffed and over the years I watched her career become less of a job and more of a lifestyle. The trust and connection I saw her develop with the people in her care obviously made it worth it. Personally, I never felt the management appreciated her or her sacrifices enough and their unsympathetic dismissal seemed par for the course.

While I let Jess work out her frustration on the earth, I turned my attention to cutting cribbing. Someone yelled from an open window up the street for us to quit with the yard work as it was ten o'clock at night, to which I replied, "Or what?" The Peterborough police force had been decimated by Sigma. All that remained were rookies pulled out of the academy early and senior management working from home. The dispatch centre, now an amalgamation of all Peterborough and Kawartha Lakes 911 services, was working on weeklong, two-person, lockdown shifts. The dispatchers brought in their own cots and bedding and an emergency services kitchen dropped off meals at the door. Basically, if it wasn't an active murder or kidnapping in progress, the cops probably weren't coming. And maybe not even then.

"Have you heard from your dad?" Jess broke the silence between us.

"No, but you know him. Probably out fishing." It was getting harder to believe my own lie. It was three weeks since I had been able to get him on the phone at his cabin. When he retired a few years ago he cashed in his Southern Ontario real estate in exchange for northern seclusion and the best pike fishing in the province—and half the land tax he was quick to point out.

Jess traded her shoveling for side bend stretches. In the moonlight I could see the sweaty 'V' that had soaked through her shirt between her lean shoulder blades. Her messy ponytail, rolled up track pants, and look of steely determination on her porcelain doll face made me smile.

"What about you?" I asked. "Heard from your mom and dad?"

"Not since they crossed the border. I still can't believe they actually left." Jess's parents had forfeited their condo in Peterborough for the Florida Panhandle. As a family, they used to go down every few months to stay with her aunt but, since COVID, they hadn't been able to. Her mom felt an enormous sense of guilt when her sister's husband, a Florida senator, died of Omicron (Sigma's precursor). Unable to bear the thought of her sister being alone, Jess's mom and dad decided to make a run for it as border restrictions tightened. Besides, they said, they wouldn't survive electrical blackouts in their condo as her father relied on a home dialysis machine. They hoped the power would be more stable at the late senator's house. I had reservations but I imagined the combination of her sister's finances and access to the private American healthcare system wouldn't hurt though.

I set down my saw and climbed into the hole with Jess, pulling her against me.

"It's just...a lot. You know? It's a lot at once," she mumbled into the crook of my neck. "I'm exhausted." I nodded, holding her weight as her knees wobbled, her body threatening to cave in.

"You've been living in sixth gear since the pandemic started. I know it feels like you don't have a lot to show for it right now, but you know what you got that no one else does?" She shook her head between quiet sobs. "Me.

You've got me, and I will do anything to keep you safe. I will die for you. Right here, right now, if I had to." My words didn't soften her anguish.

"I don't want to die alone!" she cried. I instantly recognized my verbal misstep.

"Ok, let's make a deal." I changed my tactic. "If the ship is going down, we go down together. You and me until the end. Ok? You won't die alone, I promise." We both knew it was an impossible promise, but the longer we stood there, the more regulated her breathing became.

"Let's call it a night. Popcorn and a movie? I've got my laptop charged so no interruptions." I kissed her sweaty forehead and we climbed out of the hole together. As Jess got cleaned up, I put fresh sheets on the bed, her favorite thing to climb into after a shower. Then I made a bowl of popcorn—fresh kernels, not a bag, and real butter—and set up her favorite movie to rewatch while falling asleep, "The Biggest Little Farm."

"This always makes me think of Will and Vanessa," she sighed, curled up in a mountain of pillows beside me. "I wonder how they're doing."

"I talked to Willy last week. They're doing ok. I forgot to tell you they said hello and that they miss us." She nodded wearily. It wasn't long before soft snores echoed from her side of the bed—she had fallen asleep wrist deep in popcorn kernels.

Pausing the film, I reopened my files containing the plans for the bunker. I had calculated that it would be ready in about two more weeks but, with Jess home to help, it could be as early as next Friday. All that would be left was to finish gathering the supplies to stock it, which would be right up Jess's shopaholic alley. I had squirreled away a Ziplock bag of cash in our freezer for just such an occasion.

It was a habit passed down by my father and his father before that—a remnant of the Great Depression, although apparently my grandfather kept his in an outhouse. Many stores in Peterborough were no longer accepting plastic and ATMs were not reliably stocked. Cash-in-hand was king again, and if it could buy Jess a little reprieve from her mental torment, so be it.

IV

One afternoon at the end of June, black and green smoke appeared on the horizon. The power had been out for a week and, according to an old army buddy who worked for the city's fire department, no one from utilities was showing up for work anymore. People were either sick, dead, or scared. He stopped answering his cell phone too a few days later.

As evening fell, I could see the silhouette of tall flames while standing in our backyard. It appeared the downtown waterfront was on fire, which was confirmed when a change in wind brought the sickly smell of burnt oatmeal with it. The fire had reached the Quaker Oats plant.

Jess, struggling under the weight of her emotional baggage, had rarely been getting out of bed. Occasionally I'd coax her out to show her progress on the bunker or to ask her opinion on something, which she would offer begrudgingly before pulling the comforter back over her head.

A low point as a carbon dioxide reservoir? *Sure, Nathan.*
A dug-in garbage can to hold water? *Ok, Nathan.*
RhinoWrap? *Whatever, Nathan.*
Plants for oxygen? *Go ahead, Nathan.*
Ventilation blast valves? *I. Don't. Care. Nathan.*

Unable to wait any longer, I sat on the end of the mattress and rubbed her feet until she woke up. I knew what was about to happen was going to be hard for her. For us. For anyone left alive in the city.

"What do you want, Nathan?" she mumbled, brushing away strands of black hair from her face. It stung a little to hear how suspicious she was when I tried to be nice—not that I blamed her. It was just so obvious that she wasn't used to it, so much so that it she was uncomfortable. It made me feel like a huge dick. I'd been so wrapped up in my own shit since my last tour that my behavior as her partner, well, it wasn't something I was proud of. Since we were home together all the time now, I promised myself I'd do better. I didn't bother telling her though—I made that same promise to her many times before. This time I would just show her, turn my feelings into actions as my therapist coached, but it was becoming apparent it was going to take longer to win her back than I realized.

"It's time," I told her softly.

"What do you mean? For dinner? I'm not hungry." She pulled her feet away, scrunching her body into a ball.

"Jess," I knelt at the side of the bed in front of her. "There's a fire headed our way. The bunker is ready. It's time to go." She opened her eyes and stared at me, as if trying to decide if I was real or just another nightmare. I kissed her forehead to assure her that I was real, and serious.

"A fire?" She slowly sat up, massaging her jaw and temple.

"I've been watching it since this afternoon. It looks like it started at the waterfront. The wind is pushing it this way and I haven't heard a single siren."

"Ok." It was all she said, her eyes seeming to look right through me. Her body language was permeated with defeat. I was worried about her.

"Put the last of your things together. I'll do a sweep to see if we missed anything." I left her to get ready. I had already packed up the essentials, but something Will had said on the phone suddenly inspired me, so I packed a few extra things into an outlawed plastic shopping bag. As I passed by the front window of the house, an unnatural orange glow and the distant sound of crackling quickened my step. Upstairs, Jess started sneezing.

"Nathan!" she yelled. "Oh my god, Nathan, I can smell it. Oh my god—Nathan—come up here!" I heard her slide open one of the windows that led out onto the roof. Stepping onto the shingles, a gust of hot, toxic air hit us, forcing us to pull our shirts up over our noses. We could usually see the clock tower on Market Hall from where we stood, but everything was obscured by a growing wall of flames and thick, impenetrable, black smoke. As I reached out to hold Jess, the goosebumps on her arms pricked against my skin. We stood dumbstruck, minutes passing like hours. As the fire found its way through natural gas lines, explosions shot up into the sky in a shocking display of pyrotechnics. For a moment my brain was tricked into thinking I was back in Afghanistan. The muscles in my body braced for impact. I instinctively felt for my sidearm.

"Ok, let's go." Jess broke the trance, leading me back inside. "Meet you down there in ten minutes, I guess." She sighed, too tired to scream. I shook off the lingering combat hallucination like a bear emerging from an icy lake. My priority right now was Jess's safety and, having given myself a task, my thoughts came back into focus.

Exactly ten minutes later Jess was at the door to the bunker. For someone who was usually running late, her punctuality was a gift to me. She knew that strict adherence to plans was something that helped me feel under control, even when my internal world was spinning. I suppose she noticed my flashback earlier.

Smiling ironically, I hopped back over the fence from collecting her a bouquet of our neighbour's prized tulips. There hadn't been any sign of activity there for weeks so I figured the flowers wouldn't be missed.

"Welcome to Fort Jess," I said as I pulled open the door. Snake plants and battery-operated candles (nice touch, Willy) cast zebra striped shadows on the back wall. Her favorite band, The Lumineers, played from my laptop speakers, which I managed to keep trickle-charged with a portable solar bank. On the floor I had arranged a nest of pillows and blankets around a charcuterie board filled with cheeses, fruits, veggies, cured meats, and organic candies. Jess was something of a health food nut, so I had sourced locally as much as possible—which had quickly become the only option anyway. A packed bong and a cooler of beer and wine completed the scene. As Jess took it all in, a whimsical smile spread across her face, a smile I hadn't seen since we were dating—before life got so messy.

"If we're going down, this is where I want to go down," she said as I locked the bunker door behind us.

The next day we could hear buildings collapsing above ground. At one point the bunker got so hot we had to wrap our naked bodies with wet sheets to stay cool. In case of toxic smoke and fumes, we decided to wait a week before opening the bunker to assess the damage. We tried to pass the time playing cards, reading, writing ridiculous poems, and giving each other long, full body massages. However, the rate we were going through batteries and food, and the smell of the compost toilet, started to ruin the mood.

On the sixth evening we cracked the hatch to test for air quality. Although we were met with the scent of destruction, we were able to breathe. What we saw through that thin line of dusk was the total loss of our home. We could see clear across where it once stood to the twisted and charred chunks of metal that used to be our cars in the driveway. We hadn't been able to buy gas for them anyway, but the sight was nonetheless jarring. We closed the door and spent the rest of the night quietly wondering what else the morning light would bring.

V

"We can't stay here," Jess said aloud, echoing my own thoughts. Our neighbourhood no longer existed, razed to the ground. As far as we could see, the whole city had been reduced to piles of smoking rubble. The pink and blistered body of a cat bolted past us down the street. Jess crouched down and retched uncontrollably, clinging to my pant leg to steady herself.

"What are we going to do?" she sputtered, wiping her mouth with the back of her hand.

"We'll figure it out," I said, faking confidence while helping her to stand. I didn't really have a contingency plan for this. For starters, we were now in the middle of a food desert. The bunker was never meant to be a long-term survival option and we had eaten through most of our stores already. Ten cans of soup did not a survival plan make.

"I guess the good news is," I offered, "shit has officially hit the fan and we're still standing." Jess's frozen expression didn't change. "Let's put together our bug-out bags, ok?" I hoped to shift her attention from trauma to task. It worked for me in the moment sometimes. Other times diversion was just avoidance in a monkey suit, prolonging the inevitable. Jess followed me back into the bunker like a freshly whipped zombie.

"Only the necessities," I reminded her as I stood my two

old army packs against the wall (that I absolutely did not illegally keep after discharge, if anyone's asking). "Try to keep it light. The heaviest items should rest against the middle of your back and shoulder blades. It's not how much it weighs—it's how you carry it." Jess systematically packed the bags as I moved around the bunker collecting whatever I thought might be useful for a long journey—not that I had any idea where we were going.

"Nathan," Jess eventually said, "I need to go to work."

"What do you mean? I thought everyone was being sent home from Bonny Acres?" I was puzzled.

"Management *said* everyone was being sent home. But... I just...I have this feeling? I need to go check. I can't explain it...I can't stop thinking about it." As much as I could appreciate the experience of unshakable feelings, I was deeply afraid of what we might find when we got there, but I simply couldn't think of an argument that would dissuade her. The folks she worked with meant the world to her. And really, we had nowhere else to be. A memory from when I was a teenager suddenly occurred to me.

"You've given me an idea." The surprised look on her face told me she had been preparing for a battle. "Will used to have a couple of four wheelers, we would take them deer hunting."

"And?" She stared at me expectantly.

"And I don't remember him saying he ever sold them. In fact, I'm pretty sure they were still at his parent's place when he was visiting last, in that shipping container his dad converted." Will's parents, Mike and Ethel, lived on the opposite side of Peterborough. They treated me like their own son, but I hadn't done the best job keeping in touch the last few years, just like with almost everyone else. It would be a half day's walk to their place but, since they were on the other side of the river, there was a chance they had survived the fire. Will said they had been very cautious about self-isolation throughout the pandemic and were still alive and hibernating the last time we spoke in May. It wasn't the best plan, but at least it was forward momentum and Jess seemed genuinely jazzed about it.

"So, go find Will's parents, see if we can borrow the quads, and then check on Bonny Acres?" she confirmed. Bonny Acres was about thirty kilometers outside of Peterborough, south of Norwood. I figured even if we couldn't get the quads, but we were able to find food, we could walk the rest of the way if we had to. Either way, I didn't really see any harm in making the trip if it would put her mind at ease. After that, her guess was as good as mine regarding our future.

Shouldering our bags and donning preemptive full-face respirators, we walked off in the direction of Will's old house. It was the first and only time I didn't mind the slight restriction to my vision where the mask sat against my face. The landscape was disturbing enough without the added panorama. The city we had grown up in was reduced to a wasteland of torched and smoldering concrete shells. A plume of ash billowed from beneath our footsteps. We decided to walk down the middle of the trafficless road to avoid being crushed by unstable walls.

As we approached the core, I caught a glimpse of a disheveled man and woman standing in the middle of what used to be a subsidized apartment complex. They appeared to be washing and drying dishes, placing imaginary plates into imaginary cupboards above their heads. I caught Jess's elbow, cautioning her against making contact. We simply had no way of knowing if they were infected—or trustworthy. We passed by with caution and yet the couple waved to us as if we were just regular neighbours on a noontime stroll, maniacal smiles on their sooty faces. We politely waved back before continuing our way toward the river. The spectacle was a stark reminder of the many ways shock and trauma can manifest. I wasn't sure how they even survived as the downtown hub appeared to be where the fire was the hottest, but the answer was soon revealed.

A few small clusters of people sat forlorn along the bank of the Otonabee river, in which they had sought refuge during the fire. Unsure where to go now, they seemed resigned to waiting for rescue that I suspected was never coming. At least the river provided them with a source of water. A child, maybe five years old, and his father fished from the shore using rudimentary fishing poles they had created from nothing more than a chunk of iron pipe and thin wire. A woman, maybe the boy's mother, grilled a couple of small sunfish over coals. A few articles of mud-stained clothing drooped from the branches of surviving bushes along the river's edge. The whole scene was shrouded in an eerie silence. Some folks stared at us as we passed by while others seemed oblivious to our presence.

Luckily, the Hunter Street bridge was intact, so we were able to make our way across without having to go for a swim ourselves. Less fortunately, the river had not been successful in blockading the fire. As we pressed on, any obvious signs of life faded behind us. A lump began to form in my throat as we neared Mike and Ethel's subdivision. The route was so unrecognizable that the only thing assuring me we were in the right place was muscle memory from all the times Will and I walked to his home together after school. His mom would always have grilled cheese sandwiches on fresh bakery bread waiting for us, which I'd give my left arm for right about now.

"Mike, you're a goddamn genius," I muttered as their property came into view. The house was a total loss but, in the backyard, virtually untouched save for smoke damage, was the shipping container. There was no evidence of their travel trailer or their jeep in the driveway. "Maybe they went to their cottage," I told Jess hopefully. I reached for my phone to tell Will the news, but the lack of service bars was a harsh reminder that calling out was impossible.

"Door's locked," Jess said, stepping back from the metal can. Snapping my fingers, I pointed at a nearby clay flowerpot where I suddenly remembered Will hiding a key years ago. Jess picked up the pot and in the middle of a perfect ring of ash lay the brass key. Jess hopped up and down gleefully before thrusting her hip toward me in an invitation to join her in the "Backpack Dance," to which I simply had to oblige. I don't know who started laughing first but soon our respirators were completely fogged up as we swung our arms back and forth, faster and faster. Maybe it was delirium, but it felt good to let go. To laugh. To have something to celebrate—even if it was just a tiny piece of metal in the palm of her hand.

Finally able to get hold of ourselves, we removed our masks, wiping sweat from the superimposed creases around our faces. Easily fitting the key into the lock, we swung open the container door and were greeted with the faint smell of stale grease. Will's two quads were parked safely inside beneath tarps covered in a fine layer of dust and ash. Four full jerry cans of fuel sat beside them in a neat row.

"*Thank YOU!*" I shouted to Mike and Ethel, wherever they were. As we searched through the sea can, we also found some old camping gear. No longer on foot, we could accommodate a few additional luxury items such as a two-person tent with a floor and a door, instead of my rustic single pup. I also found a collapsible fishing rod and a small tackle box of lures while Jess triumphantly held up a half can of bug spray and a bottle of sunscreen. Then she really hit the jackpot with the discovery of a portable camp stove, complete with untapped propane bottles. The only thing missing was helmets, which wouldn't have concerned me in my younger cowboy days, but now I had Jess to think about and we had no idea where to find the closest ER doctor. We would just have to be careful.

As we packed up to leave, I also spied a can of fluorescent orange spray paint and decided to leave a note in the unlikely case that someone returned.

I. O. U.
Nathan

VI

With a summer's afternoon sun behind us, we decided to leave the smoking city for Bonny Acres immediately. We would look for a place to spend the night along the way where we could hunker down and consider our next steps. Unsure what the highway would bring us, we decided to try our luck on the Lang-Hastings trail. The air cleared as we made our way out of Peterborough and through forests and fields untouched by the fire. Startled grouse flew out from the underbrush, and Dog-Day cicadas hummed in harmony with our machines. Grassy meadows bowed in the breeze and puffy white clouds dotted the electric blue sky. I was almost lulled into feeling like it was just a nice day for a ride. A few miles out from Bonny Acres reality set back in so I pulled over to stop on the side of the gravel path.

"You sure this is what you want to do?" I asked Jess as she pulled up beside me. She nodded energetically. "You know what we might find, right?" She nodded again, eyes steady and lips pursed in determination. I had to give it to her, the girl had grit.

As we approached the facility's roundabout, I pointed out a farmhouse across the road. The driveway was gated and, judging by the height of grass in the laneway I suspected no one had been home in a while. It might make a suitable candidate for the evening. As we pulled up onto the sidewalk in front of the entrance to the care home, I noticed that there were no vehicles in the parking lot. I wasn't sure if that was a good sign or a bad one.

"There should be more PPE inside the main doors," she informed me, retying her ponytail beneath her respirator.

"Mind if I go first?" I asked as I removed my handgun from my bag and tucked it into the waist of my jeans. At least if there was something dangerous or gruesome in there, I might be able to shield her from it. She accepted the gesture and waved me past. The doors of course were locked so I punched a hole in the glass with a rock. With a shirt wrapped around my forearm I reached through it to unlatch our way in. Then we outfitted ourselves from the boxes of gloves and gowns that were still stacked in the foyer. Dark and quiet, the place seemed deserted. There was no paperwork or telltale cups of coffee at the reception desk and, although a couple of forgotten spring jackets hung haphazardly in the front closet, there were no outdoor shoes on the rack.

"Maybe I was just being paranoid. Maybe they did get everyone home..." Jess started to say when we heard shuffling from one of the hallways. I put my arm in front of her as she automatically stepped forward to investigate.

"Please?" I asked again, drawing my gun. "Let me?" She conceded, following close behind. I cautiously moved in the direction of where we heard the sound. Doors on either side of the hall opened into empty bedrooms, revealing the remnants of hastily packed belongings. Beds remained unmade and unclaimed clothing drooped from half closed dresser drawers. A film of yellowish-grey dust had settled on everything. My heartrate exploded. I bit down hard on the inside of my cheek to ground myself, salt and blood-tinged saliva filling my mouth. The neurotoxic dust of

Afghanistan disappeared.

Around the corner something crashed and someone, or something, let out a long howl. Keeping my body concealed behind the wall, I cocked my head to try to get a visual.

"Short, roundish, man...I think. Knocked a picture off the wall," I whispered to Jess. "Fuscia sweater—"

"Oh my god—it's *Rose!*" She forced herself past me. Apparently, it was my turn to follow. I found it odd that she didn't say anything as she crouched down a few paces in front of the wailing man. His head bobbed slightly as he punched himself in the side of the thigh.

"Bad...bad...bad..." he repeated to himself. After a couple minutes he looked up at Jess, appearing to notice her for the first time.

"Jessi?" he asked, his eyes growing wide.

"Yes, Rose, it's Jessi."

"Jessi!" he screeched, throwing his arms tightly around her neck, tears wetting both of their cheeks.

"Are you alone?" she asked, pulling back slightly, unwrapping herself from Rose's vice grip.

"Rose—bad, Rose—bad," he repeated, frantically patting his chest.

"What the hell?!" Jess mouthed to me.

"Rose—bad, Rose—bad." He continued tapping his chest, rocking slightly back and forth. His small black eyes were locked intently on Jess. I was certain he wouldn't be letting her out of his line of sight anytime soon. I wasn't sure what to make of the entire situation—I was still stuck on the fact that someone had named this man Rose.

"How long?" I finally thought to ask them both.

"I'm not sure," Jess replied, nonchalantly hanging the framed canvas back up where it belonged. Like magic, I saw agitation leave Rose's body and his repetitive speech abruptly stopped. "The concept of passing time is kind of lost on him without timers," she explained. "He has Down syndrome. Maybe we'll find more clues if we look around. Or maybe you can look while I help him get back to baseline?" Feeling a little overwhelmed and disconnected, I gladly accepted her offer of escape. I proceeded to clear the rest of the facility, thankful for no further surprises.

"The last entry in the staff logbook was June 8th," I told Jess when I returned to find them sitting on sofas facing one another in the common room.

"More than two weeks," Jess mused while setting Rose up with a juice box. "I don't think we need to worry about PPE with him then." The staff had truly performed a miracle at Bonny Acres. They boasted not a single outbreak among the residents in the past five years. It was a testament to their enhanced cleaning practices, pre-shift self-screening, and elective social isolation outside of work. That wasn't to say they hadn't lost any staff to the virus, but staff who were sick stayed home—an option made easier due to the COVID-19 disability compensation clause fought for by their union. The new health policy had undoubtedly saved lives—for the interim.

"How is he even alive?" I whispered.

"The snack cupboard, I think," Jess said incredulously.

"Ok, but why is he still here? How could anyone do that? What are we going to do with him now? Why would anyone name a guy Rose?" An endless parade of questions was churning in my head. Rose in his fuchsia sweater and khaki cargo pants stared at us across the room, intently sucking on his apple juice.

"We'll figure it out," she replied bluntly. I got the feeling I wouldn't have much say in the *"we"* matter.

VII

Rose stared at me calmly but defiantly from the edge of his bed. Sparse black hair jutted out from his chin all the way around to the top of his head, which made him look like a cheeky hedgehog. Jess had tasked me with trying to help him pack up his room, hopeful that my voice might inspire him whereas she had been unsuccessful for the past week.

Rose had been living at Bonny Acres since the day he was born to his mother, Rachel. After leaving the foster care system Rachel had come to live at the facility as a young woman. She had then fallen in love with a fellow resident, Bose, who was several years her senior. When Rachel was discovered to be pregnant, there was significant debate about the best course of action. Thanks to staff advocacy and a successful GoFundMe page that helped cover child-rearing costs, it was decided that the child would be raised on site. The decision sent shockwaves, mostly positive ones, through the realm of assisted living. Unfortunately, Bose died before his child was born.

"Sooo, is that your mom and dad?" I pointed out a picture on his dresser, reaching for anything to cut the painfully awkward silence. Rose's face lit up like sevens on a slot machine.

"Rachel," he said, coming to stand beside me. He pressed his thumb against the glass where a tiny woman stood smiling in a polka dot dress and modest veil. She shared Rose's dark, almond-shaped eyes, and slightly drawn-out face. "Bose," he called the man next to her in an oversized blazer, also smiling but somewhat stooped over a walker. I recognized the setting where the happy couple stood as the facility gardens. A single tier wedding cake sat on the table in front of them. "Rose," he said, turning to show me the 't' he had made with his pointer fingers.

"Oooooh, Rachel plus Bose… equals Rose! It's a portmanteau!" It clicked in my brain like a clue on Jeopardy. "That's pretty cool, my man." Jess already told me about Rachel's death five years ago and how difficult it was for Rose to lose his only real family just as the pandemic began.

"I found something," Jess beckoned me in a hushed voice from the doorway. She was leafing through a staff logbook when I joined her in the hall. "They didn't leave him—he hid."

"Oh, sure. You mean they just never bothered to look for him."

"No, they did! I guess when everyone was leaving, he got scared. This is the only place he's ever known. My boss came back to check multiple times after everyone was gone but never found him. She's the one who filled the cupboard with food, just in case." This revelation could be swallowed much easier than the assumption he was abandoned, especially knowing Jess had left her contact info as a potential adopter. Then again, with the power out there would have been no way for her manager to reach her even if they had found him.

"So, he's afraid to leave. That explains why we can't get him to pack, especially when we don't even know where we're headed. We need to rethink our approach. Jess, we need a better plan." We agreed to reconvene for a strategy session after she prepared Rose a supper with more substance than pudding cups and granola bars.

As I walked back up the lane across the road, a sunset filled the darkening mauve sky behind me. It lit up the old farmhouse windows like gold. I was so distracted by the striking effect that I did not see the small black wolf until it had fully stepped from the shadows of the woodshed. I reached for my sidearm, but I hadn't brought it with me. The animal was close enough that I could see the golden sunlight reflected in its eyes. As we stood there assessing each other, a strange feeling of familiarity overcame me. It seemed that the beast and I knew each other somehow.

"Remmington?" I asked, immediately feeling like a total fool. The canine tilted its head, its large black ears cocked in my direction. The resemblance was uncanny. I tried to remember if I had eaten enough that day. Maybe I needed a glass of water or something.

"Is that you, pup?" I whispered. I silently hoped Jess was on her way behind me so she could verify the mirage, but we remained alone, our gazes locked together. The animal was clearly a wolf, but it could easily be mistaken for a close relative of Vanessa's therapy dog. Either way, its intense stare was unnerving. I was about to try to scare it off when it let out a long, low howl and took off across the field, running east. The emerging full moon shone on its silver back and, just before it disappeared from view, it glanced back at me again as if to say something.

Then it was gone.

Perhaps it was a coincidence, perhaps the stress was finally getting the better of me, but the encounter had given me a strange inkling.

"What do you think about going to Nova Scotia?" I asked

Jess when we sat down at the kitchen table together later that evening.

"You mean like, for a vacation?" she replied sarcastically.

"Think about it," I went on, although not entirely sure where I was going until the words fell out of my mouth. "Willy and Ness were getting set up to be self-sufficient before the pandemic was even a thing. If anyone is surviving, and I don't just mean on the banks of the Otonabee River, I bet it's them. And if not, we could probably at least make it through the winter at their place. You saw their pantry. And we can't stay here." I gestured vaguely at our surroundings. The roof leaked, there was no water except for a stream a kilometer away that would surely freeze, and once the non-perishables at Bonny Acres ran out—there would be no food.

"Are you serious?" She stared at me as if I had suggested we fly to the moon. I didn't think it was the right time to tell her that I got the wild idea from a golden-eyed wolf.

"I am. Very serious. Didn't you say Rose loves animals? Maybe moving to a farm will be right up his alley." Jess opened and closed her mouth without saying anything. "I know it will take longer on the quads but, I bet we could be there in a couple weeks." Jess leaned her head back in her chair and closed her eyes, uncertainty filling the room. I wasn't sure if she had fallen asleep or simply willed her conscience to escape for a parallel universe.

"Ok," she finally said, seeming bewildered by her own voice. "Let's go to Nova Scotia."

"Let's go to Nova Scotia," I echoed. It was an insane idea, but it was the only one we had. The only thing more insane would be sitting around waiting for a miracle to save us.

"Oh, before I forget—did you know that Rose's name is a portmanteau?"

"Um, what? What's a poor man toe?" Her tittered response cleared the air.

"Rose's parents, Rachel and Bose, his name is a combination of theirs."

"Ohhh, I get it! I guess back in the day the staff tried to talk Rachel out of calling him Rose. They told her it was a girl's name, but she wouldn't have it. They even tried calling him Ramone for a while, hoping she would too, but she never did. I'm not sure that anyone realized it was a port-man-toe or whatever you called it. That's really kind of beautiful. When did you get so smart?" Jess got up from her seat and came to sit on my lap, her head resting in the crook of my neck. Her hair smelled unwashed, but I kind of liked it.

"It suits him somehow," I told her.

"It does. And I seem to remember lots of rose bushes at Will and Vanessa's farm too, from that summer we went together. Didn't she make us rose petal jam?" she mused. "Maybe it's a sign." I kissed the top of her head to stifle a snort.

"Mmhm, maybe it is."

VIII

"C'mon, what's wrong Rosie?" Jess asked, with just a hint of exasperation, as I turned the four-wheeler off again. Although we had made positive headway on the idea of travelling to Nova Scotia together, we couldn't seem to get Rose onboard with the first step—a sleepover at the house across the road. I had officially never met a more stubborn individual which, coming from an army guy, was saying something.

We were trying to take things slowly, considerate of the fact that Rose had never spent a night away from Bonny Acres and now here we were, possibly taking him away forever. The last two days had been spent choosing which belongings to put into his sole suitcase. We also brought over the ATVs to show him what we would be riding on. He was so excited by the machines that his fevered clapping nearly tipped him over, but now that we asked him to try getting on one, he clamped his hands over his ears and confronted us with a resounding "NO."

"Ok," Jess eventually groaned with defeat. "You want to *walk* there with me, then?" Rose nodded agreeably. I tried to suppress my frustration, but it was shaping up to be a long walk to the east coast. I crawled the machine back up the lane with Rose and Jess following behind. I couldn't make sense of it. It didn't seem to be the noise of the engine that bothered him. He had walked around the machines while they were running and now, as he trotted along only a few feet behind the wheels, he was right back to grinning and giving me a thumbs up. Rose was turning out to be quite the onion.

Back at the house we prepared a big pot of one of his favorite meals, cheesy macaroni, and after dinner we planned a game of Go-Fish. Earlier in the afternoon I had lugged containers of water back to the house on foot, not wanting to waste any fuel. The experience made me wonder how pioneers managed to get anything accomplished. I imagined their whole day was consumed with the task of just staying alive. While we played cards, I used the kitchen woodstove to heat up the water, pot by pot, until a few inches filled the bottom of an old clawfoot bathtub. The ration would have to do because we could all use a little freshening up.

After Jess helped him with his bath, Rose approached me with a metal razor he found in the medicine cabinet. He stroked his stubbled cheeks, clearly suggesting I be the one to help him shave. I tried to redirect him to Jess's expertise, but he was adamant and, for another reason entirely, Jess found the situation hilarious. She knew damn well that shaving another man would be a first for me. Not many men had worked at Bonny Acres over the years, so I supposed Rose was looking for something to bond over. I inspected the razor he handed me and found it clogged with rust.

"If we're doing this, we're doing it right," I told him. Jess got him seated at the table with a warm, damp cloth on his face and clean towel around his neck. Luckily, a hardened box of baking soda had been left in the cupboard and a piece of steel wool sat under the kitchen sink. As Rose prepared his skin, I restored the razor blades. Giving us the kitchen to ourselves, Jess busied herself setting up the tent in the living room. I could hear her giggling as she peeked back at us from time to time.

"Ok, my man, *hold still.*" Taking about three times longer than it would to do my own face, Rose was eventually revealed as a brand-new man. After checking himself out in the bathroom mirror, he bestowed me with a double thumbs up. Even I had to agree, he looked pretty good.

"Woot woot!" Jess called her approval from the next room. "What do you think Rose? Is it Nathan's turn?" Rose carefully considered the reddish-brown beard I had been working on since returning from my last tour in Syria. He gave her proposal a thumbs down and scored a couple points with me. I had considered shaving it myself so my respirator would have a better seal, but laziness won. Dramatically tucking a strand of hockey hair behind my ear, I stuck my tongue out at her. Rose and I endorsed our newly established boys' club with a fist bump.

We decided he and Jess would test out the tent in the living room first, but the latest development led to a change of plans. I sensed he was desperate for male companionship, so I offered to take the first shift. On our journey we wouldn't always be able to count on roofed accommodations, so it seemed pertinent to try to get Rose to sleep in the tent while it was still an option. However, our worries on this particular challenge were unfounded. When Rose's head hit the pillow, I might as well have said, "Timber!" He spent the entire night sawing logs. I, as usual, did not.

The next morning, after a breakfast of butterscotch pudding and plain oatmeal, I decided to try a different approach to get Rose on the ATV. First, I had him sit on it without it running, which was not a problem. In fact, he grabbed onto the handlebars and pretended to drive it like a mad man. Taking the next logical step, I got on the machine behind him. Reaching under his arms I took control of the "steering," and we pretended to drive on a wild and bumpy obstacle course. *So far, so good.* Then I told Rose I was going to turn the key in the ignition. I felt his back muscles tense a little but after a few seconds we were able to continue with our game of pretend. Jess stood beside us cheering us on. With a nod of her approval, I put the machine in gear.

As soon as Rose felt the wheels begin to turn, he full-on barrel rolled off the machine. Landing roughly in the dirt, he crawled away on all fours as fast as he could move.

"What happened? Are you ok, my man?" I called to him, shutting off the engine. He shot me a look of daggers, again clapping the sides of his head.

"I think I've got it," Jess said, disappearing into the house. She returned with a pair of fuzzy winter earmuffs, left behind by the previous owners. When she tried to give them to Rose, he pushed them away, the furrow deepening between his brows. We were stumped. I slowly got off the quad, resigning myself to the fact that we probably wouldn't be leaving today either. Rose followed us back inside the house but instead of taking up his usual spot on the couch, he began flipping open cupboards in the kitchen. A few moments later he held up a large silver pot triumphantly.

"What in the world..." Jess began as Rose took his aluminum prize and marched back outside. From the kitchen window we watched as he climbed back on the ATV and placed the pot on his head.

"Oh my god, it's a helmet! He wants a helmet!" she shouted as we raced out to catch him before he could drive away.

"Safety first, eh, my man?" I asked, trying not to laugh while taking the keys. "Ok. Alright. We can work with that." Despite our hopes, there were no certified helmets to be found in the farmhouse. Deciding to meet in the middle until we could find something better, I fashioned a chin strap around Rose's pot with a bungee cord. At least if it didn't offer him much actual protection, it was less likely to fly off and hit whoever the unlucky bugger was riding behind him.

"Now can we go to Nova Scotia?" I asked as he adjusted his new headgear. I couldn't believe the design of it was remotely comfortable. He knocked on the side of his pot with his knuckles a couple times to show me how secure it was. Then, to the relief of both Jess and I, he gave us a double thumbs up.

IX

We set our expectations low for the first day, pointing our internal compass somewhere around Tweed. We were able to stop and refill our gas cans along the way, borrowing fuel from vehicles parked at an abandoned municipal depot. Even though we were fairly certain no one would mind, our new free-for-all approach was something I personally needed to come to terms with. I was formally trained to protect property, not steal it, and I worried that the subconscious guilt of our larceny might become stifling. Jess insisted that if we "practiced gratitude" and believed our cause for "borrowing resources" was worthwhile, we should sleep shamelessly. The fact that I couldn't sleep at the best of times was something we were able to exploit—I was a natural choice for nightwatchman. I'd doze during the morning while Jess prepared breakfast, and in the evening after we stopped travelling for the day. The arrangement also allowed Jess and Rose more room in the tent at night, and I had the accommodations to myself during naptime. With Rose tolerating the tent well, we decided to camp as long as the weather was fit. Without the Ministry of Health releasing the latest COVID guidelines to our Facebook feeds, we had no way of knowing how much social distancing was still in play. We decided to keep it simple—no contact with anyone or anyone's things unless it was necessary for our survival.

Forty-eight hours into our journey and we had only seen one smoke sighting that might have been a cooking fire. We also heard another vehicle as we approached a spot where the trail intersected the highway. At the first sound of rumbling on the pavement, Jess, swerving like Mad Max, signaled for us to follow her behind a nearby culvert. While we took cover, she dramatically shushed both Rose and me so she could listen for several minutes after a white cube van had passed by.

"Just a couple of regular anthropophobics out for a rip, eh, bud?" I teased Jess after she gave the all-clear.

"Seriously, where do you come up with this stuff?" She rolled her eyes at me, lovingly I assumed. Our planned route might take longer, but the sounds of human activity nearby made us glad of our decision to stay off the beaten path.

After dipping off the highway past Sharbot Lake, we entered a never-ending tree tunnel. With nothing but foliage and mosquitos to keep us entertained, we flew through that section of trail. It must have been at least a forty-kilometer hollow beneath the Great Lakes-St. Lawrence Forest canopy. We were eventually spit out in the lakes district north of Frontenac Provincial Park. There we were greeted with beautiful views as we passed in and out of quaint communities, which I imagined were normally summer hotspots. As sweat soaked through the back of my shirt where Rose was dutifully wedged against me, I found myself craving ice cream or chip truck fries like a common tourist.

We were both really impressed with how Rose was handling the adventure. Jess made sure to always include him in the plans we made for the following day. It gave him the time he needed to process. Through her patience and consideration, he seemed to have found a way to genuinely enjoy himself. His resilience was inspiring, especially when Jess explained the finer points that many people with Down syndrome struggle with—like change in their routine. Sometimes I tried to put myself in his shoes. Sure, he had known Jess as his support worker for a long time within the walls of Bonny Acres, but I was a virtual stranger. Plus, every passing kilometer must be a new experience of sights, smells, and emotions—all from the back of a bumpy ATV. I could often hear him *"Ooohing"* and *"Ahhing"* when the clouds looked particularly nice, or a deep valley appeared beside us, or we stirred up a flock of geese.

When we told him we would be passing through Ottawa the next day, he surprised us by making it quite clear that he had a request. Through a somewhat complicated game of charades, he informed us that he would like to meet the prime minister. Apparently, Rose was a news buff and was often found napping in Bonny Acre's common room while tuned into CPAC, the Canadian Parliament channel. The staff assumed it was just background noise but, clearly, he had picked up a few things.

After explaining to Rose that the prime minister probably wasn't seeing visitors at this time, it was decided that seeing the parliament buildings would be a satisfactory substitution. I was a little nervous to travel that far into the city but who was I to let my fear deny him this, truly, once in a lifetime opportunity. The Trans Canada Trail wrapped around the place anyway—literally taking us to the back door. We parked our ATVs right on the lawn overlooking the canal. The parliament flags had been abandoned at half-mast.

"Did you know they used to mop horse urine on it to

make it turn green faster?" I asked as Rose marveled over the green copper roof. He and Jess returned my fast fact with a look of disgust. Rose's attention was quickly diverted again by the Hill's cat sanctuary. The felines seemed to be faring well considering they had unceremoniously found themselves in charge of their own dinner recently. Rose managed to lure one of the tabbies into his arms before digging out a disposable camera from his backpack.

"I don't remember him packing that," Jess smiled, shaking her head in amazement. I desperately hoped that I lived long enough to see the photo developed—Rose standing in his glory in front of parliament, an aluminum pot/helmet strapped to his head, and not another soul in sight save a grumpy orange cat tucked under his arm. I could imagine it hanging in a frame somewhere titled "Last Man Standing," or something. The folks at National Geographic might have even given it an honourable mention.

After completing our self-guided tour, we sat down on the overgrown grass for a quick picnic lunch of nuts, dried fruit, and pepperettes. With Rose's bucket list item complete, I suggested we try to get beyond the concrete congestion of the city before nightfall. Although we hadn't seen a soul, I felt like eyes were watching us from every shadowed corner and empty doorway. The abandoned metropolis was not only a stark reminder of everything humanity lost, but with so few trees it was also hotter and stuffier than the rest of the trail. It felt like the walls, and hydro lines, and traffic poles were closing around me like a fist squeezing the breath from my lungs. I kept my eyes averted from the crumpled piles of clothes on the sidewalk. I wasn't sure if Rose was aware of what the lifeless fabric contained, and I was thankful that he didn't ask.

When we reentered farmland, I came to fully appreciate the tension I had been holding in my body as a sigh of relief escaped my lips. Just the visibility alone afforded by the wide-open fields felt safer. That was, until someone fired a god damned rifle at us.

X

"Get down!" I shouted as a bullet whizzed over our heads. We had stopped for a piss break outside Mont-Laurier. Rose dutifully hit the dirt beside me, pulling his pot down over his eyes. Jess scrambled down from the side of the road into the ditch, hiding herself among cattails. The Trans Canada Trail had been intermingling with Highway 117 for the past couple of days, so we had opted for the hardtop over the gravel to save fuel. We assumed that the highway would be less trafficked in this neck of the country.

Crouched behind my ATV, I slowly removed my gun from my bag, deliberately unclenching my jaw. No shots followed so I suspected it was just a warning. I instructed Rose to get into the reeds with Jess as a precaution—you could never be too careful in rural Quebec, from what I had heard. Tucking my weapon into my waistband beneath my shirt, I raised my hands overhead and turned to meet the aggressor.

In the distance an old woman stood at the edge of a field. She wore a long navy-blue dress and a white cap covered most of her hair. Her face was tanned and weathered, like a construction worker after spending one too many summers in the sun. A high-powered rifle rested on her hip. She didn't say a word, but her eyes told me everything I needed to know.

"Just passing through!" I called out, to no reply. Taking a moment to further assess our surroundings I realized that the fields we were approaching had been worked recently. It looked like the first cut of hay had been taken off and raked into stacks. Shielding my eyes against the sun I could see a cloud of dust trailing a horse and buggy travelling up the sideroad behind her. Undoubtedly, they heard the single shot and were coming to investigate. Clearly unhappy that I hadn't gotten on my way, the woman unleashed what sounded like a torrent of threats in a dialectic mashup of German and French. She then proceeded to put a bead on my forehead.

"Time to go! Get on the quads but do it slow with your hands up," I told my comrades on their bellies in the swamp. The appearance of Rose and Jess did not interrupt the woman's verbal tirade. I motioned that we would be on our way, hoping we would be able to get past the next intersection before more trouble arrived. "Let's get out of here, quickly."

As we flew down the highway, the woman kept us sighted in. Her dress billowed out behind her making her silhouette look like a scarecrow from hell. When we reached the sideroad the buggy was close enough for us to see the driver, a clean-shaven man wearing a straw hat, suspenders, and a look of grave discontent in the wrinkles around his eyes. Another rifle lay conspicuously on the seat beside his thigh. Rose waved at the steaming horse excitedly as we drove past. He tapped me on the right shoulder which was our established signal that he wanted to stop.

"Not today, my man, not today!"

The next field we passed was filled with manicured rows of strawberry plants. They were dotted with a handful of young, conservatively dressed, harvesters. A couple of naked babies tramped around between them, their faces and hands stained red with berry juice. Everyone stood to watch as we drove by, some of their mouths hanging open. Rose waved eagerly at them as well, the star of his own parade. Again, Rose tapped me on the shoulder, but I shook my head no. I didn't think Grandma and Grandpa would be too happy if we stopped for a meet and greet.

Having put a bit of distance between us, we stopped beside a river near Mont Tremblant to make camp for the night. I fashioned a clothesline between two trees while Jess washed the clothes soiled by their earlier swamp adventure. Rose, clearly unhappy with the way the day's decision making had evolved, sulked beside the fire while stirring a pot of soup for dinner.

"It's kind of ironic, isn't it?" Jess said to me. "Everyone used to think people that lived like that were backwards, stupid even. Yet, here they are, just going about their lives like nothing happened."

"Something to be said for simplicity, I guess," I contemplated. "And staying connected to your roots." What I couldn't figure out was the overt hostility. My only interaction with Mennonites had been at farmers' markets. They always seemed like friendly enough folk. Certainly not the kind to meet you on their doorstep packing fire power, which I didn't realize their culture even allowed for. I wondered if something had happened. The way the old woman had looked at me, fearful yet furious, was haunting.

As we cleaned up after supper, I suddenly heard the sound of hooves on the pavement leading to our encampment.

"Stay calm, I think we're about to have visitors," I warned Jess and Rose. My nervous system hadn't let me put my gun away today, so I casually began to polish it. Surveying our campsite, I was satisfied that we were each in a position with multiple exits. Jess moved around the fire to be a little closer to her ATV as the sound drew nearer. She took out our masks and passed them around.

"How about a song?" I asked. Jess looked at me like I had lost my mind, but Rose perked up for the first time since I kiboshed his hangout plans.

"If you all will shut your trap,
I will tell you 'bout a chap,
That was broke and up against it, too, for fair..." I started.
"He was not the kind to shirk,
He was looking hard for work,
But he heard the same old story everywhere...." Rose joined in with a low hum, tapping on the log he sat on like a drum.
"Tramp, tramp, tramp, keep on a-tramping,
Nothing doing here for you;
If I catch you 'round again,
You will wear the ball and chain..." Rose waved to Jess encouragingly, to which she rolled her eyes.

"Keep on tramping, that's the best thing you can do," she finally added her soprano to our band. I wasn't really sure if the tactic would work for humans as well as bears. I just hoped that we wouldn't startle whoever was approaching and maybe our voices would give an impression of friendliness. Had anyone ever heard a villain singing Joe Glazer around a campfire? Exactly.

An unfamiliar whistle joined in our ditty as a horse and rider trotted into the light. Dressed in navy pants, a beige work shirt, and leather suspenders, a teenage boy stepped down from his chestnut steed. He had a blue bandana tied over his mouth and nose, but his demeanor was not threatening. Rose, unable to contain himself, jumped up from his seat to greet the stranger and, more importantly, his horse.

"Rose," he introduced himself, patting his chest emphatically.

"Dan," the young man returned in a heavy potpourri of German and French. With the minimum customary pleasantries out of the way, Rose pointed earnestly at his tall dark companion.

"Un moment," Dan replied, holding up his pointer finger while he rummaged around in his pocket. Pulling out a small, auburn, glass bottle, he poured liquid into his hands and rubbed them together before offering it to Rose to do the same. "L'alcool. Fait à la maison."

Rose looked at Jess for instruction, but she had already retrieved our own stash. Hand sanitization complete, Dan stepped back several feet, indicating that Rose could approach. "Eli," he told him. Slowly Rose extended his fist for Eli to smell. After the horse offered his own consent, Rose proceeded to stroke the white star on his nose, clearly in heaven.

"Est-ce que tu parles français?" Dan turned to ask me, leaving Eli's reins in the hands of a delighted Rose. *Now that's a trusting fella,* I thought to myself. Despite my elementary school attempts, my command of Canada's other official language was not remotely passable, so I pointed him in the direction of Jess's French heritage. Although they were technically speaking the same language, their accents were wildly different resulting in a lot of "ums" and "ers" as they slowly introduced themselves. Unable to participate, I occupied myself watching the interaction between Rose and Eli. They both looked so comfortable and relaxed, more so than I had ever seen Rose before.

"He's from the settlement we passed," Jess interpreted, confirming my suspicions. "He came to apologize for his family, and he brought us food from their farm."

"Well, that is unexpected," I said, turning to Dan. "Mercy bow-coop, Dan."

"Nathan is welcome," he returned, his eyes smiling. Dan then stood to fetch a bag of goodies from his horse's pack and Rose gave him an appreciative thumbs up.

"His elders are very scared of outsiders. He said they haven't lost anyone on the colony to COVID," Jess explained.

"No one?" I was baffled.

"No one. They heard of what was happening everywhere else, so they decided to self-isolate, like, *hard*. Really strict, no one in or out," she went on. "The older, orthodox members think the pandemic is an act of God, only infecting nonbelievers and sinners."

"Oh. Well, it is something of a miracle that *none* of them died. But isn't it really dangerous for him to be here then? With us?"

"It would certainly be frowned upon. But he's vaccinated. They all are—they see vaccines as one of God's gifts, but the younger generation is antsy to loosen the self-imposed restrictions. They are more skeptical about the pandemic's origin. And it's been a long time since they talked to anyone from the outside, so he decided to risk it. He hasn't seen traffic on the highway in weeks." Dan returned to us with a large bag containing fresh buns, strawberries, jams, pickles, various root veggies, and cured sausages. Overwhelmed by the friendly offering, Jess began to cry softly.

"I wish I could hug you!" she told him, opting to blow him a kiss instead. Caught off guard, Dan looked at me wide-eyed. His obvious discomfort made me laugh.

"De rien," he replied sheepishly before returning to his horse once more. From Eli's second pack he presented an oddly wrapped gift to Rose. It was hard to imagine what the oblong parcel could be and, clearly in on the surprise, Jess simply winked at us. I made a mental note to brush up on my French. Carefully untying the twine and removing the brown paper, Rose found what looked like a brand-new ATV helmet in his hands. He turned it over and over, inspecting it in the firelight. A huge grin was obviously plastered on his face beneath his mask. He showed his new possession to Eli before holding it up for me and Jess to see—which let us know exactly where we stood in the order of things. I don't think either of us minded one bit.

"Awesome! Try it on, bud!" I congratulated him. The helmet's shiny black and green paint didn't appear to have a single scratch on it. Fitting easily onto his head, Rose flipped down the full-face visor. He looked like a bonafide spaceman standing next to his new, more rustic, friends.

"Apparently Rose's pot was the talk of the supper table tonight," Jess told me. "Dan bought this helmet for dirt biking with his friends from town. He doesn't figure he'll be out riding anytime soon so he wanted Rose to have it." I stood to give Dan a fist bump, immeasurably grateful for all the ways he had shown us kindness. He and Jess spoke for a few more minutes until it was time for him to head back before someone noticed he was missing. Rose walked alongside him and Eli until they made it back onto the road. His grin didn't leave him, even in his sleep.

XI

"I knew it! I knew you were up to something!" Jess hollered, playfully wrestling me to the ground from the log I was sitting on beside the fire pit. She grabbed the book I had been studying from my hands.

"Word-A-Day," she read out the title. "I knew your man-toes and anthrophobes and whatever else had to be coming from somewhere! Where did you get this?" I was busted.

"Remember me telling you about Aadhill? It was his."

"Um, maybe, was that Aaban's dad? From Afghanistan?"

"Ya, that's right. While we waited out the fire fight, I had one of those daily quote books in my pack, so I read from it a few times. Aadhill seemed interested so we traded. He had a couple of basic English books in his bunker collection too. That was one of them," I told her, tapping the book she was now leafing through while sprawled out on the ground, her head perched on my chest.

"He could speak English?" she asked.

"Well, not really," I laughed. She planted a kiss firmly on my lips.

"What's today's word?" she wanted to know, brushing the dirt from her leggings as she stood.

"Sidh," I told her. "It means a mound or hill where fairies live. An old Irish word or something. I dunno, sounds silly to me. I find the words only stick in my brain if I find ways to use them."

"Challenge accepted! This will be fun. Why didn't you tell me about it?" I shrugged, feeling a little self-conscious. I had never been known as a book-smart kind of guy. "Alright, go get some rest Mr. Dictionary. Rose and I will start breakfast." Jess patted me on the butt as I headed for the tent. "Maybe we can find you a copy in French next!" she teased. She seemed to be in an exceptionally good mood this morning. On his way back from a wash in the river with just a small towel folded around his waist, Rose gave me a high-five as we crossed paths. He had his quirks, but the guy had grown on me.

Our goal for the day was to get to the other side of Montreal. I'd driven through the city before but couldn't seem to remember much about it other than a lot of construction, traffic, and road signs I didn't understand. I assumed travelling the highway would be unavoidable in places because we had to get over the island's bridges. We discussed the merits of skirting around the city altogether, but I was starting to feel antsy about our timing. It was already August and we had blown past the "couple of weeks" I thought it would take us—and the entire province of Quebec still loomed ahead. Not to mention, my back was constantly aching from being on the quad all day only to be followed by sleeping on hard ground. Despite the trip's highlights so far, I was ready to kick my boots off at the farm.

As we approached the city, we could see that some areas had suffered from unattended fires as well. It was nothing like the loss endured in Peterborough, but a few unlucky subdivisions were still smoldering. It was a cloudy day, and an unseasonably cool breeze blew in off the water. The ambience did not feel welcoming. I wished we could just drive right through without stopping, but there were a few staples we needed to restock. Hopefully we would find muscle relaxants, too.

The first grocery store we stopped at had been picked clean aside from some unappetizing cuts at the meat counter. The smell of rotting flesh was so thick I could almost taste it from the front door, which had been previously left pried open. Forced to try our luck elsewhere for food and drink rations, we thought we would at least be able to get gas out of the handful of abandoned cars in the lot, but our siphon kept coming up dry. I didn't think it was a coincidence that they had all inconveniently gone empty at the same time while parked at Sobeys. Other travelers had beat us to it.

We decided to try our hand a little more off the beaten path. As we rode along a ridgeline away from the main highway, Rose tapped me on the shoulder. I assumed he spotted another store but when I stopped the quad he just began rummaging in my backpack. Finding my binoculars, he climbed onto the seat with a look of excitement which quickly turned to concern when a gust of wind made him wobble unsteadily. Motioning for me to stand in front of him so he could hold onto my shoulder, he mustered the courage to stand up tall on the seat of the ATV while he scanned the St. Lawrence River.

"Oh. My. God," I heard him mutter after a moment as he passed the binos down to me without taking his eyes off the water. His utter look of amazement intrigued me.

"What?" Jess cried, "What is it?"

"It's…" I was at a loss. "It's amazing!" Void of human activity, the city's canal had quickly replenished itself with a family of eleven humpback whales—from what I could count. I watched in awe as a huge whale, at least sixteen meters long, breached the waves. Its calf followed close behind. A pod of dolphins raced alongside them playfully, leaping through the mist created by the giant animal falling back through the surface of the river. The water they swam in was so clear that, despite being rough, swirling schools of fish could be seen darting around wildly. Wordlessly I handed Jess the binoculars while Rose and I stared at each other in disbelief. Her hands trembled as she took in the view.

"That's the most beautiful thing I've ever seen," she finally breathed. Rose and I nodded in agreement. "It's hard to appreciate how much destruction humans have caused until you see something like that—the way it's supposed to be." We passed the binoculars back and forth between us several more times, binging on the visual feast.

"I hate to be Debbi Downer," I finally said, "but we should probably get moving. We're losing daylight." Reluctantly we climbed back on the quads and continued in our pursuit of something to eat. Stopping at a No Frills, we were only able to find a few overlooked cans hidden beneath shelves. Everything fresh was now so far past its best-before date that it was unrecognizable. Resources were dwindling at an alarming rate.

"I'd fight someone for a greek salad right about now," Jess sighed as she slung her half-full bag onto her back.

"You might be out of luck on the feta, but you know who probably has cucumbers and tomatoes?" I reminded her delicately. "Will and Vanessa." She gave me a tired but grateful smile in return. The journey was evidently starting to take its toll on her as well. Keeping morale up needed to be prioritized, even if I was starting to feel emotionally and physically drained myself.

"Let's check out the subdivision behind the store," I suggested. "Maybe we can find gas back there and be on our way." Jess and Rose silently followed my lead. As we drove around the back of No Frills, I noticed an *'ATV Trailer for Sale'* flapping on a hydro pole in front of a red brick house. "Wouldn't that be lucky!" I shouted to Jess. "We wouldn't have to stop as often if we find a good haul!"

We parked the quads and walked around the home to its large double door garage. The inground pool that took up the rest of the backyard was a sickly green colour and a few frogs floated in it—belly up. Rose wrinkled his nose and shielded his eyes from the sight of the watery grave. It was certainly an unfortunate contrast to the magic we had witnessed earlier.

The door to the garage was locked but from the window I could see the unsold trailer still inside. It was the perfect size, about four-by-six feet, and in great condition. One of us could even ride in it if we needed to. Suddenly Jess appeared on the other side of the door having found her way in through another window that was unlocked. She opened the door for Rose and me and we set about looking the trailer over in better detail, ultimately deciding it was worth "borrowing." As we opened the main door so I could back my quad up to it, a noise from the roadway caught us off guard.

Brappp brappp BRAAAPPP preceded one long squeal, followed closely by a second.

"Fuck!" I screamed, immediately cluing into what was happening. I raced out to where we parked—the machines were gone and all that stood in their place was Rose's lone suitcase. I chased the fading sound of the engines down a side street, catching a glimpse of the thieves.

"STOP!" I yelled after the figures. One wore shorts, a t-shirt, and flip-flops, while the other wore jeans, an old hockey jersey, and Rose's helmet. Rage flowed through me.

My gun was in my bag.

The pair turned another corner and I barreled over a series of backyard fences to try to cut them off. Lunging from the sidewalk, I managed to get a grip on my pack with one hand, a balled-up corner of the guy's jersey in my other, and a leg up over the wheel well. The thief swerved trying to shake me loose. Realizing what was happening, their partner in crime pulled up alongside us and threw the second pack straight at my head. It ricocheted off my skull.

"Nice try, motherfuckers!" I snarled like a wild beast, reaching for the throat of the driver. Suddenly I was falling, coming to land on the pavement with a crunch. The thief had undone the pack's buckle, which was all that remained in my hands. Staggering to my feet, I watched as the thieves gained unsurmountable ground.

The quads were gone.

XII

As I walked back shamefully with just our packs, I saw that Jess had sunk down on her heels on the sidewalk to cry. Rose had his arm around her shoulder, snot dripping from his reddened face. I picked up Rose's suitcase from the road, just as angry with myself for being so careless, as with the universe for being so heartless.

"Let's go," I said, unable to dull the edge in my voice.

"Go? Go where?" Jess sobbed, wiping her face on her sleeve. "What are we going to do Nathan?" I hated how vulnerable I felt. Frankly, I didn't know what we were going to do but what I absolutely didn't want to do was stand in a Montreal subdivision in the middle of a mass extinction event and blubber over stolen quads.

"I saw the Crowne Plaza on our way in. I don't think it was more than a few blocks back. Let's go get some rest for the night, in a real bed. We can talk about what we're going to do later. It's not going to get solved right here, right now. So, let's just go." With every ounce I could muster, I tried to curb the gruffness in my tone. I was highly aware that the rage pounding inside me had nothing to do with the two people standing in front of me, but they were also uncomfortably close to my line of fire. The voice of one of my psychologists reminded me to breathe: four counts in through the nose, hold for seven, out the mouth for eight...and repeat.

"But—" Jess started to argue.

"It will be fine. We'll just have to be smarter," I said matter-of-factly, sounding far more certain than I felt. Rose took Jess's elbow, helping her to stand. I refused to let them carry any of the bags, determined to feel the full weight of my foolishness. We trudged in the direction of the Plaza in somber silence, disrupted only by the odd sniffle.

The hotel windows were dark, but it stood in an area of the city untouched by the fires. I expected the revolving doors to be locked but they swung open easily with a push. Inside the place looked immaculate, it wasn't difficult to imagine someone about to appear behind the reception desk. Rose looked around with incredulity at the opulent décor filling the mile high ceilings. A mischievous grin spread across his face when he spotted a sign for the water slide.

"Don't get your hopes up, my man," I told him, "Remember the last pool we saw?" The smile disappeared and I immediately felt even more terrible for being his source of disappointment. "We'll check it out later though, just in case, ok?" I offered.

"I guess we should find a room on the ground floor," Jess interjected. "Something close to an exit. Maybe with a door into the parking lot."

"I like it," I encouraged her. "Tactical thinking looks good on you." She turned to face me abruptly.

"I don't know how you do it," she said, which somehow sounded accusatory.

"Do what?" I wanted to know. "Think tactically?"

"No, how you just turn it off. What just happened was fucked up, Nathan! We could very likely be totally fucked—permanently, completely, fucked!" Her voice simultaneously increased an octave and a decibel. "And you're just walking around, bossing us around all nonchalant! Like nothing even happened!"

"Whoa. Let's take 'er down a notch." I raised my hands in surrender.

"I don't want to take it down a notch! I want to scream! I want to cry! I want to rip my hair out! I want to...I want to punch something!" She slammed her fist into the drywall, hitting it hard enough to leave a small crack. *"God damn it!"* she screamed, squeezing her now throbbing knuckles between her thighs.

"Hey, hey, hey, it's going to be ok." I pulled her toward me, but she fought back, pushing me away.

"How do you know, Nathan? You *don't!* Nobody does!" I stood back, giving her space as her shouts reverted to sobs.

"You make me feel stupid for crying!" Her shoulders heaved as she gulped for air in between words. *"What the fuck is wrong with you?* Are you made of goddamn *stone?"*

"I never said I don't feel like crying," I told her gently. "Guys like me, well, we are the way we are so people like you can be...human, for lack of a better word. I wouldn't have lasted very long in the military if I sat down to cry every time something didn't go my way. I'm sorry if I made you feel stupid but *I'm not better than you*. My way of coping isn't even healthy—you know that better than anyone." Jess slid down the wall coming to sit on the floor. I crouched in front of her, taking her hands in mine.

"I'm a mess too, Jess. The only reason I'm here today is because of *you*. Because of your patience, and because of your heart. Because you *feel* things, and you don't give up on people. Even difficult assholes like me. A lesser woman would have kicked me to the curb years ago! War didn't kill me but transitioning back to civilian life nearly did. Many times. Sure, surviving in perpetual chaos and uncertainty *seems* heroic. And chasing the grim reaper's shadow around every corner might *sound* brave—but there's a price to pay when the dust settles. A big one." Jess looked up at me through bleary eyes. "To me *you're* the brave one. Who you are on the inside matches exactly who you are on the outside. I just...I can't...I'm not tuned in that way anymore. Sometimes I know the stuff I feel inside doesn't match the situation, so I try to smother it. That way I won't hurt someone by accident. I know it's hard to connect with someone who either can't make heads or tails of their own emotions or doesn't show them at all. But I'm working on it. I'm trying."

"I know, I'm sorry," she cleared her throat. "I love you so much. I'm just tired, and scared."

"Me too, babe, even if I don't say it. But I have told you before—you're my ride or die. It's you and me until the end, whether you like it or not. And Rose too now I guess," I added. She rewarded me with a small laugh, finally letting me in for a hug.

"Um, Nathan?" she said after a moment. "Where *is* Rose?" It appeared he had wandered off during the commotion.

"Rose?" she called, panic creeping in. *"Rose!"* she yelled louder.

"Jess, it's going to be ok, we'll go look for him," I assured her. "He can't have gone far. In fact, I think I know where we should look first." I pointed in the direction of the pool.

"I don't even know if he can swim!" she said, breaking into a sprint.

"Oh, yep, ok, we can look a little faster then," I ran past her, whipping open the doors to the waterpark area.

"Rose, NO!" Jess screamed as we made our way along the pool deck. At the top of an alarmingly tall and twisting

green slide, we could just barely see his figure. Standing in his tighty-whities he had just dumped water from one of the lounge's ice buckets down the tube. With superhuman speed, Jess was already halfway up the stairs calling his name over and over. The last thing I saw before I dove into the cloudy pool was Rose giving her a double thumbs up.

"Whoooohoooooo!!!" echoed from the mouth of the slide as my head reemerged from the water. Rose came flying out of the entrance with a smile the size of Texas. I swam toward him aggressively, as he doggy-paddled to the side of the pool with ease.

"Whoohooo!" he hollered again at Jess, who found she was now the one standing alone at the top of the slide.

"Ya, Jess, *whoohoo!*" I joined in between fits of sputtering laughter. Although it wasn't sparkling in clarity, the pool's chemicals had kept the sterile water entombed in time. Rose and I gave her the thumbs up, knowing full well she couldn't turn us both down.

"Rose, I'm going to get you for this!" Jess shouted down before getting onto the slide herself. We spent the rest of the day soaking up the entire waterpark to ourselves. I wondered how much it would have cost to rent it out privately pre-pandemic. We had certainly gone from rags to riches in a matter of minutes.

"Tequila?" I asked Jess as we got settled in our room down the hall. The minibar was somehow still intact. She shook her head no, which surprised me as it was usually her favorite choice of poison on the rare occasion that she indulged in hard liquor. "Ok, how about whiskey?" She shook her head again, coyly. "Well, I'm having one. I think we deserve a drink," I told her, a little miffed that I had miscalculated her mood.

"Oh, we do. We definitely deserve it," Jess agreed. "But I

actually have to tell you something."

"I haven't got all day you know," I teased, flopping down beside her on puffy mounds of white, bamboo comforter. The whiskey burned where it touched my lips.

"I wanted to tell you yesterday..." she went on. I propped myself up on my elbow, sliding my hand up the back of her fresh shirt.

"And?" I made small circles on her skin with my fingertips. She was always so soft.

"And... you're going to be a dad!"

XIII

Several more whiskey shots followed Jess's revelation, but only by me. According to her missing-period-math, she was about eight weeks along which meant we were in the bunker when the magic happened. I was mostly ecstatic—with a side of bone crushing fear. We knew we wanted to be parents someday but sitting in an abandoned hotel with no ride and no concrete plans for the immediate future was quite the time to make it official.

Rose had taken the room next to us and seemed content to entertain himself when we told him that we needed alone time. We soon heard telltale snores coming through our adjacent wall. All too aware of Jess's fragile emotional state, I tried to keep the conversation positive. We bantered about baby names, and I was not overly surprised when she said that the forerunner for a girl was 'Rosie.' For a boy I suggested 'William,' a tribute to my best friend.

"What if we just stayed here?" Jess suggested.

"You mean, live in Montreal?" She nodded.

"Maybe not forever, but until things settle down. Maybe we could make it work. You saw how happy Rose is," she added. Not wanting to start another argument unnecessarily, I agreed to give it some thought. It was probably the fatigue but half of me didn't think it was a terrible idea, and yet it didn't sit right with the other half either.

"I don't know, Jess. Resources seem to be drying up around here. And we don't know anyone," I reminded her. "I don't think babies are supposed to grow up with just their parents. Oh, and a middle-aged uncle I guess."

"Uncle Rose!" Jess laughed. "I love that."

"So do I, but that's not really my point. They'd never have friends their own age."

"But there are people here..." she said after thinking about it for a moment. "Maybe we could meet them somehow?"

"All we know is that someone stole the quads. They might have just been passing through too and took the opportunity when they saw it. Or maybe they are just shitty and not the kind of people we'd want to raise a family around."

"True," she conceded. "But we don't know if Will or Vanessa are at the farm, either. How do we know it's even still standing?" She motioned toward the window where flattened sections of charred city blocks could be seen in the distance. I sighed deeply—she was right too. The only thing for certain was that we didn't know anything for certain.

"How about a foot rub for the pregnant lady?" I changed the subject, pulling her ankles toward me.

"Now that is a plan I can endorse!" She laid her head back on a pillow and it wasn't long before she joined Rose's orchestra. Starting to feel groggy myself, I pulled a corner of the bedsheet over my chest.

Incessant barking filtered in under the bedroom door. Rubbing my eyes, I tried to get my bearings. Oh right, the hotel. Jess stirred in her sleep beside me. "I'll go check in out," I whispered. Standing up made the room tilt like a not-so-fun house. I hadn't had any booze in a while and probably needed to hydrate.

The barking got louder as I approached the door to the hallway.

I stuck one of the complimentary cups under the bathroom tap, forgetting that there was no running water. Maybe there was something to drink in one of the lobby vending machines.

I stepped into the hall and found Remmi standing at the edge of the canal. She barked at me expectantly, her telltale black ears reeling me in like an air traffic controller. My feet felt like concrete. A steady breeze blew, and tiny white flakes peppered my face. Snow? In August?

"What's wrong Remmington?" I shouted. The howling wind filled my throat, making me cough. Remmi, falling silent, turned her attention toward the canal. Overcoming my lead feet, I found my way beside her, following her gaze. White-sided dolphins leapt into the air from the roughening water. Their waving flippers transcended into a synchronized dance. Faster and faster, they swam in a circle creating a whirlpool between them. Frost formed on the edges of the riverbank, icy feathers cracking the surface of the water. One by one the dolphins dove, the last one disappearing just as the St. Lawrence completely sealed over—a tomb of ice. Remmi darted away from me out onto the rink.

"No! No, Remmi! Be careful!" I shouted after her, gingerly testing my weight on the freshly formed ice. Unable to support me, I sank into the dark and freezing water. Somewhere below, a white light beckoned. As I swam toward it with curiosity, I realized it was the fluorescent lights of a grocery store. The shelves were filled with frost covered boxes of cereals and loaves of bread. I reached out to pick up a melon, but it crumbled into ice cubes between my fingers.

Barking from between one of the aisles, Remmi grabbed my attention before turning to run from me again. As I chased after her the aisle began to lengthen, the space between us growing instead of shortening. In the distance I could barely make out where she was headed. A familiar old, two-story farmhouse with a red steel roof was bathed in a warm glow. Will and Vanessa stood smiling on the porch. The front yard was filled with apple trees, *their branches bending down under the weight of their fruit. Wherever an apple touched the ground, another small sapling had sprouted. Vanessa crouched down, opening her arms to embrace her dog.*

"Nathaaan! Nathaaaaaan!"

XIV

"Nathan," Jess shook my shoulder. "Nathan! It's lunchtime." Opening one eye, I peered at my surroundings suspiciously.

"Water," I moaned, my head pounding.

"We just used the last of it to make spaghetti. I'll go replace it from the canal after we eat. Rose found us a couple of ginger ales in the lobby though." She pressed a can of pop into my hand.

"What time is it?" I wondered aloud. Only a crack of sunlight made its way into the room from between the blinds.

"I just told you, Big Poppa," she teased. "It's lunchtime."

"Oh, wow…" I groaned, falling back into the bed after guzzling my drink. Unaccustomed to the carbonation, I inadvertently let out a giant burp. "Excuse me."

"Impressive," Jess retorted. She pulled the curtain open a little wider, allowing fresh air to flow into the room. "I don't think I've ever seen you sleep so long. You must have needed it. I think we all did."

"I feel like a bag of hot garbage," I told her.

"Look at you all open and in tune with your feelings!" she poked fun at me. "Maybe a swim this afternoon will help. Rose and I have already been twice." I smiled at her from beneath my forearm shielding my eyes from the light. After lunch I offered to go get the water. I needed to clear my mind and figured the walk would do me good. I brought my nine mil for company. Last night's dream bothered me. My guts told me it contained a message, but my brain said that was ridiculous—it was just an elaborate figment of whiskey and stress. How would I ever explain it to Rose and Jess? They'd lose their confidence in my ability to lead, to keep us safe. Then what?

I stepped into the river to fill our Nalgene bottles, half expecting ice to form around my ankles. The water felt refreshing against the sticky summer air, which was filled with the sound of bees pollinating wildflowers that grew along the bank. Wading out a little farther, I focused on the feeling of the current against my calves. I closed my eyes, willing my mind to take a break from its constant chatter. Filling my lungs deeply, I breathed into the rhythmic ebb and flow. I wanted to be more diligent about practicing the breathwork my psychologist had prescribed. It helped, but only if I practiced.

A past conversation with Will and Vanessa around their kitchen table floated to the surface of my consciousness. Vanessa had wanted to know what the food situation was like when I was in the middle east—what we had eaten in the military versus where the locals got their food, and so on. It turned into a lofty discussion about global food security, including inner-city food deserts. I realized how much I missed those chats, but really how much I missed my friends. *What would Willy do?* I asked the universe, half seriously. At that moment, a bumblebee landed on the rim of one of the bottles I held. Looking closer I noticed that its legs were thick with yellow pollen, or 'plant sperm' as Vanessa joked once. I blew on its wings, encouraging the insect to be on its way so I could drop in the purifying chlorine tabs.

On my way back to the hotel I checked the ignitions of the few vehicles parked along the route. Only one had a key stashed above its visor, but the tank was empty. The city had already been pilfered hard. I knew I was going to have to convince my crew that we needed to keep going, I just wasn't sure how.

As I reentered our room and saw Jess sitting by the window, her skin awash with a glow I hadn't noticed before, I knew that honesty was going to have to be the best policy. It would be the first brick I would lay in the foundation of my own family—the promise to be brutally genuine with each other, even when it was hard.

"There are decent looking sideroads along the main highway up to about Saint-Pascal," she said, flicking the map of Quebec in her hands that I recognized from the front foyer. "It doesn't make sense to follow the trail anymore because it crosses back over the St. Lawrence and I'm pretty sure the ferry we would need to take back again isn't an option. I think the sideroads will give us enough cover and there probably won't be much traffic when we're forced back onto the Trans Can.," she rattled off at me.

"You mean, you still want to go to the farm?" The surprise stopped me in my tracks.

"I thought about what you said, and you're right. It takes a village to raise a child and I believe when you say that our village is waiting in East Dalhousie." With that the flood gates burst open. I told her everything from the wolf sighting, to the battle between my brain and my intuition, to last night's dream. She didn't call me crazy, she just listened. Nothing felt logical about what was happening anyway. If an invisible bug could nearly wipe out the human race, why couldn't a wolf bring us a message? We agreed to continue hedging our bets on our friends' Nova

Scotian homestead.

Over the next few days, we fell into a routine of looking for our next mode of transportation, eating as well as we could, and exercising. Rose and Jess even took a self-led tour of the city's Jewish public library, so we gobbled up new reading material in our downtime.

When we weren't able to find anything to drive within a couple hours walk, we began hotel hopping our way out of the city. Along the way we found Atmosphere, an outdoor sports store, which provided us with warmer clothes, more water filtration supplies, mini propane tanks, and a handful of MREs. Still unlucky in the wheels department by the time we reached the outskirts, we communally decided to leather-tramp it—"Into the Wild" style. Hopefully we would find something along the way to speed up our journey. It was almost September and, as Jess gleefully reminded me, she'd be hauling around a pregnant belly before we blinked. Knowing Quebec's weather in October could be unpredictable, I wanted to make sure we were all tucked in somewhere nice and warm before the first snow.

XV

"I think I smell a campfire," Jess said with wry optimism. We were huddled beneath a tarp I had strung between trees. It had been raining for days and everything we owned was wet, right down to the gusset in our gitch. We were still managing a few kilometers a day, but our energy was running black, along with our food and our propane. It was impossible to get a good fire going with the saturated timber supplied by the forest. All of us now suffered painful blisters from our perpetually sopping shoes. Houses were few and far between on the route we had chosen. It was great that no one had bothered us, and the scenery was pretty, but otherwise it seemed to be a curse. Without the ATVs we had to ditch some of our supplies—including our nice tent.

Every time we stopped somewhere to dry out, I immediately started to feel anxious. The trip was simply taking too long. At one point a gravel pit had gifted us a pickup truck which we had enjoyed for about half an hour until we ran out of fumes. We reluctantly abandoned it where it sputtered to a stop. Then we discovered bicycles in a shed, complete with helmets, but they were another false start because no one had taught Rose to ride. We tried our best over the course of several hours, but he simply couldn't get the hang of it. He was actually a liability behind the handlebars, even with head protection.

"I smell smoke too," I confirmed. Rose patted his grumbling stomach. The MRE labels boldly claimed they contained enough calories, but they never felt like they completely filled the void—and we were thirty-six hours away from only having the packaging left to eat.

"Let's go see. Maybe we can stay there for the night?" Jess pleaded. Although she was strong and healthy herself, this was not a good environment for a developing baby, or Rose for that matter. Over the past few days, we both noticed a shift in his demeanor. He didn't complain but he walked with his head down, watching the road pass beneath his feet. His smiles had become few and far between, and there had been no thumbs ups. He had also started refusing to eat some of the MREs. Although asking strangers for help made me extremely uncomfortable, I had to admit it was time to call in the cavalry. Or rather, try to find them.

"This way, I think." I led us down an overgrown trail into the woods. It could have been mistaken for nothing more than a deer trail, but my trained eye noticed faint boot prints along it. *This is how it ends,* I thought to myself. *This is where we find the zombie horde and we all get eaten alive.* Although the smell of smoke grew stronger, the path was longer than I anticipated. It was impossible to see where, what, or who we were headed toward for more than five feet in advance.

*"Blackbird, blackbird,
Singing the blues all day
Right outside of my door.
Blackbird, blackbird,
Why do you sit and say,
There's no sunshine in store?"* A voice rang out from between the tightly knit branches.

"*All through the winter you hung around,*
Now I begin to feel homeward bound..." the raspy singer crooned.

"Stay close behind me," I whispered to Jess and Rose, crouching down to get a better vantage between the tree stumps.

"*Blackbird, blackbird,*
Got to be on my way,
Where there's sunshine galore. ..." Fingers drummed on a bucket rhythmically.

"*No one here can love and understand me,*
Oh! What hard luck stories they all hand me—Hey! Hey, bear! Heyyy, bear!"

From where I squatted, I could see a man standing under a covered porch. He looked about fifty years old, wearing a plaid shirt and jeans with patches in the knees. He banged aggressively on the bottom of a white five-gallon bucket, staring intently in our direction but evidently unable to see us. He had a long reddish beard with a mustache that hung down over his upper lip. He hawked a wad of chewing tobacco expertly into a spittoon at the bottom of the steps. I motioned for Jess and Rose to wait where they were, opting for my cloth mask over my respirator for the sake of clearer communication. Clearing my throat I stepped into sight, my hands held out in front of me in an offering of peace.

"No bear, sir, just my companions and I seeking shelter from the rain."

"Holy hell, boy! You scared the foreskin right off me! I thought you was Jeff—I mean, a black bear that comes around here once in a while. What in the hot damn are you folks doing out here in this weather? It's been raining since Jesus was a cowboy!" The man put his bucket aside, waving for us to join him on his porch.

"We hate to bother you, but the hospitality is much appreciated," I said, turning back to my crew hidden in the bushes. "Ok, it's safe to come out."

"Hold up, hold up, hold up!" The man suddenly held up his hand to stop us from coming any closer. "You folks ain't sick or somethin', are ya?"

"No, we've haven't been in contact with anyone for...almost a month now I guess," I assured him.

"Then what's with the masks?" he stroked his beard, obviously concerned.

"Um, habit I guess?" I confessed. "It feels like the polite thing to do. Can't be too careful these days, right?"

"You gotta be more specific," he said, crossing his ropey, tattoo-filled arms in front of him. "Been a while since I had any company with news." As I looked closer at the man's accommodations, I noticed it didn't have any power or telephone lines. The rustic cabin was constructed of hand sawn logs and there were no hints of modern amenities or decor. A pair of antlers hung above the entrance and the smoke we smelled came from a modest woodstove I could see glowing through the window.

"How long would you say exactly..." Jess asked, wide eyed.

"Ohhh, now you've gone an' stumped me, little lady." The man scratched the top of his balding head in thought. "Somewhere's 'round five years I reckon."

"Oh my god, he doesn't know." Jess and I stared at each other for a moment. I slowly pulled the mask down from my face.

"Do we ever have a story for you," I told him.

"Well, isn't that God's sweet timing!" he exclaimed. "I was just about to catch up with Holden Caufield. I reckon he can wait, hell—that little runt's been waitin' a decade already. I love a good yarn!" He extended his weathered hand toward me. "Albert Johnathan Kellington McGuigan at your service. But you can call me John. Close the door behind ya folks, don't wanna give Jeff any weird ideas."

XVI

"Thirty percent you say, eh?" John sat back hard in his wooden chair. "I'll be damned."

"That was the last estimation I heard, before the power went out," I informed him. "They said the number of survivors could be as low as fifteen percent within the next month. That was back in June. They called it a mass extinction event."

"You've gotta be shittin' me." He combed his calloused fingers through his beard. "Humans—the whole lot of 'em—just up and gone like a fart in the wind? I'd be half inclined to call ya liars if ya weren't sittin' here in front of me."

"I wouldn't blame you," Jess said. "Sometimes I still have to remind myself of everything that's happened when I wake up in the morning. My brain just can't keep up. It's a lot to accept. It happened so fast."

"If what yer sayin' is true," he pondered, "exactly how many horseshoes y'all carryin' in yer arseholes?" Splitting a pot of rabbit chili between us, we filled John in on the bunker in Peterborough and all the events that followed. To his credit, it did sound like a fantastic tale of bullshit.

"Trust me, I wouldn't be dragging this thing around if I didn't think I needed to." I pulled out my full-face respirator from my backpack as evidence. John instantly looked as if he had seen a ghost.

"Now, now that's quite the thing. Quite the story indeed," he stammered before abruptly standing to leave. "You, ahem, you folks just relax here. Get your stuff dried out by the fire. I think this old dog needs to take himself for a walk." Jess and I exchanged puzzled glances. We watched as he headed around the back of the cabin and disappeared down another inconspicuous trail leading further into the woods.

"Maybe he had to go to the bathroom?" Jess shrugged. "This chili is to die for though. Right, Rosie?" Rose had helped himself to a second bowl, mopping up the first with the last of the fry bread John had whipped up for us as well.

It was starting to get dark and there was still no sign of John. Not having been officially invited to stay the night we were leery to lay out our sleeping bags. However, our full bellies and the prospect of dry bedding was enough to brighten our moods a little. Rose and Jess played checkers on a board they found while I tended the small fire. I spied a copy of White Fang amidst John's bookshelf and decided to give it a test drive. As I leaned my back against the wall by the woodstove, a photo fell from between the pages.

A serious young John wearing a freshly pressed military uniform looked up at me from the creases. Beside him stood a slightly older man, probably not more than twenty-five, wearing the same uniform. Their eyes and prominent cheekbones suggested they were related, maybe even brothers. I turned the photo over and found *'John and Samuel, 1990'* written on the back. Like Tetris, the pieces started to come together. No longer in the mood to read, I replaced the picture and lay the book beside me. Half-listening to Rose and Jess's game instead, I let my eyelids droop, suddenly very tired.

Another hour or so went by before we heard John

coming up the steps. After a mumbled apology about his absence, he insisted Jess take his bed for the night. She politely tried to decline but he simply would not have a pregnant lady sleeping on the floor on his watch. Rose, whose oddities he had graciously accepted from the start, was given the couch. He had something different in mind entirely for me and him on the porch.

"Been a while since I used 'em, but they should hold," he said, holding up two balled up hammocks. After shaking the bug carcasses from them, he attached a carabiner to the end of a rope and tossed it over an exposed beam. Within a couple minutes the hammocks hung securely beneath the porch roof, their mustiness permeating the air.

"Do you partake, young fella?" he asked, passing me a joint from his shirt pocket. "Might as well give the slings a minute to air out." I lit the pinner with gratitude and took a couple of deep puffs, noting the earthy overtones. "Homegrown," John winked. I suspected he didn't know that growing your own marijuana in Canada was legal now too.

"You really haven't seen anybody for five years?" I started. "How do you get by out here all by yourself?"

"Well, my old pal Rick used to drop me off a parcel ya see. Couple times a year he'd bring coffee an' whiskey an' socks an' such. I don't need much. He hasn't been by in a while though. You folks got me wonderin' if maybe that 'rona virus did him in," he explained. "I thought he just got tired of my old ass. Not that I blamed him. Never been the best friend." I nodded, unfortunately able to empathize more than I cared to.

"Was Rick in the military too?" I asked. "I saw a picture of you in uniform."

"Mice in the corn wouldn't get by ya, eh, boy? Ya, Rick

was infantry. He lived down the backroads like me growin' up, in Kinmount—heard of it? Anyway, we signed up together, lookin' for adventure, I guess. Misadventure more like!" John grew serious as he drifted to a far-off place and time. "Probably only reason Rick put up with me so long is 'cus I saved his ass once— we were boots on the ground for Desert Storm. Rick got himself caught up in some sort of pesticide. Biowarfare bullshit. Had to drag the poor bastard halfway to Britain by the scruff. Nurses said he wouldn't have made it if I didn't get him out of there when I did, but he was never the same after. Couple guys nicknamed him Jitters, but I never did." He paused to take another long toke. "If we're being honest, that's why seein' your mask there earlier gave me a lil' spook. Reminded me of my crew of bullet catchers in the Gulf. Hadn't thought 'bout that in a while."

"That's incredible, John. Thank you for your service. Did your brother serve too?" I asked quietly. John nodded, his eyes growing a little misty.

"Best pilot in the air force at that time. Shot down in '91 but they never found his craft. MIA. Presumed dead. My poor mother never believed it though, not even the day she died. Always said he was walking round with a head injury in the desert, forgettin' who he was," he sighed. "Been a long time since I talked 'bout this crap with anyone. Sorry if it's heavy."

"Nothing I can't carry," I assured him.

"Ya, I wondered 'bout you. Got that same look about ya. Eyes of a man who's seen some crazy shit himself," John probed back.

"Afghanistan. 2012 and 2014. Syria after that."

"Well then, bravo zulu." He passed the dwindling roach to me.

"When did you move out here?" I asked, diverting the conversation from ruminating on my own service. "Why Quebec, of all places?"

"This property belonged to Rick. He let me put up a tent out here one summer—and I guess I forgot to leave!" He chuckled wistfully. "I tried to fit in as a civi after the war but couldn't make sense of it. Still can't. The way people live these days, man—total soup sandwich. Everybody's got these fancy cars, and jobs, and houses—the world is their oyster—but nobody got *time*. So, their kids hate 'em, their wives are shackin' up with the neighbourhood street meat, and instead of doin' somethin' about it they just complain about bills, or how the grass needs cut again, or some other superficial shit—until they die." I sensed there were more personal details to John's diatribe, but figured if he wanted to share them, he would.

"A man's only value is in his pocketbook it seems, and that don't add up to a nickel's worth of respect in my mind," he said with disgust. "The rat race just ain't worth the sacrifices we made. I don't recall signing up so some brat could cry over a dent in their sedan while steppin' over my men asleep on the sidewalk. What's left of 'em. The nonsense could drive a man mad…" John paused. "Remind me—what were we talkin' bout, soldier? My gum flappin' got away on me, been a long time since I bent somebody's ear… Oh yes, so, then I decided to build this place—every log is from this here forest. I offered to buy the land from Rick—my folks left me a lil' somethin' when they died—but he wouldn't hear tell of it. Gave me the deed for my birthday one year. He was a real good friend. Standup fella. Wish I could have said goodbye." The rain clouds finally started to move off and slivers of star-filled sky peeked down at us. "I still dunno what the point was—all that fightin'. Sittin' here, it's like an insane dream. A nightmare."

"Roger," I nodded, sympathetic to the fact he was referring to more than just the Gulf War conflict.

As we sat together in contemplative silence, my stoned brain dredged up news footage from 2022. Hundreds of thousands of people had descended on Ottawa to rally for "freedom" against vaccine mandates. Constituents of the self-proclaimed "Freedom Convoy" were outraged that their "right" to do-whatever-the-fuck-they-wanted had been violated. To emphasize their discontent, they used their jacked-up trucks—decorated in inverted Canadian flags and "Fuck Trudeau" stickers—to block paramedics from entering hospitals. And for what? So a bunch of dicks could pollute a hot tub in the middle of Wellington Street while innocent people died? As I watched it unfold, I thought my molars might explode into my gums like shrapnel. More stories emerged of protesters bullying Shepherds of Good Hope volunteers and taking meals meant for the homeless. Then, free take-out in hand, they danced on the Tomb of the Unknown Soldier. Again, for what? Was this the "liberty" my military brethren fought and died for? *Fuck no.* I was glad John was sheltered from it. Some aspects of civilization certainly hadn't progressed in his absence.

"I hope we haven't disturbed your peace too much, showing up unannounced like we did," I offered.

"Nah. Ya'll seem ok in my books. My mother would be glad I had the company," he said looking up at the stars. "Probably don't sleep much, do ya?"

"No, not really," I half chuckled.

"May as well look like we tried, eh." He zipped the bug net closed over his hammock and turned his back to me.

"See ya at zero dark thirty, soldier."

XVII

"Headin' for Nova Scotia you say, eh?" John asked over breakfast the next morning. He had treated us to a feast of sourdough pancakes topped with apple butter. "You folks still got another thousand k's I reckon." He brushed crumbs from his beard onto the floor.

"Yes," Jess sighed. "I imagine The Proclaimers would be proud."

"I would walk 500 miles…" he sang to her, the dishes on the kitchen table rattling in time to the stomping of his foot. Rose joined in, snapping his fingers, and Jess couldn't help but smile a bit.

"Something like that, but I don't remember them mentioning all the blisters." Jess removed one of her socks revealing large red welts on the sides of her toes and heels.

"Oh my, my—workin' on a case of trench foot, are ya?" John ruffled through a drawer before coming up with a pair of scissors. He clipped a leaf from an aloe vera plant sitting on his bookshelf. "Courtesy of my mother," he said as he passed it to her, clear goo emerging from the freshly cut limb.

"That feels a little better already, thank you," Jess said as she gingerly applied the natural ointment. Not wanting to miss out, Rose whipped off both his socks. His feet were in even worse shape. John handed him a leaf of his own.

"Rule number one of the infantry—you gotta take care of

your leg stems." He wagged his beard at us. "Don't be shy there, Nathan, it's time for show n' tell." I winced as I peeled the wool socks from my wounds. A couple of spots were brewing a greenish-grey slop. "MmmMmmMmm—bit of infection setting in there, soldier. Lick of honey for you." He produced a sticky jar full of yellow liquid.

"Um, you want me to eat it?" I asked, feeling like a moron.

"Well, ya can," he laughed, "but make sure you save a lil' for your foot gremlins too."

"If you say so," I shrugged. "You wouldn't happen to have any Band-Aids too, would you? Our first aid kit ran out."

"Well, not the kind in a fancy package," he said, taking a box off the shelf mischievously. "Here ya go, folks." He handed each of us a menstrual pad. Rose looked at him with sheer disgust.

"It ain't dirty, boy!" John laughed even harder while handing him a piece of tape.

"Actually, that feels a lot better," Jess said, stretching her newly tended feet toward the fire. "Yep, much better." She examined one of her shoes sitting next to the woodstove. "These aren't quite dry yet though."

"I'm not one to tell ya how to go about your business, folks," John addressed the group, "but my unsolicited advice is ya stay another night." He turned to clear away the breakfast plates, giving us a moment to discuss. His shoulders squared up when we concluded that he was probably right. A runaway infection could be a first-class ticket into a grave if we weren't careful.

"You sure we wouldn't be imposing?" Jess asked, standing to take over washing the dishes.

"No bother at all, little lady," John hesitantly patted her

on the shoulder. "Now you folks can meet Big Mac, Milkshake, and #6. C'mon, the dishes never run far around here." Unsure of what was to come next, we followed him down the same path we watched him disappear down yesterday. After a few hundred meters the forest opened into a pasture complete with a small log barn.

It turned out Big Mac, Milkshake, and #6 were John's cows. Rose was absolutely delighted.

"Moo?" he asked John.

"Yes, moo," he replied, raising one eyebrow. "You never met a cow, boy?" Rose shook his head. "Well, yer in for a treat." Rose followed along closely behind John, gingerly stepping between cow pies. Big Mac and Milkshake wore halters and were clearly used to being handled. Milkshake lowered her head so Rose could scratch behind her ear which made him giggle. #6 was a calf, perfectly matching the fawn colour of its parents. He jumped around, kicking up his hooves, showing off for his audience just like a little kid.

"This is where your dairy comes from?" I asked naively.

"Dang straight, cream right from the teat! They make a pretty good mozzarella. Oh, and pastrami too! Whatcha say to pizza for dinner?" Rose wiped away a bit of drool from his lip. I wasn't sure he realized that the pastrami was probably from the suspiciously absent #5.

"I think you've said the magic word," Jess laughed. "Pizza is Rose's favorite. It's what he always asks for on his birthday."

"Well happy birthday, Rosie boy! No guarantees on the delivery time—the chef actually does gotta fetch the tomatoes from the garden around here," John replied. "Come along." Leaving the bovines to happily graze, he led us to the most chaotic garden plot I'd ever seen. On a south facing slope, covering about an acre, cucumber and squash vines overtook nearly every nook and cranny of the tilled ground. Peas grew up tasseled corn stalks, and the tomato bushes hung so heavy with fruit that some were rapidly returning to the earth while still clinging to their foliage. Flowers and herbs filled with butterflies fought valiantly for their own piece of sun, and several beehives buzzed nearby.

"It looks like a sidh," Jess whispered, coming to stand beside me.

"A Sid?" I wasn't sure what she meant—Sid the Kid and Sid the Sloth were the only things that came to mind.

"From the Word-A-Day book. We never used sidh, and I think this looks like one," she squeezed my hand.

"Now *I'm* impressed." I squeezed her back. "Sidh, eh? I forgot all about it. If fairies were looking for real estate, I could definitely picture them setting up shop here."

"Garden got away on me a little this year," John confessed, slapping a fly from the top of his head. "Danged arthritis. Whoever said gettin' old is a privilege must have been goin' senile."

"I'm amazed at all you've accomplished here," Jess told him. "It's really inspiring. So much hard work."

"Didn't feel inspiring when I did it," he chuckled. "Just necessary." Rose approached John, pointing out a swath of prolific bush beans.

"Beans?" he asked politely.

"Go right ahead, boy. I'm just about ready to never see another bean again myself. Usually change my mind a few weeks into winter though. Maybe you can help me out and do a little pickin' while yer in there? Be nice to get some pickled for the lean season." Rose, clearly glad of his assignment, waded into the food forest with gusto. After tying a knot in the sleeves, John tossed him his shirt as a satchel to collect the pods into.

"Nice fella," John said to Jess and me from the corner of his mouth. "Funny name though."

XVIII

One extra day at John's place turned into two, and then four. By the fifth day everyone's feet were in much better shape and discussion about hitting the road resumed.

"I been meanin' to talk to you 'bout that, soldier," John said as we sat together on the porch after a delicious toasted-sandwich supper. I was worried he was going to ask us to stay indefinitely. It would be a difficult offer to refuse as I think we had all fallen a little in love with the guy, but there was still the baby to think about and John was no spring chicken. As difficult as it would be for us to leave his slice of paradise, I also wasn't looking forward to letting him down. He constantly reminded us of how much good our presence had done for him.

"I got somethin' for ya'll. Guess ya could say it's my parting gift."

"Oh?" I asked, a little surprised.

"Yep, should shorten yer journey quite a bit. Reckon you could make it to yer destination within a day or two if ya don't get caught in any tourist traps..." He had garnered all our attention. "Thing is, I'd kinda like to strike a trade." The three of us nodded simultaneously, encouraging him to go on. "You seen the state of the garden. I've been dreading gettin' my veggies put away for the winter. They are for Big Mac and Milkshake too ya know. It's gettin' to be a lot on my own, 'specially with this dang back." Pausing for emphasis, he rubbed his lower back. "I also still got firewood to split an' stack. So, I was thinkin'—" He paused again, clearly enjoying the attention. "Maybe you'd like to have my bus."

"Your bus?" I was dumbfounded. It simply sounded too good to be true. Maybe John had lost more of his marbles than we realized. Even if he really had a bus in working order, which I was skeptical of, we'd already had problems finding fuel. I couldn't imagine how much diesel we'd need to fill a bus tank and I presumed that, no matter what year it was, it was going to be a guzzler. My mind was spinning.

"Yes, my bus," John nodded, a toothy, yellow-stained grin emerging from his beard.

"Your bus?" Jess echoed, equally in shock. "Like, a school bus?" Rose clapped his hands excitedly.

"Sure, back in its day. It was a little project I worked on when I first retired," he told us.

"That's awful generous of you, and we don't mind helping you out with a few things before we get on our way," I told him. "But does it really still run? And honestly, even just getting fuel has become an issue. I don't want to sound ungrateful but—"

"Oh, she runs! One of my little winter hobbies was keepin' 'er goin'. Never really knew why though, no plans to take 'er anywhere. And the fuel she takes, well, that won't be a problem either. Long as yer in farm country." I didn't know what else to say. I was floored. "Well, c'mon then, let's go have a look before the daylight totally fucks off."

We followed John down another side trail I hadn't noticed before. A little way in it opened into a glade and beneath a great oak tree sat the distinct outline of a bus. It was hidden under mismatched tarps that were covered in fallen leaves in various states of decay.

"You really have a bus," I said, still bewildered. "What makes you think we won't have trouble finding fuel though?"

"Biofuuuuuel," he explained, wiggling his fingers at me like a magician. Then he started to remove the tarps. The bus, no longer school bus yellow, had been painted camouflage to match the Quebec Forest that surrounded it. Minor rust outlined the body, but it otherwise looked to be in decent shape.

"Biofuel?" I asked.

"Biofuel," he confirmed. "You see, Big Mac and Milkshake are good for more than just John's belly." He motioned for us to look in a small shed behind the bus. A lock hung on the doors, but it wasn't secured. Inside were several large steel barrels attached together with a series of hoses and valves. Beyond that, I had no idea what I was looking at, but I could definitely smell manure.

"It's a bio digester!" he clarified, sticking his head out the window from the driver's seat. "Made 'er myself." The clarity he presented was completely lost on me. "What are ya waitin' for? Climb aboard!" The inside of the bus was surprisingly nice. There was a queen-sized bed and a pull-out couch, as well as a stove top, and even a small shower.

"Well, I'll be damned," were the only words I could find.

"It's *amazing!*" said Jess, flopping down onto the bed. "*And* it's comfortable." Rose pointed curiously at a small hole beneath the mini fridge. A wooden sign hung above it read *'Chester'*.

"Ah yes," said John a little sadly. "Even made a built-in litter box back then for my old pal. Fancy lil' cat, always wearin' a tux. Never liked to travel though. Bet you woulda liked him." Rose walked to the front of the bus and wrapped his arms around John, picking him up off his feet in his embrace. The surprises just kept coming.

"Oh, oh, there, there, now, son. By golly put me down— no need for theatrics!" John squirmed but quickly learned that the key to his escape was to simply hug him back. Satisfied, Rose jumped off the bus and held up both his hands indicating that we were to wait there, which wasn't really a problem because I still wanted to hear the thing run. As John turned his attention back to the key in the ignition, Rose disappeared down the path back to the cabin.

With a single turn, the engine jumped to life. Jess threw her tanned arms around John's neck.

"Oh my god, how can we ever repay you? This is the best, most unexpected, gift I couldn't ever have imagined." He patted her arm.

"Like I said, there's a few strings attached to this old girl." He smiled at me in the rear-view.

"Thank you," I mouthed.

"Yes! Yes! Yes! Anything you need!" Jess exclaimed. John proceeded to put it into gear demonstrating that it could in fact drive. In all its unusual glory, it was flawless. I simply couldn't believe it. His obligatory horn honking summoned Rose from the bushes with his disposable camera in hand.

"I think I know what he's after," I said. "Are you up for a photo John?" Standing together outside the camo bus, Rose, John, and Jess hung their arms around each other's shoulders. I hoped that the cheap camera was able to capture how their smiles shone in the fading afternoon light.

"Alright, off with the lot of ya," John shooed us away. "Busy day tomorrow and I want to check a couple things over here— without y'all distractin' me." We took the hint, leaving John to his emotional tinkering.

"Thank you, thank you, *thank you!*" Jess called to him repeatedly over her shoulder as we walked back to the cabin.

XIX

For the next couple weeks, we settled into a routine of getting John ready for winter. Jess worked in the garden harvesting, separating out the best vegetables for seed collection. She'd bring them to the porch for John where he would begin the process of saving them. After harvesting each crop, he would teach her how to properly store them in his earth cellar or show her the best place to put them for curing. He had pre-prepared trays of sand for roots like carrots. "Keeps 'em crisp as a hooker's panties," he bragged. Things like garlic, onions, and herbs were strung from the rafters in his living room, turning the whole place into a dynamic scent-scape.

Rose discovered a knack for splitting kindling after I showed him the way around my hatchet. He didn't seem to mind the monotony and only stopped to take breaks when it was time to milk Milkshake, or for lunch. It wasn't long before he had proudly accumulated enough kindling for several years. As his final task, John then taught him a few simple preservation recipes. One afternoon they surprised me and Jess with virgin Bloody Marys. John said they wouldn't get us drunk but at least they'd "curb the scurv" (which evidently referred to vitamin C deficiency). Not only were the glasses rimmed with seasoned salt, but they were also garnished with all the pickled fixings Rose had been working on so diligently—beans, pickles, and pearl onions. I wasn't usually one for mocktails, but I couldn't remember ever tasting anything so fresh and delicious, even if the pickles weren't quite ready.

I took the ax for myself, welcoming the physical activity and the time alone. I hadn't had much quiet time with my own thoughts since the trip began. My goal was to drop and buck enough trees to keep John going for the next three or four years. I wondered what would happen to him after that. Luckily his cabin was small and surprisingly well insulated, so it didn't take nearly as much to heat as a standard home. As a bonus, between the sweat and the outdoor air, I was sleeping like a three-toed sloth.

"I'd say you folks have more than held up your end of the bargain," John told us one late October night. The fall colours had peaked, and frost had started to linger in the mornings. "Old man winter is gettin' near, or so my dang back keeps tellin' me." He pulled the keys to the bus from his pocket and slid them across the table to me.

"I still can't believe you are giving us your bus. Does this place have an address?" I asked him, tucking the keys into my own pocket.

"Oh, no, not officially. The less the government knows 'bout this place the better!" he snickered. "Used to rent one of those mailboxes in town but it was a costly way just to get fire starter, so I gave that up years ago. Nope, I'm a hard fella to get a hold of—except I'm always home. Maybe when the COVID war is over you folks can stop back in sometime. I wouldn't mind hearin' more of yer crazy tales from the road."

"Absolutely," Jess assured him. "And you can meet the baby!"

"Ah, yes," he smiled wistfully. "Be nice to meet the wee lad or lass you two put together."

The next morning as we packed up our things, John presented one last gift to each of us. To me he handed a small envelope of marijuana seeds and his copy of White Fang. I opened it to find the picture of him and his brother still inside.

"Can't wait to read it, thank you," I told him, busying myself looking for the best place to put it in my pack, unable to meet his eyes for fear I might crack. I noticed that he turned away rather quickly himself.

For Rose he had put together a sack of food complete with various pizza toppings like sauce, cheeses, and pastrami, as well as samples of the pickles and jams they made together. This time he didn't resist when Rose went in for a hug, in fact I think he held on a little tighter.

To Jess he handed a square package wrapped in butcher's paper and tied with twine.

"You really didn't have to," she told him. "You've done so much for us already." He waved her off, sitting down at the kitchen table to watch her open it with a gleam in his eye. She peeled back the paper to find a book with finely sanded wooden covers, neatly bound together with paracord. When she turned the book to show me, I saw it had been beautifully carved with the image of a bear cub and the words *'Baby's First Year.'* Then neither of us could contain the flood waters.

"But when..." she blubbered, holding her gift against her chest. John just grunted, trying to hide the fact he was wiping his face with the bottom of his shirt. "We will treasure it," she told him. "I wish we had something to give you in return!"

"Oh, I don't need nothin'," he replied humbly. "You've brought me more entertainment than the strip clubs in the Gulf. And those bitches took all my money!" I had noticed that when John felt uncomfortable his language devolved even further into lewdness. Completely undeterred by the derogatory subtext, Jess stood to give him a hug of her own.

"I'll never forget you," she told him.

"It's not much but I actually do have something for you," I said, removing from my pack the thick winter socks I had scavenged from Atmosphere. I had planned to leave them somewhere for him to find after we left. He seemed like the kind of guy who might refuse the act of kindness on principle, but with enough eyes on him in the room I figured he'd have a harder time resisting. And he did.

"Warm as a couple a' seal pups! My leg stems will be glad of ya in December. Thank you, soldier." He clapped me appreciatively on the back.

"Well," I said slowly. "I guess we best be hitting the trail." John accompanied us to the bus, insistent on carrying Jess's pack. He explained one last time how to take care of the biofuel system and offered a few troubleshooting solutions should we need them.

As I drove the bus out of the clearing, Jess and Rose sat at the window waving fervently. I honked the horn a few times for good measure. As we turned the corner out of sight, we could hear John crowing over the hum of the engine.

"I'm looking over a four-leaf clover
That I overlooked before
One leaf is sunshine, the second is rain
Third is the roses that grow in the lane
No need explaining, the one remaining
Is somebody I adore
I'm looking over a four-leaf clover
That I overlooked before..."

XX

We arrived at the New Brunswick border within a couple of hours. A pile of burnt tires barricaded the road but a well-worn path in the grass skirted around them. If we could ignore the abandoned vehicles randomly scattered across the highway—but no actual traffic—it might have felt like we were living on easy street. But as the kilometers streamed behind us, the interior of the bus remained muted. We were all waiting for the other shoe to drop. I suddenly found myself driving an LTV on the rugged roads of Syria, swerving to avoid the shadow of a suicide car bomber.

"Bunny!" I reassured my passengers as I clawed back to reality. The flashback was distressing, but this time it came with the realization that my symptoms were, slowly, beginning to recede. The distemper affixed beneath my skin since Afghanistan reared its head less often. The involuntary, recurrent memories were less potent. *I even made a friend*, I thought, glancing at Rose in the rearview mirror. Was some semblance of recovery possible? I took a long, deliberate breath.

"Let's stop at the tourism office to stretch our legs," Jess suggested, fully aware that there was never a suicidal rabbit. "Maybe they still have brochures." I gave her a funny look in the rear-view mirror. "I know this is going to sound horrible. I just—I want to forget about everything for twenty-four hours. John gave us a little win—can we celebrate that for a minute? Can we pretend that everything is going to work out somehow and go back to worrying tomorrow?" I wasn't sure how she planned to accomplish such a grand suspension of disbelief, but if it offered her a little respite, I didn't see the harm. It would be good to give our developing baby a break from the worries of the world too.

"Just remember to be careful," I reminded Jess and Rose as they headed toward the office—my late father's voice coming from my lips. There were certainly a few stories I would like to tell him right about now. I went to take a leak behind the building and the irony of my modesty made me snicker. There probably weren't too many public indecency tickets being handed out. When I promptly returned to the bus, I learned that Rose and Jess had found brochures indeed—armfuls of them.

"We've taken a vote," Jess informed me. "We want to do a little sightseeing." Boy, did they move fast. I was irked that they had come to this decision in my ten-second absence, but it would have been two against one regardless. Weren't they eager to get to the farm? There had already been so many delays. The bus was working fine for now—but what if we got stranded again? My heartrate ticked up a notch.

"We will basically be going right past anyway," she coaxed, sensing my apprehension. "We might never get the opportunity again. For all we know, we could die tomorrow." She wasn't wrong, but I wasn't convinced that the best approach in this very moment was to throw caution to the wind. I knew that committing to an internal landscape of perpetual terror, guilt, sadness, and anger was no way to honour the dead—but forgetting what happened, even for twenty-four hours, felt premature. "Old-Nathan" instinctively, and protectively, wanted to dig in his heels, but "Trying-To-Be-A-Better-Partner-Nathan" wanted to practice making compromises. Jess and Rose stared at me patiently as I duked it out with the voice inside my head.

"Be-A-Better-Partner-Nathan" won the SmackDown.

"For the record, I hate this idea. But—" I sighed, punctuating my resignation, "we can make a couple stops *on the way*. Where do you have in mind?" Jess smiled at me warmly while Rose pointed at an advertisement for the world's longest covered bridge in Hartland. Trying not to let them hear me gripe, I nodded and retook my post in the driver's seat.

I had to admit, it was a pretty long bridge. I couldn't imagine needing to see it more than once, but I guess I was kind of glad we added it to the itinerary. Rose got me to take a picture of him giving Jess a piggyback underneath it. It was another photo I hoped I would get to see developed someday. When we had our fill of the architectural wonder, we decided to pick a place to park for the night. There were zero excuses for me to drive tired, and Jess simply wasn't comfortable tagging in on such a large vehicle—and neither of us were comfortable with the idea of Rose taking over.

"How about we aim for somewhere around St. John? Then we can see the reversing falls," Jess proposed. "Then tomorrow we can do Fundy National Park or Hopewell Rocks!" As much as I hated the delays, I loved watching her get excited about things. Despite all our current obstacles, she was in a completely different headspace than she had been coasting in for the last few years. Gone was the burnout from work. Gone was the frustration and disappointment with me. Gone was the resentment toward her parents. Even if it was fleeting, or fueled by hormones, or a coping mechanism—it was like she was seeing the world through new eyes for the first time. Tragic shakedowns can force people to live in the moment—and sometimes that contains a strange gift. *YOLO,* as the kids used to say.

Rose held up another brochure with brightly painted buildings on it.

"Oh, oh! And Sussex!" she said, examining it more closely. "It says here that it's the mural capital of Atlantic Canada. Great idea, Rose!"

"Cheese and rice," I grumbled, climbing back into the tour bus driver's seat. It was only another two and a half hours to St. John. The bus topped out around eighty kilometers an hour so, even without the tourist quagmires, we wouldn't have been breaking any land speed records.

The area around St. John was filled with green, rolling hills and bountiful farmland. A brief stop was made at a former dairy operation to top up the biodigester from its decomposing manure mountain. Rose was disappointed that none of the animals were available for a meet and greet, but we did find a couple abandoned potato plants that we dug up for supper. After stopping for the night, Rose went to put his toes in the bay while Jess and I grilled the taters, smothered in John's gift of butter and cheese.

"Are you having fun?" Jess asked, cuddling up beside me on the couch while we waited. I was indeed having a little fun. "Want to make another baby?" she whispered in my ear, running her hand up my inner thigh. I didn't think that was how it worked, but figured it was worth a shot. Afterall, our species practically depended on it.

XXI

The next afternoon we made it to Hopewell Rocks. Before I even parked the bus we could hear the sound of music, and chanting. It was carried up on the ocean air from the beach below. Peering over the embankment we could see a party taking place. A group of people wearing various combinations of linen, leather, tie dye, and bare skin, danced around a large bonfire. A group of drummers formed an even larger circle around them. One of the female drummers with feathers braided into her long blonde hair was chanting. There were people of all ages, from the very old to the very young.

"What do you think?" I asked Jess. Rose was already halfway to the stairs that lead down to the ocean floor. "Hold up, my man. We gotta take a vote." His vote was, of course, a thumbs up. "Is it really worth it? What if they're sick? Or...nuts?" Jess thought for a minute, watching the festivities.

"What if they aren't? What if they have news? I think we can safely say hello, from a distance," she countered. Just then one of the dancers happened to look up and notice us. The drumming came to a stop. The woman who had been chanting shouted something, but it was too distorted by the wind. Everyone began to wave at us to come down.

"Sorry," Jess said, slowly adding her thumbs up to the vote.

"Son of a biscuit eater," I muttered under my breath. I was certainly getting practice on my fake swear words on this trip, and at this rate I'd be an ace by the time the baby came. I reluctantly placed my pistol in my waistband again. "Ok, Jess—but only if you wear your respirator. And Rose double-masks. I mean—please?" Grabbing hand sanitizer off the bus, I caught a glimpse of my father in my reflection in the door.

The dancing and drumming had started up again by the time we reached the shore. Before we could caution him, Rose had taken off his shirt and was running to join the dancing, the checkered flag trailing behind him. Although he remained outside the circle, his eccentric contributions to the choreography made him an instant hit. Jess swayed beside me to the rhythm while the group played for another half hour.

"Hello, friends!" The chanting lady approached, brushing sand from the folds of her ribbon skirt. She stopped eight feet in front of us and bowed slightly with her hands in prayer.

"Hello, nice to meet you," Jess said, holding out her arms warmly to "air hug" the young woman. I suddenly realized how long it had been since she had any female companionship. In Peterborough, before the pandemic, weekly girls' nights had been sanctified in our house. When they couldn't meet in person, she made a point of connecting with her friends over Zoom a couple times a week. Frankly, it had kind of annoyed me. They would always be cackling and talking over one another, and somebody was always spilling wine somewhere while they professed their undying devotion to each other. I found it all a bit over the top, grating even. Now, witnessing her brief exchange with this stranger, I saw that my attitude had been selfish. Some women just needed other women in their lives to thrive.

"What's everyone celebrating?" I asked, trying to be amiable.

"Samhain! Have you heard of it?" she asked us cheerily.

"Samhain? Nope. Sounds like something from my Word-A-Day book," I joked lamely, feeling totally out of my element. Jess squeezed my hand supportively.

"Maybe," the woman pretended to ponder. "It's a Gaelic Festival to celebrate the end of harvest. Everyone is welcome though. You can be my guests!"

"Nathan's heritage is Irish!" Jess said helpfully.

"Then maybe he will find his ancestors here," the chantress mused dreamily. I wanted whatever this chick was smoking. "My name is Samantha. We were going to do yoga next if you'd like to join."

"Absolutely!" Jess kicked off her shoes enthusiastically. "C'mon, you could use a good stretch too." I declined, posting myself on a piece of driftwood not too far away instead. А tall, lean man with coffee coloured skin and a seashell necklace led the group through a series of poses. Samantha patiently helped Rose as he repeatedly fell out of posture. It still managed to look like a postcard—the bonfire and yogis on the beach against a backdrop of towering red rock spires, crowned with their own mini forests. Shore birds circled inquisitively overhead. I watched with amusement as a green crab picked away at the carcass of a starfish. We certainly weren't in Ontario anymore.

After completing their practice, Samantha and Jess returned, jabbering like they had known each other for years.

"They want us to stay the night," Jess proposed.

"Samhain doesn't end until sunset and there's a big feast planned." I knew I was in a trap even before its jaws closed around me. I smoothed my beard, pretending to think about it but ultimately just delaying the inevitable.

"We have beer," Samantha added slyly. And the trap snapped shut. The festival goers had begun packing up their things and we were instructed to follow them to their tiny house commune just a few kilometers up the coast. I was relieved to learn it was right along our route to Nova Scotia.

"Can we make a pact?" I asked Rose and Jess before getting off the bus again. "Samhain today, but East Dalhousie tomorrow. For sure. Deal?"

"Bet you'll never forget that new word!" Jess said, offering me a pinky promise.

The evening passed by in a whirlwind of booze, weed, food, singing, and dancing. Someone had homebrewed enough beer and mead to inebriate a stadium. I winced when someone put a glass of the stuff into Rose's hand. The residents were strictly vegetarian, and some were vegan. Although I was thankful for the free feed, I found some of their food choices more palatable than others. Kale salad, for example, was not my friend, but kale chips were tolerable. Eggplant, no. Sun-dried tomatoes and basil on a cracker, yes. As the edible portion of the evening wound down, I decided that although I could appreciate their food philosophies, the amount of kale in their diet was something I simply couldn't get onboard with. Everybody's skin and hair looked great though.

Striking up a conversation with Damien, the lead yogi from the beach, I learned that the partygoers believed the threat of the virus had passed. They hadn't seen anyone visibly sick or dead from the disease in over a month—but there also hadn't been any foreign traffic passing through. Their community, not unlike the Mennonites we had seen, had extraordinarily survived the pandemic almost unscathed. I was starting to wonder if there were grounds for a ringer of a school science project in these pockets of, what seemed like, Sigma immunity.

Damien also told me that although the group came from all sorts of backgrounds, they helped each other celebrate the traditions that were important to each of them. There were First Nations, Muslims, Pagans, Jews, Christians, atheists, agnostics, and Catholics living peacefully among them, to name a few. This Samhain was particularly special to them all because they had agreed it would also be the day to celebrate the end of the virus.

"I don't want to sound like an ignorant white dude," I broached with extreme hesitance. "But how is that different from, you know, people wearing a headdress at Halloween or...black face?"

"It's not cultural appropriation if you're invited," he clapped me affably on the shoulder. "You can't imagine the pain that would have been prevented if more 'ignorant white dudes' had the balls to ask questions like that. I wouldn't call you ignorant. More like, curious. We are most often curious when we care. Black face, though—it's just offensive no matter how you spin it. Even well-intentioned costumes can hurt others because the initial concept was rooted in evil." He went on to tell me about how they named their communal home "Sundry Turtle Island." It paid homage to Indigenous land rights but also the common thread that had forged the residents' greatest strength—diversity and inclusion. *Now that,* I thought, *is a sort of freedom worth fighting for.*

"I guess it's like one big party all year here then, eh?" I

joked.

"Work hard, play harder, my friend," Damien laughed as we fist bumped. "I often feel like a perpetual birthday party attendee—spirit style. Don't get me wrong, there are still disagreements and tension on occasion, like most families, but we are proud of how we have learned to navigate them. Impatient or inflexible folk probably wouldn't enjoy it here very long."

Around zero two hundred hours, I noticed Rose getting a little too comfy reclined on a haystack. Someone had put a sleepy barn kitten in his arms and an empty beer glass lay beside him.

"Bedtime for you, my man." I shook his leg to wake him. He looked at me with what I suspected was a goofy grin behind his mask.

"Chester," he said, patting the black and white fuzz ball on its head.

"Ok, well we'll have to find who Chester belongs to in the morning. For now, you need to get to bed," I told him.

"Ok, Nathan. Help?" He held out his arms weakly. Damien helped me walk Rose back to the bus, the kitten nestled into the pocket of his sweatshirt. I made sure he downed a couple of glasses of water and that both he and Chester knew where the washroom facilities were located before tucking them in on the couch.

"Our friend might be having regrets when the sun comes up," Damien said prophetically, to which I unfortunately agreed. This time it was my mother's face that floated up from my memory bank—disappointed after discovering I spent a night out drinking in my youth. It didn't feel judgmental like it had back then, just concerned. How the tables had turned.

I found Jess by another bonfire, wearing nothing but her

respirator, a new tie-dye bikini, and a hula hoop around her waist. I noticed that her naked belly now protruded like a grapefruit—and it was fucking beautiful. Instead of crashing her party, I tried to relax into the scene. Damien passed me another glass of beer, which helped. Giddy from the socialization, Jess eventually collapsed beside me in a heap of impassioned exhaustion. Cradling her in my arms like a delicate sack of flour, I escorted the love of my life back to John's bus.

XXII

"Maybe it was all that organic food, but I actually feel great for having stayed up so late," Jess boasted as she slurped on one of the green smoothies Samantha had thoughtfully dropped off for everyone. However, "great" was not a word anyone would have used to describe Rose. I put my sunglasses over the poor bastard's bloodshot eyes. He didn't even move beneath his cocoon of blankets, a bucket strategically pinched between his knees. His new tuxedo kitten was stretched out, totally unconcerned, beside him. Damien told us the feline had come from a recent litter on Sundry Turtle Island. The cats were responsible for keeping the mice population under control in one of the communal barns. The child who took care of them noticed how much Rose loved the kitten and wanted him to have it. The vote we held as to whether Rose should keep it had been unanimous. I hoped Will and Vanessa wouldn't mind another mouser.

"Maybe it was the food, or maybe it was all the hula hooping," I teased Jess, discovering yet another piece of spinach between my teeth. "Did you have a good time?"

"The best," she smiled, reminiscing. "At least we have a place to go now if the farm doesn't work out." Ready to hit the highway for one last push into Nova Scotia, I honked the horn goodbye to the residents of the tiny house commune. They returned peace fingers and blew kisses.

Samantha and Jess drew smiley faces and hearts for one another on opposite sides of the grimy bus windows. Jess was right, it was reassuring to know that there were still good people alive out there.

Besides stopping at the Shubenacadie River for Rose to refresh himself, we made a beeline for the homestead. The closer we got to the centre of the province, the more familiar our surroundings became. When we hit Trunk 10, I knew we were home. Even the obvious signs of human devastation zipping by us hardly triggered me. My knee developed an uncontrollable, anticipatory shake and even Rose perked up from the excitement in the air. He held Chester II up to the window to see the sights as I described them.

"And that there's "2 Papa's Pizza." Oh man, they made the best dough boys! And that's where the New Germany Farmers' Market was held. And up a little further is the fire hall..." My heart was racing when we turned onto Cherryfield Road.

Please, sweet baby Jesus, let them be home, I prayed, superstitiously crossing my fingers. The farm didn't come into view until we were at the bottom of its long driveway. The entrance had been barred with a pile of logs, but I could tell that the fields had been recently tended— a good sign.

"Oh my god, they got solar power!" I hooted. It was a sustainable addition I knew Will and Vanessa had been dreaming of for years. Shielding my eyes against the afternoon sun, I could see the outline of a black dog with tall, pointed ears running across the apple orchard toward us. I opened the bus door for Remmington. Cross my heart until the day I die—that damn dog looked up at me from the steps and winked.

Part Three

"Peace. It does not mean to be in a place where there is no noise, trouble, or hard work. It means to be in the midst of those things and still be calm in your heart."
-Anonymous

I

I was in the hoop house harvesting the last of the long-season melons and cutting back the vines when Remmi suddenly bolted out from under the tarp. She had been content laying in the path while I worked, getting up every so often to make sure she stayed close beside me. Setting down my shears, I stood to stretch my legs and lifted a corner of the plastic to see what had drawn her away. An unusual rumble could be heard down the road. Ryley and Morgan flew past me in a torpedo of dark fur, barking like crazed animals.

Honk honk honk honk honk...honk honk! A loud horn sounded that I didn't recognize. Will, Paul, and Travis stepped out of the barn from where they had been working on trimming the alpacas' nails for the winter. I threw up my hands to tell them I didn't know what was going on. Jo-Anne and the kids, who had been in the house doing schoolwork, stepped out onto the porch.

"It's a bus!" Jo yelled over to me. "A big...camo...bus!"

"Do we know anyone with a bus?" I asked the men who had come to meet me halfway across the pasture, but they shook their heads no. I didn't think so either.

"I'll go grab my gun," Travis told us quietly, making a one-eighty for his camper.

As we approached the road, we could see the three dogs

dancing around a man with a rough reddish-brown beard. Two more people emerged from the bus, another man and a woman. They appeared somewhere between twenty and forty years old, and they all wore cloth masks. The shorter man was cradling a black kitten.

"Can we help you, folks?" Will called, coming to a stop a couple hundred yards back.

"Depends! Is there any room at the inn, brother?" The man with the beard called back.

"Well, I'll be damned," Will said under his breath.

"Is that...is that you, Nathan?" he stammered. I clapped my hand over my mouth, stifling a scream.

"Only God's greatest gift!" Nathan replied. Will and I ran the rest of the way to the roadside, forcing ourselves to stop a few feet back. Unable to form a coherent sentence, I just pointed frantically at the culvert, reminding Will to get the decontamination kit.

"Nate! Jess! Guy I don't know! Holy fuck balls—how did you get here? I can't believe you're here! Is this real? Is this real life?" Will found his words again before I did. We hastily put on surgical masks from the decon kit, desperate to hug our friends. Jo-Anne and Travis had met Nathan on occasion when he came to visit, but the others must have been mystified by the unfolding spectacle. Like a released pressure valve, I morphed into the star of my own melodrama—a wailing, sniffling mess.

"I'm so glad you're here," I sputtered, pouring hand sanitizer into Nathan's hands before clamping my arms around his torso like a vice. I wasn't sure I'd ever be able to let go again. "But how? And—where did you get this camo rocket? I have so many questions!"

"I'm so glad you guys are alive! Man, it's been quite the trip, I tell ya," Nathan's own voice cracked.

"Nice to see you, Nathan!" Jo-Anne waved from the porch. "And that must be the infamous Jess, is it?"

"Hello, Jo!" Nathan and Jess waved back. "Seems you've got a few new tenants since I was here last," Nathan said to Will, elbowing him in the ribs playfully. "And solar! You guys finally got solar!"

"It's a recent addition—just finished hooking it up this morning, if you can believe it," Will told him. "All thanks to Paul there." Paul gave him the two-finger salute from where we abandoned him halfway up the orchard. His cheeks reddened slightly with embarrassment from the attention.

"Those your rug rats, Travis?" Nathan waved at the kids who were hopping up and down beside Travis, who had just returned with his shotgun. He unloaded the bullets and put them in his pocket.

"The boys are mine, little blondie there belongs to Alex and Steve—not sure where they're at," he replied. "Nice to see you again, Nathan! Good thing you retired when ya did, eh?"

"Amen to that, brother." Nathan went on to introduce his companions. "This is Jess—some of you have met her before—and this is Rose, and the fuzzball is Chester II."

"Rose, eh? How very Jonathan Van Ness!" I said to the slightly balding man with a patchy black beard and a pink hoodie. My comment was met with a blank stare.

"Rose was one of the residents I worked with at Bonny Acres. We picked him up along the way and he's been with us ever since—a natural born traveler," Jess explained while Rose held out his kitten to show me.

"Well then, Rose, welcome to The Misfit Farm!"

II

"Wow, you guys have done a buttload of work," Nathan said, admiring the new barn. Steve had just finished hanging laundry on the line and Alex was taking an afternoon nap. I was a little surprised, and annoyed, when he declined the opportunity to meet our new guests, but he said he'd catch up with them at dinner. Steve, on the other hand, was elated to be introduced.

"Tell me news from the road! I want to hear *everything*. What's it like out there? Did you see anyone? All the way from Ontario—how incredible!" he gushed. Jo and Paul had gone into the house to begin preparing a celebratory feast while Travis and his sons worked on removing the logs blocking the end of the driveway.

"If we had known you were bringing a whole dang bus, we woulda made room in the barn for you!" I told Nathan and Jess.

"Honestly, we didn't know what our plans were from one day to the next. We only got the keys to the bus—let me see—" Jess counted her fingers on one hand. "Wow. Three days ago. That doesn't seem right."

"Three days, three lifetimes, who even knows anymore?" Nathan said, rubbing the back of his neck. "Honestly, Alex might have the right idea. I'm thinking a nap might be in the program for me as well. It just hit me like a load of bricks."

"How do you feel about hammocks?" I asked. "I mean, I know you have the bus, but the boys have got everyone convinced that sleeping in the greenhouse is the cat's ass. Or 'snackin' and relaxin' as they call it. It's not too hot in there today."

"Who could argue with a tagline like that?" he replied. Jess nodded too, starting to look sleepy herself.

"I don't want to be rude," she said. "We just got here."

"That's alright," I told her. "We'll have lots of time to catch up over supper. In case you didn't notice," I stuck my thumb in the direction of Alex's trailer, "we actually take rest pretty seriously around here."

"Work hard, play harder," Nathan said with a knowing smile.

"Something like that," I replied stiffly.

"I'll escort you to your suite," Will changed the subject with a sweeping mock bow.

"As for you, Rose," I offered, "I know a little girl who will be dying to meet your kitty. If you wouldn't mind." At first, he stared after his two companions looking lost, like a puppy being left home alone for the first time. Jess turned back to give him an encouraging thumbs up, so he wordlessly followed me back to the house. Only the cabinet containing our preserves gave him pause. He spun various jars around, appearing to admire the contents. I somehow managed to keep my poker face steady when he sniffed a couple of the lids.

"Norah!" I called into the living room which had been permanently converted into a one-room schoolhouse. "You have a special visitor!" She tossed the worn copy of Anne of Green Gables she was reading onto the couch. The one-on-one time with Jo had been like pouring rocket fuel on her reading and writing skills.

"Oh, hello," she said to Rose as I handed her a mask and sanitizer. "I'm Norah, nice to meet you." She held out her fist for him to bump. Instead, he pulled Chester II from his pocket, promptly handing them over to her.

"Wow!" she said. "I wish that's what happened every time you met someone new! Pow! A kitty!" She held the small creature against her shoulder, rubbing her cheek on its fur. "Oh, it's sooo soft! Is it a boy of a girl?" The cat's gender was apparently something Rose hadn't considered yet as he was clearly stumped. His face read like he had forgotten to call his mother on her birthday.

"That's ok, it doesn't matter," Norah assured him. "Does it have a name?"

"Chester II," he told her confidently.

"Nice to meet you, Chester II," she told the cat who was clearly enjoying being fawned over. "Can we play with him? I mean...them?" Rose nodded enthusiastically. "Awesome! I've got paper in here we can make into little balls. Oh! And tape, and string, and maybe a little stick..." I slowly backed up toward the doorway where Will was waiting after having tucked in Jess and Nathan in the greenhouse.

"Can you believe it? Like, did we do magic 'shrooms last night and then forget or something?" I whispered.

"I was just going to ask you to pinch me," he replied.

"There isn't room in the barn for the bus though, that's for sure," I reverted to worry. "And we're getting pretty filled up in here."

"Actually, I already thought about that," he informed me.

"You did?" I feigned shock.

"Ok, don't make a big deal about it. I get good ideas sometimes, too." He exaggerated his pout. "But seriously, what about the neighbour's house? I know I mentioned it to Keith and Tracey but who knows if we will see them again. There wouldn't be power up there right away, but it's got a woodstove and good bones. Plus, they've got the orchard and blueberry fields on their property. It would be nice to have someone maintaining it over there come spring. Maybe Paul knows where we could get another solar system."

"They *are* staying right?" I suddenly realized we hadn't asked. Nathan had a habit of being unpredictable. His decisions often seemed swayed by hidden mystical forces—or more specifically, his post-traumatic stress disorder. When Jess said she didn't know what they were doing from one day to the next, I knew she was referring to more than just their recent road trip. Nathan's flakiness and self-absorption caused him to lose some friendships in the past. An ace in the otherwise shit-hand we had all been dealt, was that Will and my experience with PTSD helped us be more tolerant of his mood swings and run-aways. The key, for us, had been not to take anything personally. His choices and actions reflected his internal world—not us as people—and he was usually pretty good at apologizing once he had time to process.

"Yes, I think he's staying," Will laughed. "I doubt this is just a pitstop on some crazy COVID bus tour," he paused, rethinking his words. "We'll confirm at supper."

"Putting them up at the neighbour's place is a really good idea though," I reassured him. Sighing out a mixture of content and buzzing anxiety, I leaned against my husband's strong body. He wrapped his arms around me supportively and we turned our attention back to the living room shenanigans. Norah and Rose had devised a whole ensemble of toys for Chester II, who looked like he had just discovered cat heaven. They took turns coaxing the kitten with a ball and string through a rudimentary obstacle course. Their imaginative play transcended the need for spoken language, and I thought it was delightful.

III

With the help of Jess, Jo and I, the kids went absolutely bananas for Christmas. All over the property, trees were adorned with wildlife-friendly decorations—strings of popcorn interspersed with cranberries, balls of lard rolled in seeds, dried flowers and herbs braided together, alpaca fiber pompoms, and rags turned into ribbons. My solar string lights were also commandeered as they were no longer needed in the greenhouse. Paul had hardwired the structure to the solar panels, which meant we could use my—*our*—legitimate grow lights. The plants I had started growing in there quickly showed their appreciation for the regulated temperature and proper lighting with prolific growth. There had never been a tastier fresh, garden salad than the ones we had that December.

The farmhouse had two Christmas trees—one in the kitchen and one in the living room turned schoolhouse—and the RV barn had four. The kids wanted one for each direction with the biggest one standing in the north, chosen to stand guard over the presents. They even insisted on decorating the huge birch tree in the middle of our neighbours' yard (now Nathan, Jess, and Rose's). Jess didn't want a tree losing needles in their house because bending over to clean was becoming increasingly difficult with her expanding waistline. The birch had been their compromise. However, wreaths on every door were non-negotiable.

The adults decided to draw names for gift giving, but the kids insisted on making something for everyone. In the weeks leading up to December 25th, Jo reduced their formal lessons to just three hours a day to better accommodate their present production line. Travis, Alex, and Steve, eternally grateful for the leadership she had shown in their children's education, fully supported the decision. They agreed there was value in allowing them to steer their own ship on occasion, especially when it came from a place of love for the people around them.

The kids created an elaborate schedule for their "adult elves," so the gift recipients wouldn't ruin their surprise. My favorite personal assignment was helping them with the interior decorating and furnishing of Rose's kitty condo. It had a built-in litter box which thoughtfully contained the mess caused by the wood shavings he had opted to use. There was also a cat bedroom with a luxurious cat bed, stuffed with alpaca fibre. Hung above it was a portrait Norah had drawn of Rose and Chester II, which the boys had even framed. No detail was overlooked, and I couldn't wait for Rose to see it Christmas morning.

Rose was truly thriving under his new routine. In the morning he would walk down to the farmhouse with a change of outdoor clothes in his backpack. Paul would help him with basic trade training workbooks, while Jo taught English and Social Studies to the kids. Then they would all make lunch for the rest of the adults, their "culinary art lessons" as Jo would remind them when they grumbled, which was rare. It was Rose's favorite class by far, although it took a while for Jo to teach him to keep his fingers out of the dishes they were preparing— or to at least not double dip. However, he was a whiz with the kitchen timers and showed a real affinity for spices. I looked forward to introducing him to my herb garden in the spring.

In the afternoon, Rose would head outside to work on either firewood or the sawmill with Travis, Nathan, and Will, and Steve on occasion. He was becoming quite the force with Nathan's hatchet, and he took great pride in the mountain of kindling he had assigned himself to. Travis took to calling him 'Beaver' or 'The Beav,' which caught on like Velcro among the men. Jess was confident it was the first time Rose had been given a friendly nickname, as opposed to just being called names. She could tell it made him feel like he was really one of the boys. We all watched with pride as his confidence, motivation, and ingenuity soared.

Alex, however, had become a difficult blip to ignore on everyone's radar. He spent most of the day in his trailer, rarely joining for communal meals or work tasks. Steve tried to reassure us that he was "just going through some stuff," but his lack of contribution or even a hint of gratitude had become irksome. He had been noticeably losing weight and any attempt at conversation with him was often met with one-word answers. His eyes and hair looked dull and if anyone asked him to do anything, he visibly prickled.

Steve and I had tried everything we could think of to unburden whatever was threatening to swallow him up and yet we hadn't been successful in the slightest. Steve worried that our efforts were pushing him farther away. At this point it seemed that the most compassionate, and proportionally the hardest, thing we could do was let Alex struggle. We had reached the limit of what we had to offer. Ultimately, we were resigned to a stalemate until he decided that he wanted help.

Travis was especially starting to lose his patience with

him, which came to a head Christmas morning. We began the morning with a breakfast spread in the farmhouse, knowing that gift opening was going to take time. I think the only thing that got Alex to the table was Norah's persistent excitement. When Jo and Paul got up to start clearing the dishes, Travis told Alex he'd like to speak with him privately. Begrudgingly, Alex followed him outside. Moments later the anger in their voices could be heard from the kitchen. Only Travis returned, shaking his head in frustration. Jess and Jo knowingly ushered the kids from the room.

"What happened?" Steve demanded.

"I'm sorry, Steve—I just told him it would be nice if he helped clean up. Everyone's been catering to him a lot around here without so much as a thank you, let alone a helping hand," Travis confessed. "I didn't mean for it to turn into a fight, but everyone's always pussy-footing around the guy. Figured some tough love was in order."

"On Christmas morning?" Steve pushed his chair back and stood to go after his partner. Travis held up his hands helplessly to the rest of us.

"Let's give them a minute," I suggested. "Maybe he'll come around."

"Who wants to play Kids Against Maturity?" Will said, directing everyone into the living room to play the twins' favorite game. It was hard to know what to tell the kids, so we simply did our best to show them that they weren't alone and that, despite Alex, their home was stable and loving. An hour or so later Steve returned to the farmhouse to give the all-clear for present opening in the barn.

"Yahooo!" yelled the boys, throwing their cards into the air before racing outdoors. They were clearly disappointed when Alex beat them to playing the role of Santa. Travis gave them a look that told them not to make a fuss about it and, thankfully, they were quickly preoccupied with the pile of gifts being set before them. Although the adults had drawn names for each other, we had each brought something for the kids too. They certainly deserved to be spoiled.

"Oops, this one is for Jess," I said, returning the gift that Alex had handed me.

"My apologies, my love," he replied, patting me on the cheek. It was the nicest thing he'd said to me in months, but also jarringly out of character. It wasn't the only mistake he made with the name tags either and I couldn't help but notice his eyes were a little glassy. He was also doing odd things like clumsy pirouettes, and I swore I heard him slur his speech a couple of times.

"I think he's high," Nathan said, pulling me aside.

"There's definitely something going on," I agreed.

"I think it's more than just weed," he pressed. "He's either on drugs he shouldn't be, or not on drugs he should be. Maybe it's time for a formal intervention? I know you said he won't listen to you or Steve, but maybe if we all raised our concerns? Strength in numbers?" I told him I'd run it by Steve, and we agreed to keep an even closer eye on Alex in the meantime. Not wanting to spoil the day completely for the kids, we turned our attention back to the task at hand—wrapping paper. Rose meticulously collected and folded each piece, mostly handmade or whatever I had left over from before the pandemic. Chester II swatted at the paper hilariously from Rose's sweater pocket. The kids were saving their kitty condo gift for last, which was currently hidden in the root cellar.

There were already several other oversized gifts emerging from the cellar. Rose and Nathan had made an elegant wooden cradle for Jess and the baby, and the boys had made a stylish bookcase for Norah's growing collection of favorite reads. Paul had also mysteriously acquired a spinning wheel and wool carding set for Jo, which we learned had belonged to his late mother. She was ecstatic to resurrect an old hobby and thanked him with a long kiss under the mistletoe.

"Ewwwwww!" the boys shrieked, which was even funnier when I reminded them that the decoration had been their idea.

Next, Will and the kids presented me with a beautifully handcrafted seed storage chest, and both Travis and Steve were given ornate lockboxes for their guns. When it was time for the adults to exchange their gifts with the person whose name they'd drawn, I noticed that Paul didn't receive anything. I overheard Alex give him a lame apology and tell him that he "forgot." In his humble and gracious way, Paul shushed him and told him not to worry, the day was about the kids anyway. Maybe Nathan was right—maybe a full-blown intervention was in order.

It was finally time for the kids to present Rose with his kitty condo. Unable to find a big enough box, they had wrapped it in layers of old feed sacks, pieces of cardboard, twine, and newspaper. It took Rose several minutes to open it, his eyes growing to the size of dinner plates when he finally did. Unable to find any words—despite the fact that his language had been steadily improving—he gave each child their own thumbs up. Then, with a smile as bright as the sun, he invited them for a hug with open arms. The three of them swarmed him. The boys were now strong enough that they picked him up clear off his feet, just like Rose was known to do to them. Chester II promptly gave his own stamp of approval, making himself at home in his new cat bed.

"Hey—where are you going, Beaver?" Nathan called as Rose headed toward the door of the barn. Rose motioned that he would be back shortly. "Alright, well, I know we drew names," Nathan cleared his throat as he stood up, "But I have one more thing for everyone." Evidently, he had found our neighbour's old yarn collection, because he had knitted everyone a pair of socks. Jess began laughing uncontrollably.

"I was wondering what you were doing going down to the basement all sneaky every night after you thought I was asleep," she gasped for air. Her pregnant belly was shaking like a bowl full of jelly. "In a million years I would never have guessed that you were down there learning how to knit!" Nathan turned several shades of red.

"First rule of the infantry," he shrugged with a smile. "Gotta take care of your leg stems."

Winter air blasted into the building as Rose returned to the barn. He held up his disposable camera triumphantly. Familiar with the drill, Nathan helped him gather everyone in a group, their new socks pulled up over the hem of their pants at Jess's insistence. In the middle, Rose stood with his arm proudly around his kitty condo where Chester II had promptly fallen asleep, oblivious to the activity around him. There was only one photo left so Nathan turned the camera around, giving a thumbs up in the most epic Christmas selfie of 2024.

IV

The next morning a nor'easter from hell blew over the farm, coating every surface in a layer of ice an inch thick. Tree limbs crashed to the forest floor under the weight. The wind whipped snowdrifts around the yard, which quickly rose to the bottom of the windowsills. Everyone was on deck making sure that the livestock had enough food, water, and bedding to survive. Extra bundles of wood were brought inside for the stove to beat back the cold. We couldn't even speak to each other as we trudged from building to building, the howl of the wind amplified by the ice rapidly transforming the landscape into a twisted freeze-frame.

Nathan, Jess, and Rose came over at first light to pool resources and effort, setting up camp in the farmhouse living room. Rose was clearly a little unsettled by his first introduction to a Nova Scotian winter storm, so Jo tried to take his mind off it by enlisting him to help her make storm cookies. Even though he was moving a little slower than usual, his face and eyes expressionless, he took his job seriously and even kept a rotation of hot tea steeping at the same time.

Every available bucket and jug were filled with water in case something happened to the solar power system. Every hour or so someone was designated to go out and keep the paths cleared between the barns. Candles and flashlights were rounded up with whatever remaining batteries were on hand. Will and I had seen quite a few bad storms at the farm, but this one was shaping up to be a contender for first place, depending on how long it decided to stay and play. Travis made sure the generator was primed and filled with fuel, leaving only a quarter left in one of the main tanks. Although it was a calculated decision, running the sawmill had taken a toll on our reserves.

Aside from keeping accesses cleared, and water buckets thawed, eventually there wasn't much left to do besides hunker down. Everyone assumed their various posts with books, games, or independent hobbies. Nathan challenged Jo to a hilarious knit-off; whoever finished the most wearable pieces before the storm ended would be crowned the winner. It was quickly evident that we would all be getting new scarves.

Nightfall came especially early under the heavy storm clouds. The epicentre still swirled above us like a stubborn old witch. I was busy in the kitchen making a giant pot of duck stew and dumplings when Will banged open the door coming back from his patrol. He yelled my name in a manner I'd only heard once or twice in our marriage—when something terrible had happened.

"There are wolves in with the alpacas!" he roared, "Willow is dead!" I had already started putting on my coveralls when I first heard my name, but his words stopped me in my tracks, an ice pick plunging into my heart. *Wolves?* There hadn't been wolves sighted in Nova Scotia for one hundred and fifty years.

"Get the guns!" I screamed back at him, the zipper on my jacket suddenly an impossible matrix. Nathan had also sprung up from the couch, knitting needles and yarn flying across the room.

"Are you fucking serious, Willy?" he asked, pulling a balaclava over his face.

"There must have been at least five of them!" Will yelled, already running back out the door. On our way past the RV barn, I pounded on the door, screaming for Travis to bring his shotgun. The wind had completely unhinged the door that led from the pasture into the alpaca barn. I could see a pool of blood spreading out in the snow where Willow lay—two skeletal wolves gorging on her still body.

"Holy fuck, it's hard to see," Nathan hollered, wiping snow from his eyes as he took aim with his pistol. One of the wolves dropped to the ground when he fired while the other took off across the field.

As we rounded the corner of the barn, we could see another wolf with its teeth clamped around KLee's throat. Blood streamed from where it had already torn her open, exposing her trachea. The big brown alpaca was screaming in terror, her eyes bulging from her head, foam dribbling from her mouth. Nathan took his shot. He missed. The wind made it almost impossible to keep his hand steady, but the noise was enough to make the wolf fall away from its prey. Like a ghost, it followed its pack mates back across the pasture and disappeared into the storm.

Gasping for air, KLee fell to her knees. Nathan looked back at me. I nodded my permission for him to do what needed to be done. The suffering animal didn't pull away when he put his gun to her head. Silently she fell into the snow, only yards away from her mother. They had been together since the day she was born. I ran to my beautiful brown eyed girl, dropping to my knees beside her. I buried my ear against her chest, ensuring she was really gone. There was no movement. I closed her cartoon eyes one last time.

"Where's Nikko?" I yelled, turning to find Will stepping back from the barn. His face was white, and he grabbed for a fence post to steady himself. He shook his head sadly at me before puking on the ground. Travis and Steve, who had just arrived, tried to bar me from entering the building.

"You don't need to see him like that," Travis said gently.

"I know you're trying to protect me," I replied, pushing my way through, "but these are *my* animals." In that moment I didn't give a damn about the complicated nuances of ownership. Poor Nikko's fluffy blonde body lay in a pile of blood-soaked hay. The wolves had gutted him. His sweet face had been left unmarred so if I focused there, he almost looked like he was just sleeping.

"Can you get a few tarps?" I asked of anyone who was listening. My voice clear and measured, years of emergency service experience arriving to begin unraveling the chaos. Travis patted me regretfully on the back and headed out to find some. Nathan and Will had already started to drag Willow back into the barn, fighting against the snow, and ice, and wind. I went back out and knelt beside KLee, not wanting her to be outside alone, while I waited for them to give me a hand. I put her head in my lap and stroked her soft ears, an act of love that would have got me spit on if she were alive.

"What in the actual *fuck?*" Will broke down again seeing the three bodies wrapped in tarps lined up beside one another on the barn floor. He screwed his palms in anguish into his red eye sockets, as if he might scrub away what he just witnessed. His eyelashes and brows had frozen white, suspending him in a look of horror. Travis also carried in the wolf Nathan had shot as there was no sense in wasting its pelt.

"I've never seen one or heard of wolves around here. I

guess they are making a comeback," he thought aloud, running his fingers over the creature's ribs. "They must have been really hungry coming out in a storm like this..." His pointer finger nearly fit in between each bone despite its winter coat, which also appeared much thinner than would be expected for this time of year.

"I bet it's because of that damn deer cull last spring," I speculated. "Big predators like wolves are probably starving all over the continent. This is what the Defenders were trying to warn everyone about. They knew something like this would start happening." My emotional side sat quietly on the sidelines, waiting for its chance to grieve later. "I'd like to secure the barn for the night. I want to shear the alpacas in the morning. Then we will have to decide what to do with them. It will be impossible to dig a grave big enough at this time of the year without a backhoe." Nathan got to work on a temporary fix for the barn door and Will and Steve helped him secure it with a couple of logs. Then we headed to the RV barn to warm up. Will and I stood inside the door holding onto each other wordlessly, our frozen clothes dripping around us like cold rain.

"What's all the yelling and shooting about?" Alex asked, opening the door to his trailer sleepily. Travis had already taken Ryan and Chris aside to explain what had happened.

"Oh, those poor creatures," Steve told Alex sadly. "The door broke on the alpaca barn and a pack of wolves found them."

"Wolves?" Alex rubbed his face looking dazed. "I thought those were extinct—"

"Alex, where's Norah?" Steve suddenly interrupted him.

"Oh, I'm sure she's around here somewhere..." he replied.

"Norah?" Steve called, starting to look around the barn. *"Norah?!"* His voice became a little more frantic when she still didn't reply.

"Maybe she's at the house," I offered. "I'll go look—Rose is probably feeding her cookies."

Alex stumbled over to Travis and the boys and proceeded to grill Ryan and Chris about her whereabouts.

"Hold up there a minute," Travis was saying to him as Will and I left. "Did you ask them to watch her? Because if not, you better lay off my kids..."

V

Norah wasn't with Jo at the house either. Everyone thought she was with Alex, and he had last seen her colouring at the table in their RV. Steve, his whole body quivering, informed everyone that her jacket and boots were gone. Ryley, who had taken up sleeping in the RV barn under Alex and Steve's trailer, was also missing. The shepherd had claimed Norah as her own and could usually be found curled up at her feet during lessons or following her around while she did her morning chores.

"Here's what we know." I hushed everyone who had gathered in the barn to organize the official search. "Norah and Ryley are likely together, and they are almost definitely outside." A small sob escaped Ryan's lips, and Jo, her own face stricken with fear, pulled him against her supportively. "Last time she was seen was in Alex and Steve's trailer approximately forty minutes ago. Steve, what colour are her jacket and boots?"

"Her coat is yellow with white fur trim on the hood, and her boots are black," he informed us, a wild look of panic in his eyes. "She had on light grey track pants," he added. "I think. Or was it jeans? Oh my god, I can't remember..." Will began to pass out flashlights.

"It is very important that we keep each other in sight *at all times*. We'll form a search line. If you can't see your neighbour's light, you need to make finding it again your priority before you continue looking for Norah. We will be no use to her if we get lost ourselves." I dictated the plan firmly. "It's kind of a long shot but Remmi has a keen nose so, Steve, if you could bring me something Norah wore recently, I'm going to try to get her to help us track. She also knows the command to find her sister, Ryley, so if they are together that might help as well." Steve ran and grabbed Norah's pajamas from the trailer. "The storm has completely erased any hint of which direction they went, so if we are all in agreement, I suggest we follow Remmi's lead."

"We're going to let a stupid farm dog lead the search for my kid?" Alex criticized, rising anxiously from his seat.

"Do you have a *better* idea?" Travis shot back, also standing with his arms folded in front of his chest. Alex shrank back, shaking his head. "Right now, it looks like the only stupid one in the room is you, Alex, so sit down and shut up for once!"

"Jo, Jess, and Rose," I said, deflecting from the confrontation. "Can you stay here with Morgan in case Norah comes back on her own?" Morgan's tall black ears perked up at the sound of her name. "Jo, keep the kitchen really warm—like, warm enough to make you sweat. And Jess, keep checking the house and the barns, Norah might be confused if she's hypothermic. Take Morgan with you when you're outside, for protection." I paused, waiting for my instructions to filter through the room. "Ok, everyone, let's suit up."

The twins insisted they be allowed to help form the search party line. Travis, hesitant at first, agreed as long as they were positioned on either side of him. Will, Paul, and Alex each took bags filled with first aid supplies, blankets, and thermoses filled with warm water. Nathan, Steve, and

Travis each brought their guns. I got to work amping up Remmi by holding Norah's pajamas and Ryley's dog bed up to her nose. I'd give her a sniff, then give her a treat, and repeat. I had no idea if she understood the task at hand but, with the clock ticking, we headed out into the blizzard anyway.

"Find your sister!" I ordered Remmi as we leaned into the wind. It was a command she was familiar with on the farm, but I wasn't sure if she'd be able to pick up any kind of scent in the sleet. At first, she paced back and forth, nose to the ground in front of the RV barn. Then she slowly made her way back toward the farmhouse.

This isn't going to work, I thought to myself, alone at the front of the group. *This is where they would walk every day for school. Remmi thinks they are over here because they aren't in the barn.*

Just when I was about to suggest we switch tactics, Remmi changed directions and began to pull me back behind the pond.

"Good girl, Remmi!" I told her, rewarding her with a piece of sausage. As we entered the forest the search party fanned out behind us. We were only able to see each other's lights about ten to fifteen feet apart, but with the nine of us we covered a fair chunk of ground. Everyone called out Norah's name, sweeping the lights through the trees. Remmi towed me relentlessly through the snow for what felt like ages. I'd occasionally have to reign her in to wait for the others to catch up. She'd look up at me every time we stopped, whining.

"I hope you know what you're doing," I whispered, giving her another treat.

After what was probably only a kilometer, my flashlight caught a glimpse of eyes peering out from a spruce tree well. I froze, suddenly remembering the wolf encounter only a couple of hours, or was it lifetimes, ago. Remmi was undeterred, dragging me toward the dark figure. The animal slowly raised its head and I recognized Ryley's tall back ears, replicas of her sisters'. I felt like I was moving in slow motion as I fought against the burden of snow which was now above my knees. As I yanked back the tree's branches, I could see a piece of yellow fabric nestled beneath Ryley's curled up body.

"She's over here!" I screamed, shoving my hand beneath my dog, feeling for Norah. She moaned when I pinched her, and relief flooded through me. Will was the first to reach us, quickly unpacking the blankets from his bag. When I moved Ryley to the side so we could pick up Norah, I realized the dog was also unable to stand.

"We'll have to carry them both," I instructed my husband who nodded, wiping snow and ice from his face. Nathan arrived beside us and picked up Ryley against his chest like a child herself. "You did good, dog, you did good," I told her, kissing her cold nose as her eyes fluttered shut. "We need to get back to the house *now*. I know it will be hard but try not to jostle either of them if you can help it. If they've started to freeze on the inside, any rough movement could stop their hearts."

Spurred on by both urgency and optimism, we methodically waded back toward the house. Jo fell to her knees in prayer at the kitchen door when she saw our lights, now grouped together, coming back from the woods.

"She's alive," I reassured her as we made our way inside. "Let's get her wet clothes off and get her in front of the fire. Ryley, too. Gently, gently. Yes, lots of blankets..." Morgan instinctively curled up beside Ryley and Remmi in front of the wood stove, slowly licking the ice from their fur and paws. I also sat wedged between them with a blanket around me, where I was able to keep a close eye on the rhythmic rise and fall of Norah's back. After half an hour of being wrapped in a cocoon of warm blankets in Steve's arms, she was able to start taking sips of warm sugar water.

"I think she's going to be ok," I said, putting my arms around both of them and kissing the child's now warm forehead. Alex stood close by, unable to take his eyes off of them, but unable to approach. "She needs you too," I whispered to him. "Go on." He stared at me for a moment as if he had forgotten who I was. *"Get your shit together and go be with your daughter!"* I hissed, snapping him into action.

I went to join the others who had gathered in vigil in the living room. Rose insisted that he serve us snacks and beverages, even though most of us didn't feel very hungry. He was right though, we could all benefit from replacement calories.

"She's keeping liquid down," I relayed as I entered the doorway. The twins' cheeks were both red and wet from crying. They had sat themselves so they could keep a watchful eye over Norah in the kitchen as well. "It all turned out ok," I reassured them, even though it wasn't the whole truth—there was still the gruesome scene waiting in the alpaca barn. I took up a spot on the couch beside the twins, realizing how badly I needed downtime while wrapped in the closeness of my friends and family. "Thanks for being such good helpers tonight, boys. I think I'm ready for bed now though." I rested my head on the back of the sofa.

"Alex has gotten out of hand," Travis said quietly to the room, which was received with a round of nods. "As soon as Norah is feeling better, I vote we deal with him once and for all."

"Ok, but what does that mean exactly? Once and for all?" I asked from behind closed eyes. "Off with his head?"

"I'm not even sure what I mean, Vanessa," he sighed, "but he's becoming a liability. I'd even go so far as to say he's dangerous."

No one disagreed.

Opening my eyes enough to peer through my lashes, I looked at Will sitting across the room. He appeared to have aged ten years since lunchtime. Worry and tension were etched into his laugh lines. His normally confident shoulders slumped forward. The grey hairs just beginning to invade his stubble were more prominent somehow. Was the drama of living in community worth it? Hadn't it been easier when it was just the two of us on the farm? It felt like a distant memory.

VI

The next morning Rose, Jo, and Paul made two feasts—one for the humans, and one for the dogs. Norah was back to herself after a long sleep and she was very, very sorry for scaring everyone. She heard the commotion in the alpaca barn and gotten lost on her way to see if she could help. Her, Chris, and Ryan opted to have their breakfast on the floor with the "hero" dogs instead of at the table, which no one minded. The boys had brought each of the canines a new fluorescent orange bandana they made for them to wear around their necks. Many hugs were shared but the conversation was quiet. Like a fish without enough water, the room's atmosphere squirmed between loving appreciation and frustration.

Alex put his hand softly on Jo's forearm when she and Paul stood to clear the dishes.

"I'll do it, Jo. Please don't get up, Paul," he said before clearing his throat. "If I could have everyone's attention for a moment? There are a few things I'd like to say..." The room fell silent, and all eyes turned to observe him. Some faces were more obviously angry than others. His fingertips were white from gripping the edge of the table and he cleared his throat a few more times before he began.

"I owe you all an apology. I know I haven't been myself for a while and, because of that, you have all been picking up after me. Last night my distraction almost cost Norah her life…" Tears began to stream down his face. Travis rolled his eyes sarcastically and Jo gave him a stern look from across the table, reminding him that the kids were watching. Norah came to her father's side, putting her arms around him. Ryley, fully recovered from her own ordeal, followed her and sat leaning against her leg. I had a feeling the shepherd wouldn't be letting Norah out of her sight any time soon.

"I've been selfish," Alex went on. "I also haven't been very nice to the people who have shown me the most kindness while facing very difficult times themselves. I'm embarrassed that I've contributed to making all your lives harder."

"And Ryley," Travis reminded him through clenched teeth. Alex stared at him blankly. "You almost cost Ryley her life, too."

"Yes, yes, of course," Alex went on. "My actions jeopardized everyone, including these magnificent creatures." He gave Ryley a quick pat on the head, who I could have sworn rolled her eyes at him too. "And I know sorry will never be enough, but I hope I can make it up to you all someday. Starting today. I'm going to get it together. I promise."

"Sounds like lip service to me," I overheard Travis whisper to Will. Neither of them looked particularly convinced by his speech. It sounded like something we had heard before. Alex stood to begin clearing the table, insistent that he do it alone. *And therein lies the rub.*

"What's the plan for the day?" Will turned to ask me. The storm had cleared and although there was cleanup to be done, my priority was shearing the alpacas. Jo expressed that she would be honoured to spin their fibre and together we would decide what special things to make with it. The alpacas had not only given us their fleece, but their manure was the primary soil amendment that grew our bounty of produce without synthetic chemicals. "Alpaca TV", as the kids called it, had also provided a source of entertainment in lieu of actual television. Jo had even taken the kids out to the alpaca barn on occasion to practice reading aloud to the animals.

"I think a funeral pyre is probably the most reasonable option," I told Will. "I thought about using them to bait the wolves away from the farm, but I can't stomach the thought of it. I can't imagine feeding them to the dogs, either." I looked over at my beautiful, furry girls lounging with the kids by the fire, never more in love with them than I was that morning. Nathan snuck Remmi an extra piece of bacon before he came to join us.

"What do you think, Nate? Could you and Travis work on building a pyre? Paul said he would skin the wolf and I'd like to help Vanessa prepare the alpacas," Will asked his friends.

"Absolutely, brother," Nathan said. "Anything we can do to make today a bit easier. Right, Trav?" Travis nodded in agreement, although his furrowed brow suggested his mind was still on Alex. Despite last night's fleeting sentiments, I was immeasurably grateful that they had both found their way to the farm. Living in community had its challenges, but we were creating something that made belonging matter—even when it was hard. *Especially* when it was hard. We finished our hot apple ciders before setting about our tasks.

At the funeral that night, Norah brought me a letter she had written for the alpacas and asked if I'd like to read it out loud for her. On the back she had drawn a beautiful picture of herself standing with the three of them under an apple tree. I told her I'd love to.

Dear KLee, Willow, and Nikko,
We are going to miss you. You were really good alpacas. I liked when you gave me kisses. Your noses were squishy, and I liked the smell of your breath because it smelled like hay and grass and apples—except when you spit. That did not smell good.
I will never forget you.
Thanks for being my friends.
Norah

"Thank you, Norah, that was beautiful," I said, passing the letter back to her. "Your writing is getting really good, and your drawing is wonderful. It looks just like them."

"You can keep it," she told me, reaching up for a hug. I held onto her a little longer than usual and was reminded of the celebration of life we held in the fall. As adults we don't always know how our words, habits, and rituals impact the children around us. It heartened me to see Norah seeking out ways to honour the things that positively impacted her. It's never too early to start practicing gratitude. *She could teach her father a thing or two.* I cringed at my own musing.

Did I tolerate Alex in hopes of a reward, even if it was something as small as a thank you? I promised him a place on the farm no strings attached, except for the shared labour we agreed on. Sure, Steve, and Norah, had been shouldering their family's share, but it wasn't so long ago that Will had done the same for me when I was adhered to the couch. Acts of loving kindness do not have conditions, unless an ego seeking validation lurks beneath. I realized that my "reward" came earlier and had exactly nothing to do with Alex—it was my own good fortune to be able to offer him support. *I guess I still have things to learn about gratitude, too.*

People slowly wandered off to bed in an aura of emotional exhaustion. Rose, Jess, and Nathan decided to head back to their own place up the road. Eventually it was just Will and me left with the fading embers.

"Do you think he'll change?" Will asked after a while.

"Alex?" I sighed. "I don't know. He seemed sincere but...I'm not sure how he's planning to pull himself out of whatever hole he's in. He needs help. Professional help. Know any good therapists taking clients?"

"That was my thought," Will agreed. "I guess his actions will prove whether or not his words mean anything this time."

VII

Winter began to give way to spring, like it always does. Planting was in full swing between the gothic arches of the hoop house again. The snow had begun to melt off the roads and plans for another recon mission were underway. We wanted to get a solar system for Nathan's house, replenish our fuel if possible, and get materials for a second winter greenhouse. Added bonuses would be staples like flour, rice, sugar, and coffee—all food stuffs that were difficult or impossible to make ourselves. Thankfully, fuel was less of a concern now that we had the Bio-Bus, and Paul was confident that if we could find more solar power materials, we could even revamp the sawmill.

Nathan and Jess's baby was due any day and Alex had become surprisingly involved in helping them get ready for an at home birth. He still suffered significant mood swings and occasionally disappeared from view for days at a time, but overall, he seemed to be trying to be more helpful and considerate. His relationship with Steve also appeared to be healing as they often spent the evenings reading or playing chess together, instead of Steve trying to take care of their household all by himself. They had begun to discuss building a permanent home for themselves somewhere nearby. Travis and the boys were hoping to do the same, although Ryan and Chris were fixated on the idea of it being a massive treehouse. Surprisingly, Travis didn't put an immediate end to their outlandish proposal. Not yet anyway.

I was teaching the boys how to sow and germinate carrot seeds when we heard an engine on the road.

"Did somebody take the bus out?" I asked them. It didn't sound like the bus though—the small motor was whining at a high throttle. Whoever it was, they were flying.

"It sounds like a four-wheeler," Ryan said excitedly. We all poked our heads out from under the plastic to investigate. It turned out he was right, a red ATV was barreling down the road toward the farm, barely making the corner into the driveway and screeching to a halt in front of the log blockade.

"Holy shit balls! I thought they were going to nail it!" Chris exclaimed. I smacked his arm lightly for swearing, although we had agreed that whatever language happened in the hoop house stayed in the hoop house. Admittedly, I was usually the worst culprit.

"Just don't get too far ahead of me," I told them as we hurried over to meet the rider, who had just removed her helmet.

"Tracey? Is that you?" I recognized my friend from the farmer's market, the same one Will had reconnected with on his first recon mission.

"Vanessa!" she cried, heading across the orchard toward me. "I'm so glad you're here—*Keith's had an accident!*"

"I assume it's bad?" I asked, to which she nodded, tears filling her eyes. It had been a few months since any real crises had happened on the farm and her expression filled my stomach with knots. "Boys, can you go get Alex? He's up at Nathan's." They nodded, dutifully running off like mini torpedoes.

"Tell me what happened." I led Tracey to sit on the

porch. Jo, having overheard, brought us out glasses of iced tea. Tracey's plaid shirt was soaked with sweat and her short brown hair was matted to her forehead from her helmet.

"We were out cutting down trees for firewood when one took a weird fall. His leg is trapped under the log and between two rocks. I've been trying to free him all morning, but his axe busted in the fall. Nothing will budge." She paused to catch her breath. "He's lost all feeling below his knee and his foot is cold. It's kind of a purply-black colour now. I think I could see pieces of bone, maybe."

Oh shit. I squeezed her hand, encouraging her to go on.

"He's the one who told me to try to find you guys. We just didn't know what else to do. I can't lose him!"

"I understand. We'll get moving right away. Jo?" I called. "Do you mind sitting here with Tracey for a minute? I've got to go find Will." Jo traded places with me on the porch and I left to start forming a plan. I could really use Alex's help on this one as I was anticipating a field amputation or, at the very least, crush syndrome. I quickly explained the situation to Will who began preparing the bus and got Travis to help clear the driveway's entrance. They loaded an ax, chainsaw, pry bar, and ratchet straps, as I wasn't sure what was available at Keith and Tracey's place. Then I went to pack my medical bags, again. *I thought I retired from this line of work...*

I had a Gigli saw that I had neither been formally trained on or used before, tourniquets, QuikClot bandages, alcohol, a kit for stitches, and IV supplies. The black cast iron frying pan hanging on the wall in the kitchen also kept calling my name, so I cleaned it and added it to my bag.

Then my heart leapt into my throat.

I couldn't seem to find any of the heavy duty pain

medication. All the opioids were missing—the oxycodone, hydrocodone, morphine, and even the Percocets. All I could find was Toradol and Advil. The knots in my stomach started to boil. I had a sickening suspicion that Alex would know exactly where the narcotics were.

Will, Travis, Tracey, and I were ready and loaded on the bus in about twenty minutes. Just as we were about to pull out, we could see the twins running back up the road toward us.

"Alex is... not coming," they said breathlessly in unison. They were both panting, bent over with their hands on their knees.

"What?! Why not!?" I demanded.

"Jess.... she's having...tractions!" Ryan spit out.

"She's having contractions?" I clarified in amazement.

"The baby is coming!" they both yelled with gusto. Everyone on the bus stared at them wide-eyed.

"Ok...alright." I attempted to collect my thoughts. "It's fine," I lied. I was feeling rusty having been away from the world of medicine for so long. It was the same feeling I had when I returned to working on the ambulance after being placed on stress leave. It was something like getting back on a bicycle—a big, scary, bicycle that could hurt someone if I forgot how to work the pedals. This situation was also different because not only would I be playing paramedic—I might also be forced to play the part of orthopedic surgeon. I mean, I *had* done hospital rounds in ortho once...thirteen years ago. There would also be no calling dispatch for backup if I found myself out of my depth. This was basically my worst nightmare. Unpracticed, ill prepared, and on my own.

"We can do this," I told everyone with all the confidence I could muster. I wanted to add, *I watched this on YouTube once*, but kept it to myself. I had enough nerves for the lot of us. Will put the bus back in gear and we headed toward New Germany.

"Has it always been like this for you two?" Travis asked.

"What do you mean?" Will replied.

"I don't know—ever since I started hanging out with you it's either chaos or calm and not a whole lot in between." I laughed in uneasy appreciation. He certainly wasn't wrong, but he probably didn't realize how hard we fought for those moments of calm. While I was working on the ambulance, chaos had become my baseline. Regular doses of adrenaline made me feel "normal." It reminded me I was alive. But, even under the noble guise of public service, constantly craving the next high demanded many sacrifices—a peaceful existence included. After my diagnosis, Will and I fought hard to strike a balance. It took years to convince my nervous system that I was safe in stillness.

As we approached Keith and Tracey's house, I laid out the plan I had been working on. I also took a blood type survey and learned that Travis and Tracey were both O negative. Despite the risks, they both consented to donate if necessary.

From where we parked the bus in the driveway, I could see the big yellow birch that held Keith hostage. Travis and Will carried the supplies, while Tracey went into the house to sterilize their kitchen in the event we needed a makeshift operating room. I also told her to stoke the woodstove and handed her the frying pan to get heated up on top of it. She looked at me horrified for a moment before quietly setting about what she needed to do.

"Lying down on the job I see," I teased as I approached Keith. Making jokes was my go-to when people ended up in precarious situations. It often helped break the ice, but their choice of response also gave me a good indication of their mental status—and will to live. An old medic had taught me that. Even if the patient ultimately died—at least it was with a smirk on their face. Tracey had already informed me that he hadn't struck his head, neck, or back, so thankfully I wasn't too concerned about a compounding spinal injury.

"Wife's been working me to the bone," Keith replied with a wink and a wince. "Figured this was the only way that woman would let me get some rest!" I was happy with his level of consciousness, but I wasn't happy with the mangled limb I could see crushed between two boulders.

"Enough with the pleasantries," I told him. "Off with your pants!" He pretended to be shocked but gave me his permission with a nod. I began cutting away his jeans from the trapped leg so I could get a better look and properly place a tourniquet.

"You think we can lift the tree off of him?" I asked Travis and Will.

"Without cutting it? Probably not," they concluded.

"Of course, it couldn't be that easy," I muttered, silently cursing Alex for the mysteriously missing pain meds. "So, here's the scoop," I told Keith. "I can give you a sedative, so you won't *remember* the pain, but you are still going to *feel* it."

"In that case, I'd like a second opinion, Doc," he joked. "Actually, the view's getting a little boring from here and I've got places to be—let's get this over with."

"Sounds good, my friend." I quietly reviewed the plan again with Will and Travis while waiting for the medication I administered to take effect. They would cut out the section of tree pinning Keith and hopefully we would be able to carry him into the house from there. If not, I'd have to amputate and cauterize his leg on the spot.

"Can I claim the movie rights to this?" Travis laughed anxiously. I held Keith's hand and blocked his face from the flying wood chips as the men began cutting away the tree trunk with the chainsaw. He screamed like a wild cat in pain before dropping into unconsciousness.

"Is he dead?" Travis shouted with alarm.

"Nope, just passed out," I reassured him. "Probably for the best. Let's get that log off him." Travis and Will picked it up with ease and Keith's "leg" came free from between the rocks. The three of us carried him up to the house, careful not to disturb his limb that now more closely resembled ground beef. It was almost unrecognizable except for a few splinters of tibia. There was no way I'd be able to save it. We laid him out gently on the kitchen table.

"Tracey, we need something for him to bite on," I told her. Although Keith was currently unconscious, I figured he might wake up again once we started with the Gigli saw. The crushed leg was full of toxic blood and if I released the tourniquet to try to save his leg, it would likely kill him. There was no doubt in my mind—the leg had to go. Tracey maintained her composure even though she was pale as a midday snowstorm.

"It's going to be ok, baby. I'm right here," she whispered into her husband's ear while placing a strip of twisted fabric between his teeth.

"I have big asks for both of you," I told Travis and Will. "Travis, I'm going to show you where to cut with the saw. You're stronger than me so you'll be able to get through faster. If you get tired, Will or I will tag in. Once the limb is off, I'll clean the wound. Then—Will—I want you ready with the frying pan. We have to cauterize the stump before

I can release the tourniquet. The faster we do this, the more tissue we can save and the less pain it will cause Keith. But first things first—PPE." I could almost see everyone's blood pressure skyrocket.

"I really need to get new friends," Travis said sarcastically. Then, we got to work. Keith faded in and out of consciousness, sometimes recognizing his wife's face hovering above him, sometimes stringing curse words together in new and creative ways. We were all relieved when the twisted lump of flesh fell away. I was even more thankful when the sizzle of the frying pan against healthy flesh stopped his femoral artery from bleeding out.

"We have to bring him back to the farm with us," I told Tracey. She nodded, having anticipated that. Even if we staved off infection, it would be a long road to recovery with our limited resources and expertise, not to mention the fact that Keith would have to learn how to get around with one leg. I wasn't sure what we would be able to find for a prosthetic.

"I'd come with you now, but we've been having issues with coyotes—and wolves, if you can believe it. Keith wouldn't want me to leave the animals, and I know he's in good hands. But—and it feels like a bizarre time to be bringing this up—we were talking over the winter about wanting to be closer to you folks. Like, permanently. We haven't seen anyone since we saw you that day last fall, Will," Tracey told us. Her disclosure was welcome news as I suddenly realized we had completely forgotten to take any sort of pandemic precautions. "We were just feeling a bit lonely then, especially trying to do everything ourselves, but now..." she paused, biting her lip while looking down at her wounded husband. Despite the smell of burnt flesh permeating the room, Keith appeared to be resting comfortably for the moment under a cocktail of sedation and minimal pain management. "This obviously solidifies it. I'm going to start packing. Can someone come let me know how he is tomorrow? Or if something changes?"

"Absolutely," I told her. "To all of that. We'd love to have you nearby as opposed to all the way over here. I'll— we'll— have someone drive over tomorrow morning, either way, and we can start getting you moved." What used to be a thirty-minute drive now felt like there was a whole other country standing between us. "Plus, I'd do pretty unscrupulous things for dairy these days."

"I think that your bus might be the perfect way to move the goats, and that was the missing link, so, it's settled. Where did you even find that thing?"

"You'll have to ask—oh my god—Nathan and Jess!" I suddenly remembered what was happening back at the farm. "Not that I want to be the one to clear out the kitchen party, but maybe we can start heading back? They're having their baby today!"

VIII

Once we got Keith settled in the farmhouse living room, we headed up to Nathan and Jess's place. Although she was eager to hear how things were progressing up the road, Jo opted to stay and tend to Keith. I was pleased to see him resting at ease on the couch. It almost looked like he was having a casual midday nap—if I diverted my gaze from the dip in the sheets where his shin and foot should be. Paul also decided to stay with them and offered to start combing my medical texts for information on amputations and recovery protocol. Their late-season companionship continued to blossom. Although I never met Paul's late wife, Annette, I had a feeling that she would approve.

I quickly picked a bouquet of tulips for Jess that had begun to bloom in the warmer hoop house temperatures. There had been many babies born on the homestead, but none of the human variety. Early in our dating life, Will and I decided that parenting wasn't in the cards for us. It wasn't a light decision and was based on a whole list of reasons, the most prominent being that I didn't want to pass on my family's mental health curse. We also believed, from an ecological standpoint, that there were too many people occupying the earth already. If we wanted to expand our numbers, we would adopt. We were also extremely concerned about the kind of world the next generation was being born into. Climate change, the disappearing middle class, and inflation weighed heavily on us. I certainly hadn't been envious of my mom-friends as they struggled through the revolving pandemic restrictions, school closures, lockdowns, and social isolation with littles in tow. Even though we held our beliefs firmly, we were still supportive of those who found fulfillment in having children of their own. I think our child-free-lifestyle allowed us to enjoy their kids even more. Well rested aunties and uncles could be a real asset.

"Just the man I'd like to have a word with," Travis met Alex at the door of Nathan and Jess's house. To my surprise, he closed his fist around Alex's throat and threw him clear over the railing of the front steps into a withered snowbank. Alex landed with a loud crunch on the icy crust that hardly gave way under him.

"What the hell, Travis?!" Alex cried, pushing his heels into the snow, trying to back away from his advances. Travis jumped over the landing after him and grabbed a hold of his shirt collar.

"C'mon man, let him go. It's not worth it," Will said with very little emphasis. Travis pretended not to hear, punching Alex squarely in the face. Blood sprayed from his crooked nose.

"What in the *flying duck* is going on out here?" Nathan poked his head out the door.

"I'll fill you in later," I told him, suggesting we both go back in the house and leave the three of them to work it out. Inside, Jess and Rose were huddled together on the couch, a distinct bundle of joy cradled in her arms.

"It's a girl," she said looking up at me, her smile beaming. I was overcome by happy tears. We all really, really needed something good to happen, and I didn't know of any better news story than a healthy baby.

"Caught her myself," Nathan said proudly, before adding, "with Alex's help, of course. Seriously, what is going on out there?" He looked back over his shoulder at the brawl taking place on his lawn.

"Later. Got something for a vase?" I asked, handing him the bouquet of tulips. "Did you pick out a name yet?" Jess gazed lovingly at her baby's new pink cheeks, and fine black eyelashes.

"There were a few hot contenders," she replied. "But I think we've settled on one... if it's ok with you."

"With me?" I laughed.

"Yes," Nathan said, coming to put his arm around my shoulder. "We thought we'd name her after your black alpaca, Willow."

"Aww, I'd love that," I sniffled. "I couldn't think of a nicer tribute. Did you know—besides the obvious—Willow also means freedom?"

"I didn't, but I love it even more. It just feels right, like a good omen. It was her dark hair and eyelashes that made me think of it," Jess said. "Would you like to hold her?"

"Yes, please!" I held the warm infant against my chest. "Nice to meet you little Willow seed." A content yawn crinkled her tiny button nose. I couldn't help but wonder what kind of world she would be growing into. What kind of opportunities would she have? What goals would she set for herself? Would this slice of Nova Scotian soil be enough for her, or would she dream of distant lands as she unearthed them from books around the farm? Willow blinked up at me, unphased by my adult worries.

A few minutes later I suggested that Rose and I go back down to the farmhouse to give the new parents time alone with their latest addition. I also still needed to go deal with Alex who was currently standing in the driveway with a block of ice held to his nose. Travis and Will stood in front of him with their arms crossed, undoubtedly reading him the riot act.

"I *know*, I'm a piece of shit!" I heard Alex say as we exited the house.

"Ok, guys, this feels wildly inappropriate—let's take it back to the farm," I suggested. "We have a lot to discuss. And Steve should be present." Travis continued to spit venom from his eyes at Alex. Rose looked back and forth between the two frantically, his lips pursed, and his eyes narrowed. He tried in vain to facilitate a handshake between them.

"Not now, Beaver!" Travis waved him off in exasperation before both men promptly stomped off in the direction of the farm, ten paces apart. Rose was hot on their heels.

"How is everyone doing in there?" Will asked, actively trying to relax his shoulders and unkink the tension in his neck.

"Everyone is doing well," I told him. "It's a healthy girl and, get this, they're going to name her after Willow." A smile crept onto the corner of his lips. "She's got Jess's black hair. A lot of it. Everyone is very happy." Not wanting to disturb their peace more than we already had, Will quickly stuck his head in the door to congratulate his best friend on his growing family. He also handed him a bag of cloth diapers from Jo who had been making them in preparation.

Back at the farm, we found Steve finishing up a woodworking lesson with the kids. They were building houses for the resident barn swallows, hopeful it would encourage the birds to move out of the hayloft. I signaled to Steve from the door, not wanting to upset the children with Alex's new facial arrangement.

"What happened?" Steve asked, stepping into the

sunlight to join us. "Are you ok?" he asked Alex, noticing his wounds, and the swelling on Travis's fist. *"What happened to your nose?"*

"We need to talk—privately," Travis told him. "Let's go in the alpaca barn, it's the only space that's free." Steve stuck his head back in the RV barn to let the kids know that Rose was in charge, and they could have free time after they cleaned up.

I hadn't spent time in the alpaca barn since the wolves attacked and I half expected to see Klee's face in the window to greet us. I really missed the animals. Their barn would be the perfect space for Keith and Tracey's goats, and I was glad it would hold life again, but at the moment it was also a stark reminder of how close we came to losing Norah. I don't think the nuance was lost on Steve or Alex either. In the building, Will and Travis tossed hay bales in a circle, and we all sat down together.

Always the first to reach for the microphone, I told Alex that he had one chance, and one chance only, to tell Steve what we already knew, or I would do it for him. Steve looked horrified, wondering what had possibly befallen his family now. Alex just looked at his hands. His fingertips were blanched from holding the ice to his face. He took a few deep breaths before finding the nerve to look his husband in the eyes.

"Hi, my name is Alex..." he began slowly and seriously. "I'm an addict." Steve's face transformed from fear to perplexion, wordlessly taking one of Alex's hands into his own. The rest of the group silently held space for them.

"There was an emergency earlier today and Vanessa needed to use the pain medication we had stocked. She couldn't find it..." He paused. "Because I took it." Alex began to cry, and I could hear Travis gritting his teeth beside me. "It just started with one, you know, to take the edge off. I needed to get some sleep. Before I knew it, the bottle was gone but the pain in my heart wasn't. It just got worse, so I took another." He attempted to straighten himself, roughly wiping the blood-tinged snot from his face. "It's not an excuse. I knew it was wrong, and you all—" he addressed the group, "you gave me so many chances to 'fess up but I was too ashamed. I knew once someone found out, I'd have to stop." Even Travis's face softened with a glimmer of empathy for his difficult confession.

"We all got demons, you know," Will spoke up. "They are much easier to fight with good people in your corner." Alex nodded.

"I know, I know that," he continued. "I turned into everything that I hated as a nurse. Just a stupid addict wasting people's time and hurting the ones who love them. It was like, I couldn't function without the drugs after a certain point. I couldn't even find the motivation to get out of bed. I just wanted to be numb. And because of that—we almost lost Norah. And now, again because of me, Keith had to suffer. *It's all my fault!* I've completely lost control." A fresh wave of sobs overcame him.

"Desperate people do desperate things," Steve said quietly. He moved to sit on his husband's hay bale and pulled him close, trying to sooth him. "You're in survival mode, honey."

"And addiction is a disease," I added softly. "It's nobody's *fault*, no more than cancer or a heart attack. We all pay for our humanity one way or another. Keith's accident with the tree would have happened regardless. If we hadn't stolen the medication, it wouldn't have been available. And yes, maybe Norah wouldn't have wandered away if you had been sober—but it also could have happened when you were in the bathroom or something."

"I know what you're trying to do," Alex replied. "Please stop. I'm just a loser. I fucking *hate* myself."

"It's out in the open now," Travis stepped in. "I think you need to take time and try to figure out how we can all move forward together. A lot of trust has been broken."

"I know, and I am *so* sorry, I truly am." He looked around at the four of us.

"Trust has been broken, absolutely, but—you're also *sick*, Alex," I said. "You're suffering from mental illness *manifesting* as a physical addiction, which I think you know. We also need to talk about how dependent you've become on the drugs and how much you have stashed away. Will you let me help you? Will you let *us* help you? You know this only works if it's something you want for yourself. Nobody can force you to get better."

"I'm ready," Alex said, his smashed nose making him look like a bully after being beaten up in the school yard for the first time. "We are Sigma survivors for heaven's sake, and I've been trashing our second chance. I'll do whatever it takes. You all deserve it. And the kids deserve it, at the very least."

"You deserve more, too," Steve reminded him, affectionately rubbing away a spot of blood on Alex's chin with his thumb. "You deserve to be healthy, too."

IX

Over the next couple of weeks, I split my time between Alex and Keith, helping them both heal. Alex and I developed their treatment plans together. He said he found it easier to suppress his cravings when he had tasks, especially if they involved helping someone else. My response was that helping himself would open an even bigger capacity for help others—you can't pour from an empty cup and all that—which he knew but hadn't yet internalized. The destigmatization of men's mental health, and specifically male caregivers, was a relatively new concept.

Because of his binging there wasn't much left for opioid medication, but we split it up the best we could. Alex received a decreasing daily dose so he could withdraw without overly shocking his system. If he stopped what he had been taking cold turkey, he risked becoming dangerously ill. There was still enough left over to keep Keith reasonably comfortable as his body adjusted to his new stump. However, the emotional pain he was suffering from the loss of his limb was not something that could be solved with medication. Only time and courage would provide a salve.

Travis, Will, and Paul helped Tracey move their things from their farm to ours, including all their goats. Rose and the kids insisted on tagging along on the trip. Tracey reported that they were actually a great addition and helped keep the animals calm during the drive. Although they were thrilled about the prospect of fresh honey, the kids weren't as keen to help when it came time to move the honeybees. Moving the hives was better suited for one of the pickup trucks anyway, and we used the last of their own fuel stash to make it happen. Tracey set up their mattress in the farmhouse living room so that she could sleep beside Keith. Thankfully it was warm enough by the beginning of April that the one room schoolhouse could be moved to the RV barn, and they could have an iota of privacy.

As Alex neared the end of his formal recovery period, he and Steve called me into their trailer one afternoon. I couldn't remember the last time I had been inside their space and noticed that it was spotless.

"I like what you've done with the place," I told them courteously. They both sat across from me smiling on the couch while I sat at their kitchen table. "Is it my turn for an intervention or something?" They laughed dismissively.

"We've been talking," Steve began. "Oh, I'm afraid she's going to think we are raving mad." He looked at Alex. "You tell her."

"We've done more than just talking. We've made a decision, and we are hoping you will support us in it," Alex explained.

"Ok, who's pregnant now?" I joked, my curiosity officially peaked.

"No, no! Nothing like that." Steve giggled. "But did you know we own a sailboat?" I did in fact know they owned a sailboat, remembering that they had taken an epic journey, just the two of them, around South America on their honeymoon. One of the pictures from their trip hung above their kitchen sink.

"I hadn't thought about it for a while I guess," I told them. "But I do recall Alex bragging about you being quite the sailor." I did my best dramatic impression of Alex swooning.

"Oh, stawwwp," Steve swatted at me. "In all seriousness—we're thinking about going on an excursion."

"Like, a vacation?" I said dubiously.

"No, not exactly. I can't stop thinking about my parents in Maine. I keep wondering if they are alive," he explained. "We were thinking of going to see if we could find them. They were living on the coast so we wouldn't actually be gone too long. We've made the trip a couple of times before."

"Would you take Norah?" I asked, anxiety tightening my throat.

"No," Steve said. "That's where we would need help. We'd like to leave Norah here because it would be safer of course, but also because we'd like time to reconnect. Just the two of us." Steve looked at Alex lovingly.

"Being out on the ocean will keep me away from any sort of temptation. And my mind and hands will be busy...sailing," Alex added.

"Sure, sure!" I winked at the pair of them. "To be frank, it does sound one sandwich short of a picnic. You won't have communication or anything," I said flatly. "I do understand the urge though. I mean, Nathan and Jess came all this way, and we aren't even blood relatives."

"I'm just not sure if I would ever stop feeling guilty if I didn't at least try to look for my mom and dad. Norah really loves them, even though she only remembers them from Skype. They'd have a virtual "date" every week. She still asks about them, and I never know what to say. I just feel...terrible. If we can't find them at least I can maybe start to move on. Does that sound nuts?" Steve asked.

"No, it makes sense," I conceded. "It will just be weird not having you here. I'll be worried sick. We all will, with no way to know if you are ok. And we don't even know what is going on over there right now, in Maine..."

"Well, we thought of something else too," he went on. "Having Keith and Tracey in your living room is probably going to get old pretty fast. We were thinking they could move into our trailer while we were gone. Our truck still has enough gas to get us to the marina and back. Maybe we can find another trailer to tow back with us on our way home."

"That's really generous," I replied. "I imagine they'll appreciate the offer. It's hard to eke out any solitude around here, that's for sure. It sounds like you guys have given this a lot of thought." They both nodded.

"Why are you asking me? Were you hoping I'd tell you not to go?" I asked them in all seriousness.

"No, not that," Alex mused. "I mean, I know we never like, elected a president or chief or anything—but if you had a fancy mahogany desk, I think everyone would agree that's how your name plate would read. No offense to Will." Now I knew they had to be pulling one over on me, I nearly spit out the tea they had just made me right on the table, unable to control my laughter. The men just looked at each other, clearly not joking.

"Oh, you're serious." I tried my best to simmer down but the thought of me sitting behind a big presidential desk with any sort of official title just cracked me up all over again.

"You're the boss, babe. I don't think we'd all be here if it wasn't for you, not like we are now." Steve leaned forward, put his hand on my shoulder, and looked into my eyes seriously. "And we will be back. I promise. A month, tops."

"I would never stand in the way of something that clearly means so much to you," I told him. "And of course, Norah is welcome to stay here—forever if she wants to. I'm going to really miss you guys. Just so you know, I'll be worried sick the whole time. It will be the longest couple of weeks in history."

Any niggling bits of the skirmishes between Alex and I melted away in that moment. It didn't matter that we disagreed, or had sharp edges, or did shitty things from time to time. Our strength as a group lay in the choice to still pull up a chair, or bale of hay, for each other anyway, *especially* when that person believed they had nothing to offer—when all they saw in the mirror was just another addict. Or a disability. Or a failed paramedic. Or an angry veteran. Or a bitter widow. Or a thief. Or a misfit. *Because healing doesn't happen in isolation.* It happens in a supportive community that never saw us as reduced to the sum of our pain in the first place. That's where the inspiration to live a full life resides. Alex had said so himself at a certain dinner party not so long ago.

"Thank you, Vanessa, thank you," Steve said, both of them enveloping me in a hug. I didn't know what they were thanking me for exactly—but I, too, was grateful.

X

Spring in central Nova Scotia is mud and blackfly season. It would be an intolerable combination if it wasn't for the beautiful temperatures for working outdoors, green grass popping up in the pasture, and bunches of tulips and daffodils colouring the yard. Flocks of geese, flying in formations larger than any of us had ever seen, were making their way back onto the fields and waterways. Kidding, duckling, chick, and piglet season were all in full swing. At any given time, Rose, Chris, Ryan, and Norah could be found with various baby animals cuddled in their sweater pockets.

Keith and Tracey had moved into Alex and Steve's trailer. Keith was learning to get around with the cane Steve had fashioned for him before they left. What was left of his leg still pained him on occasion, but he was slowly coming to terms with his new limitations. Nathan also knitted him a custom sock for his stump to help keep it as clean and comfortable as possible. It was a hard road, but I was quite proud of how well he was doing and how well the site of the injury itself had healed. Trying to reconfigure his place in the universe, Keith had even devised ways to split and carve wood while sitting down. Once he felt like he could contribute to the operation of the community, we noticed that his spirit rapidly began to heal as well.

Nathan and Jess were two of the happiest, most well

rested new parents anyone had ever seen. Rose had assigned himself as their nurse maid, ensuring they had the opportunity to take care of themselves just as well as Willow. The baby was growing like a weed. Her dark eyes seemed to hold the future of humanity within them. And, thanks to Nathan's genetics, her black hair took on an auburn sheen, just like her namesake's fleece after a summer of sun. She was somehow new and old and everything in between, dressed in recycled bedsheets that Jo had turned into clothes. Norah would not let Jess and Nathan forget that she was patiently awaiting their first playdate. She was as excited as anyone about her new "sister."

One day while we were collectively working on getting the first planting of cold hardy crops in the field, Ryan ran up to his dad excitedly. He held up the phone he had been listening to music on for his dad to see. I wasn't sure if Travis's jaw or his rake hit the ground first.

"Everybody—come here! *Now!*" he hollered. I was already making my way toward them.

"What is it?" I called.

"It's...it's a message!" He still hadn't taken his eyes off the screen. Ryan was jumping up and down, unable to contain himself. Steve and Alex had been gone for about three weeks. I wondered if they had somehow found a way to get a message to Ryan's phone. I knew intuitively that didn't make sense, but I asked anyway.

"Is it Steve and Alex?"

"No..." Travis looked up at me wide eyed. "It's the government."

"What did you say?" Nathan asked, coming to join us.

"It's the government!" Ryan shouted before doing a cartwheel—probably the first cartwheel in history inspired

by government communication.

"Here, you read it," Travis shoved the phone into my hand before rubbing his eyes vigorously. "I still can't believe what I'm seeing."

Attention COVID-19 Survivors,
On May 24th, 2025, there will be conferences held in each of the provincial capitals. If you have received this message and are in good health, you are invited to attend. On that day we will begin to pave a new way forward. Rapid tests kits will be provided prior to entry.
In solidarity,
Prime Minister Bluehorn

The garden was suddenly so quiet, we could have heard a chipmunk pee.

"Haha! Good one, Ryan! You got us!" Will went in for a high-five, but Ryan shook his head, adamant that he didn't concoct the whole thing. Chris dug his own phone-turned-music-box out of his pocket.

"I...I got it too," he stammered. "I just didn't hear it because I turned off the notifications last year." Travis started to laugh.

"Ok, I'm impressed, you two are clearly in cahoots!" He rubbed his knuckles on top of each of his son's heads. "Good game! Good game!"

"No, Dad! I swear," Chris struggled to free himself from his father's playful hold around his chin. "You know I can't spell that good!"

"I know how we can settle this," I told them. "My phone is in the house—it's been in my dresser drawer since before you all moved here. And unless *you're* in on it too," I pointed half suspiciously at Travis, "Paul and the boys wouldn't have my number." Chris and Ryan had already started marching back to the house before I had even finished, eager to emancipate themselves. Will and I shrugged at each other before racing them back to make sure no tampering could take place.

"That really does settle it, I guess," I said to the group of faces huddled in the bedroom doorway who had been patiently waiting for my phone to power up. "I got it too."

"Now *that* is prodigious," said Nathan with a smirk.

The Conference

"Perhaps the time has come to cease calling it the 'environmentalist' view, as though we were lobbying effort outside the mainstream of human activity, and to start calling it the real-world view."
-E.O. Wilson

Steve and Alex returned to the farm the same week that Ryan discovered the text from the government's emergency alert system. They were dismayed that they were unable to locate Steve's parents, but the trip brought them a sense of closure. Alex also had newfound confidence in his "perpetual recovery from opioid addiction," as he coined it. To keep his hands busy, the couple threw themselves into building a permanent home across the road from the farmhouse. In anticipation of further community growth, they planned to dedicate the ground floor as "The New Crossburn Medical Centre."

On May 24th, they eagerly joined the Bio-Bus tour to Halifax to convene with the other survivors in Nova Scotia. Rose was ecstatic at the prospect of finally seeing the prime minister, even if it was only by video. The kids begged to join—Norah hardly remembered anyone outside of the farm—but to be safe, they were asked to wait with Jo for the next road trip.

Live-streamed from Ottawa, Prime Minister Bluehorn delivered the conference's opening remarks. He, along with various other Canadian VIPs, had been given refuge in the Diefenbunker Museum—formerly known by its military designation, the Canadian Forces Station Carp. Bluehorn explained that they had successfully maintained connection with a network of global doomsday bunkers housing some of the world's brightest scholars and scientists. Through a focused combination of research efforts, the Sigma anomaly had officially been solved.

Key findings revealed by the international study were related to a popular herbicide that has been in use since the 1970s: glyphosate. The chemical was heavily applied in both agricultural and forestry sectors to eliminate competing vegetation. In Canada alone, ninety six percent of treated forests had been doused in glyphosate as an accepted broadleaf management practice. Of the one hundred and ninety-five countries in the world, the product was registered in over one hundred and sixty. It was seen to play a critical role in more than one hundred terrestrial food crops, including wheat, soybeans, and corn.

The safety of chronic exposure to glyphosate had been debated for decades. Governments assured citizens it was a benign product, while independent studies cried *"Carcinogen!"* before quietly disappearing from the public eye. As the fleet of underground scientists discovered, Sigma was the result of COVID-19 interacting with deer who were exposed to the chemical. The animals came in contact through aerial spraying, consuming sprayed vegetation, or drinking water contaminated by run off. The result was minute changes in cellular structure, and the variant escalated its transmission through those molecular discrepancies. The chemical interference of glyphosate created a physiological lock to Simga's key.

People with the highest levels of glyphosate accumulated in their bodies were the most susceptible to transmission. The high rate of mortality was attributed to an autoimmune response resulting in systemic apoptosis. Programmed cellular death is part of maintaining a healthy body, ridding it of aging or damaged cells, but when mistakenly turned on the host it was simply not survivable.

People whose glyphosate levels were little to none were either immune or asymptomatic carriers. Survivors mostly consisted of organic consumers, traditional growers, and those who lived in areas that had banned the use of glyphosate—such as Afghanistan. The theory supported Nathan's observation among the Mennonites and the residents of Sundry Turtle Island.

"In the wake of incredible sadness, and of unimaginable loss, I must remind you that we have an opportunity," Prime Minister Bluehorn said during his remarks. "We have the chance to say no to the mistakes of our predecessors. We can walk a different path. There is no reason our success as a nation, as a world community, cannot be framed by the principles of sustainability. With intention and design, we can heal the earth!" His speech was met with a standing ovation and an uncontested agreement to reexamine the foundations of government and industrial policy.

In the weeks to follow, the first national executive committee of "Earth Guardians" was formed. Membership consisted of environmental scientists, First Nation chiefs, progressive bishops from Amish, Mennonite, and Hutterite colonies, regenerative farmers, and various conservation group representatives. To her humble delight, despite having only run against herself, Vanessa was the first female farmer elected to champion the Valley region of Nova Scotia. The title didn't come with a mahogany desk, but she did receive a very official looking nametag. Alex and Steve baked her a cake to celebrate.

At the ordination of the Earth Guardians, Prime Minister Bluehorn tasked the group with developing new legislative framework that prioritized the health of the environment above all else. "Never again shall we forget that we do not live *within* the environment," he prophesized, "we *are* the environment."

The first motion passed by the assembly was to establish Mother Earth as a legal, autonomous entity, governed in trust by the EGs. "If Kitten Kay Sera could marry the colour pink in 2021, Mother Earth can have the rights to her body returned in 2025," Bluehorn told the audience. As news spread, a political comic emerged depicting the corpses of Judi Bari and Sallie McFague fist pumping in their graves.

The second motion carried was to create Major McGuigan's Law. At the encouragement of Jess and Nathan, it was the first idea Vanessa presented to the EG's. With internet access intermittently restored, Nathan tried to pinpoint the location of John's cabin, but he found a shocking blog post instead. The article, "The Cost of Company," was undoubtably inspired by John—the veteran they met on their journey east. It described a man who survived the bulk of the pandemic in his remote cabin, completely oblivious to world events. However, in the months following Jess and Nathan's departure, he ventured into a nearby town looking for a little more conversation. Unfortunately, he encountered an asymptomatic Sigma carrier at the newly established off-grid diner he stumbled upon. Although John had grown and harvested his own food without synthetic inputs, the forest in which he lived was a glyphosate treatment site. He, like the deer, was collateral damage in a war that didn't belong to him. Major McGuigan's Law would indefinitely prohibit the aerial spraying of herbicides on Canadian forests.

As lines of international communication reopened, Canada stepped forward as the fair and progressive leader it always had the potential to be. Trading in its colonial name, Turtle Island (Canadian Division) flew under the new flag of a red pine. It symbolized its peoples' resilience and dedication to consciously rebuilding from the ashes of Sigma. In the courtyard of the Nova Scotia legislature in Halifax, Prime Minister Bluehorn commissioned the planting and lifelong protection of six of such trees in commemoration of the Defenders. In front of them stood a plaque engraved with the following medicine woman's prayer:

"I will not rescue you,
For you are not powerless.
I will not fix you,
For you are not broken.
I will not heal you,
For I see you, in your wholeness.
I will walk with you through the darkness,
As you remember the light."

ABOUT THE AUTHOR

With over a decade of experience in emergency services, Vanessa Junkin has witnessed some of the very best and the very worst that humanity has to offer. After choosing to leave her career as an advanced care paramedic, Vanessa moved from Ontario to East Dalhousie, Nova Scotia, for a fresh start.

Alongside her husband, Will, she began building the Honeywwoofer Homestead. Her new home was the inspiration for the primary setting described in her debut novel, *The Misfit Farm*. When she isn't writing or boots deep on their rural property, Vanessa can be found at local markets, hanging out with her dogs, or volunteering with the fire department.

Following the advice of her late grandmother, she tries to take "one day at a time."

Manufactured by Amazon.ca
Bolton, ON